The Road to Me

Laura Drake

THE
ST RY
PLANT

The Story Plant
Studio Digital CT, LLC
P.O. Box 4331
Stamford, CT 06907

Story Plant paperback
ISBN-13: 978-1-61188-325-1

Fiction Studio Books
E-book ISBN: 978-1-945839-60-3

Visit our website at www.TheStoryPlant.com

First Story Plant Printing: April 2022

Printed in the United States of America 0 9 8 7 6 5 4 3 2 1

To the brave ones who let go of who they think they're
supposed to be
to become who they are meant to be.
To the vulnerable—the ones who say, 'I love you', first.

Huge thank you to Brené Brown, whose amazing TED Talk,
The Power of Vulnerability reminded
me of my superpower.

I was born to be a hippie.

I resisted.

Jacqueline Oliver

Chapter 1

Saturday~

I should be preparing for the show that could be the rocket fuel to propel my small business to the big time. Instead, I'm picking up my jail-break grandmother in the desert in back-of-beyond, Arizona.

It turns out, to get to this Show Low place in less than two days, I had to fly from Seattle to Phoenix, rent a car, and drive a hundred eighty miles. And the earliest flight I could get arrived here at two.

I spent the last hour driving, worrying about how much all this is costing me. I had to withdraw funds from my safety net for the plane ticket, and none of this was in the budget. No helping it, though. No one can accuse me of not taking care of my grandmother. When she broke her hip, falling out of a chair in geriatric yoga class, I had her seen by the most prominent orthopedist. He didn't take Medicare, so I paid the bill myself. If Nellie'd been in charge, she'd have had a native shaman. The rehab center is the best in the desert, but they're not used to patients trying to get away. Especially ones with fresh pins in their hip.

A deputy called last night to tell me they found her. They did a raid on a charlatan doing "sweats" in the desert. They arrested the leader, but most of the followers scattered. Nellie couldn't make a clean getaway, what with her walker. And the fact that, except for several strands of Mardi Gras beads, she was naked.

I tried to talk him into putting her on a plane, but he said he'd only release her to next-of-kin. She'd told him there was a conspiracy at the facility to sell her into sexual slavery. He didn't buy it, and he wanted a family member to come take charge.

That's me. The last of the line. I'm a failed third-generation hippie. I know where the second generation is—under a marble slab at Long Rest Cemetery. It's the first generation who's gone AWOL. Again.

I'm pretty good at controlling myself. But my grandmother? Might as well try to herd dinosaurs. My guts roil in a stew of impatience, irritation and the premonition of chaos. And under it all, the fury of a child forced to take care of yet one more adult. My mother couldn't help it—she had zero control over herself, or the booze. But my grandmother visited our succession of rattier apartments. Saw the squalor, my mother's helplessness, my desperation. And after a day or two she'd tuck me in, tell me she loved me, and in the morning, was gone.

I don't know if I resent her more for leaving, or myself, for believing every time, that *this* time would be different.

Nellie was probably headed for a convention on, "Saving the Universe Through Toe Massage," or something. She was New-Age long before it was new, trying every religion, every weird philosophy out there. Hampering her enlightenment is the fact that she has the intellectual depth of a kiddie pool, and the attention span of a caffeinated gnat.

Too harsh? No doubt. But my grandmother earned it.

Fifty miles ago, the rocks and saguaro rushing by the car window gave way to dusty evergreens and rocky hillsides with scrub grass. Being an artist, I know Leo would love this landscape. I'd text him a photo, if I hadn't just told him we are over. He's a great guy, and I really enjoyed our time together but I learned a long time ago, it's easier to end it now before he could really matter.

The temperature is better than the blast furnace I remember, but I can feel my skin parching and I miss green already. I drive past tiny towns with boarded-up stores and gas stations that, from the prices on their weathered signs, pumped their last gallon in the fifties. What would cause a person to wash up here, in the middle of nowhere? I shudder, as if my body wants to shake off the possibility of that fate.

The sign for Show Low blows by, announcing a population of a little over ten thousand. Larger than I imagined, not as big as I'd hoped. It doesn't matter. With luck, I'm in and out in an hour.

The nav system guides me onto Deuce of Clubs Avenue. I turn at a handsome split-level building, pull into a parking spot and turn off the key. I sit, trying to slow my heartbeat.

Why? The question appears out of the murk like one of those old Eight-Ball prophesies. Nellie claimed to love me. Her visits made clear she loved my mother, because Nellie took over porcelain-god duty, holding my drunken mother's hair, hugging her and wiping her face with a wet cloth while she cried. And, I remember my grandmother's smile when she'd rock me in her bony lap, reading me a book.

Which made it hurt even more when she abandoned me. My balloon of hope lost a bit of lift each time, until it was a wrinkly little thing I kicked to the back of my closet.

My childhood memories have faded from technicolor to sepia over the years, and I've relegated them to a drawer in my mind. But I haven't had as much success with the *why*. How could my grandmother profess to love me, yet leave me, a child, as the only adult in the house? I've began the trip to the desert several times, determined to finally ask. It would be such a relief to know. And just as many times, I stopped before my car left the parking lot. Because it's dangerous to ask a question if you don't know you'll survive the answer.

I listen to the tick of the cooling engine. I shouldn't feel bad. I haven't been to see her, but my not being there made zero difference. But hey, if she wants to throw that in my face, fine. *She* can learn to live with disappointment. I tighten my stomach muscles to take a blow and head inside for the Show Low Showdown.

I walk in and am smacked by the institutional smell of pine deodorizer, sweat and floor wax. When I tell the bald officer at the front desk why I'm here, his pudgy face lights up. "Ah, Nellie. She's a kick in the pants." Then he puts on his official state employee face. "Could I see some I.D.?"

"Please tell me you don't have her locked up." I pull my wallet and show him my driver's license.

"Not hardly. We've got a cot in the office behind the day room. She's been bunking there. And entertaining us with her stories."

"Nellie's got stories, all right." Most of them exaggeration or outright fabrication. "Do you mind retrieving her for me? We've got a flight out of Phoenix tonight."

He cocks his head like a quizzical dog. "You don't want to be driving back after dark. Lots of critters on the roads."

I hold my sigh. "I'll take it under advisement."

He looks like he wants to say more, but just shakes his head and clomps to the door on the back wall.

I try not to stare at the few ragged people sitting in plastic chairs that line the walls. They have no such compunction. But to be fair, in a skirt, low heels and pantyhose, I'm the one who doesn't fit in. They tend toward overalls and flannel.

The officer steps back through the door and holds it open. He's carrying a lumpy pillowcase—Nellie's clothes, I assume. My grandmother shuffles in. She is a new-age explosion, from her chartreuse and black-striped walker adorned with bells and leather bags of rocks she calls "crystals," to her oversize tie-dyed T-shirt and black tights, sagging on stick legs. Her wrinkles lift to a sunny grin. "Jack! You came! See, Easy? I told you she'd come."

Easy is G'ma's imaginary friend. I remember her talking to him when I was little.

I want to argue that she gave me no choice. I want to tell her to lose my number. I want to bolt for the door.

But I spent fifteen years being a dutiful daughter. I can stand five hours acting the dutiful granddaughter. Even if it makes my teeth grind. "Are you ready to go?"

"I'm in. Where are we going?" The walker wheels squeak their way around the desk.

The cop hovers, as if he can help by making supportive hand gestures. "You take care now, Nellie. And you come back and see us when you're in our neck of the woods, ya hear?" He hands me the dirty prison-break pillowcase.

She stops to pat his pudgy cheek. "I will, Roscoe. In the meantime, you keep these miscreants in line."

Red spreads up his neck to suffuse his entire head. "And you stay away from charlatans."

She wags a bird-claw finger at him. "Now, don't you go judging by looks. You never know who's going to give you that last piece to the puzzle." She pushes her way over to me, her dusty Converse high tops squeaking in time with the walker wheels.

When I step outside, the smell of exhaust and hot tar hit with a vengeance. I hold the door open. "Come on, Nellie, we've got a long way to go tonight." The sun is barely gone, leaving a spectacular golden orange-red horizon. It hits me that the colors would make a beautiful perfume bottle label. I snap a photo on my phone, then get her settled in the passenger seat of the car, stowing her walker and pillowcase behind the seat.

I slide in and crank the engine.

"I'm so very happy to see you, Jack. You look poised, polished, and pretty as ever." Her sparrow eyes dart over me and she sobers. "But something's wrong in your life. What is it?"

I check the mirror. The same waif as always stares back. "Why would you think something is wrong?"

The lines between her brows deepen. "Your aura is between lemon and dark yellow, with tiny tinges of brown."

"I'll talk to my hairdresser. Maybe a weave?"

"Jack, do not make light of this." Her halo of white frizz tilts as she leans in. "Your aura tells me that in your pressure to do well, you have forgotten to live. Also, you have a fear of loss."

Tell me something I don't know. But this day has been too long to go down that rabbit hole. I reverse out of the parking space and pull to the edge of the road.

"Do you think we could get a bite of dinner?" She puts her hand below her skinny ribcage. "I'm really hungry."

"We need to get—"

A loud stomach growl comes from the passenger seat. Can she do that at will? "All right. But somewhere quick."

"Oh good." She puts her palms on the dash and beams like a kid that just heard the words, "Happy Meal." "The cops rave about a place just up the road, Wally's. Good solid food, fast service."

Maybe they have a drive-through.

Of course, they don't. I park diagonally in front of an old brick building in the middle of downtown. Interior lights reveal a '50s style soda bar and red vinyl booths marching down the opposite side. It takes forever to get the walker, extricate Nellie from the car, and set her on her tottering way to the door. How could this woman have moved fast enough to escape the rehab facility?

But that doesn't matter. The only thing that matters is getting her back there. I hold the door.

"Can we take that booth there?" She points to the back of the room, though there are empty ones, closer.

I look up from checking work emails on my phone. "Whatever. Just go."

"This place reminds me of the time I went to town with Moonbeam. We'd been on the commune for six months and couldn't do vegetarian one more minute." She pulls in a deep lungful of the scent of grease. "Best danged cheeseburger I ever ate."

There's that Nellie commitment. She picks up and discards beliefs like a toddler in a toy store. She sits, and I move the walker to the corner, brush off the cracked seat, then sit opposite her in the booth.

Nellie pulls two plastic-clad menus from behind the napkin dispenser and slides one in front of me. It's covered in smeared fingerprints and what looks like ketchup.

A high school-aged girl walks over. She's wearing tight low-rider jeans and a T-shirt featuring a llama with sunglasses, flashing a peace sign. "What can I get you ladies?"

"Love your T-shirt." Nellie smiles up at her. "Can you tell me if there's anywhere in this town I can score some hash?"

"Nellie!" My head swivels, making sure no one heard that.

"Sorry, Ma'am. My mother'd switch me if I admitted . . ." She flicks a glance around. "But I've heard—"

"Nellie." My tone is a radiation level warning. "Either you order—food—or we're leaving." I sneak one more peek around. "Now."

Nellie smiles at the little delinquent. "Don't mind her, her underwear's always been too tight. I'll have a bacon burger with cheese, fries, and a chocolate milkshake."

My grandmother's skin sags off her bones. She can't weigh ninety pounds. No way she'll eat all that, but she sure can use the calories.

"Are any of your salads romaine?" I asked.

The waitress drops a hand on her hip. "We're not total hicksters out here, you know. Our Cobb has some dandelion greens in it. Locally grown."

The smell of grilling meat is heavenly, but my pants are tight already, and clothes sure don't rate a safety fund raid. "Um, thanks. I'll just have coffee."

She huffs off, and I'm left with Nellie's worried-sparrow stare. "It's the business, isn't it? I worried it would come to this when you took what you loved and made it a capitalist venture."

"Oh, don't be ridiculous." But her words hit my skin, burn through to my core and explode in a shower of sparks, singeing everything they touch. Could she be right? Just because it's Nellie, it doesn't mean she's always wrong.

I check my phone. It won't do to let Nellie know she can hurt me.

After working my way through my chemistry degree on three jobs, small scholarships and Top Ramen Noodles, Heart's

Note was born in my kitchen in stolen hours after the grind of a day job. I rushed home every evening, anxious to discover a new, unique scent.

Perfumes nowadays are exotic, designer-vogue. I was looking for a scent for the girl next door, the soccer mom, the hip forty-something. Something to make them feel special, yet still themselves. I knew if I could capture that, the women would come. It took a year and a half of late nights and take-out weekends before I had them—Adam and Eve, my signature scents. I rented a storefront in downtown Seattle two years ago. Heart's Note is doing okay, but I won't be able to relax until we hit the big time—the retail chains.

"Please don't take me back there," she whispers.

The lightning quick subject change takes me a breath to catch up. "Where, Paradise? Of course I'm taking you back. You need therapy. You need—"

"I *need* to live free."

"Oh nonsense. You make it sound like I'm putting you in a zoo. Village Breeze is the premier retirement community. It has exercise classes and crafts, and—"

"Spare me the lecture. I live there, remember?" Her eye roll would make our waitress proud.

"Well, I saw the brochure, and I think it's lovely. They even have a bridge club."

"Great. You live there." She folds her arms across her bony chest.

"Now you sound like a petulant child."

"Look at me, Jack." She spreads her spindly arms, and the beads on her wrists rattle. But her eyes . . . they're haunted. "Do I look like I belong in one of those places?"

"You're safe there. That is, when you're not running away and putting yourself in crazy situations."

"Oh please. I'm not addled yet."

"They found you in a tipi in the desert, naked, inhaling smoke and God knows what else. You could have gotten dehydrated. You could have had a stroke. You could have *died*." She shrugs. "We're all bound to die, Jack. When it comes, I'm ready. But I'm planning on living right up to that moment." She lifts a skeletal, knobby-jointed finger. "And I might add, I broke my hip in your old fart warehouse."

I sigh. "We've been over this before. The judge put me in charge of your care—"

"Sanctimonious asshole."

"You have to admit, he had reason to question your judgment with that 'Wisdom Gathering' at your house. Four hundred people in a nine hundred square foot house on a postage stamp lot? Even Woodstock had more than one bathroom."

Her smile is smug. And a bit proud. "I had no way of knowing that the word would spread. It just proves that people are seeking answers."

"In a housing development outside Palm Springs?"

"Why not? Your Jesus was born in a manger."

"Not my Jesus. I stopped believing in him and Santa about the same time." I learned early and well no savior would be coming.

Her wrinkles deepen. "Jack, your mother—"

"Don't." I hold up a hand. My stomach shrivels to a dried lemon, and I'm suddenly positive I do not want the answer to the *why*. I'll give up a precious day of my life. I'll be civil to the woman who stands for everything I distain. But I refuse to dig through my childhood with the one person who could have rescued me from the shitpile and didn't.

But still, there's the three-letter word that I can't get past. *Why?*

Thankfully, our waitress arrives with a gloppy cheeseburger to distract Nellie.

More than an hour later, we're only two miles out of town, on a road that is blacker than the inside of a bear. I'm used to strip mall lights, headlights, streetlights—in a word, civilization. The road curves as if trying to squirm away from the headlights. Seconds tick by in my head, disappearing as fast as the odds of my making the red-eye to Seattle. I depress the accelerator another micron, my fingers shining like white claws in the dashboard's glow.

Nellie's eyes are closed, but she's chanting under her breath and shaking a little rattle covered in some kind of hide. The monotonous drone is circling the inside of my skull like a manic earworm, but if I ask her to stop, she'll want to chat. I flick a glance to the console to find the radio. Can I even get a signal in this God forsaken—

A massive deer flashes in the headlights, vaulting the hood of the car. I cut the wheel to the right, and there's a click of the hooves against the windshield. Then it's gone.

My seat belt snaps tight as we bump off the road. The headlights spotlight the trunk of a tree, getting bigger. I slam the brakes, and the car fishtails in the grass.

Nellie's chant gets louder, bouncing off the windows.

The car slows.

Just as I'm sure we're going to stop in time, the sedan's back end passes us and slams into the tree with a jerk and a screech of metal.

The seat belt knocks my breath out in a whoosh.

Silence. For five seconds. Then Nellie starts chanting again.

"Are you all right?" It comes out a pant.

She just nods and, eyes closed, keeps chanting.

The engine is still running. Maybe I can get us out of here. I press the gas. The wheels spin, but we're not moving. I try again, slower this time. When the smell of hot rubber laces the air, I jam the car into park and reach to Nellie's fragile wrist. "Are you sure you're okay?"

"Yes, my chant averted sure disaster." Her eyes are still closed, her face calm in the dash lights.

Oh, for fuck's sake. I release the seat belt and scramble out. My heels sink in the grass. Holding onto the car, I flounder my way around to assess the damage.

The car is up to the chassis in wet sandy mud, and on the impact side, the metal is crumpled into the smoking tire. I look up the slope to the dark void where the road must be. "I *so* do not have time for this." Except I do, because there's now a zero percent chance of making our flight. My heels make a sucking sound as I make my way back to call a tow truck, and I add a pair of shoes to the list of things this day has cost me.

Two hours later, we're back in Show Low. The wrecker dropped us off at a cinderblock hotel with paint faded to Pepto Bismol pink. Nellie's soft snores drift in through the door between our rooms. I should be exhausted, but the restlessness buried by my busy day surfaces. I pace the threadbare shag carpet. I know from experience it won't go away.

Dammit, I hate these nights—like when you lie in bed knowing you're going to be sick and putting it off as long as possible by telling yourself it won't happen. But it always does. I need to move. I can outrun the antsiness, given enough miles. Glad I thought to pack them, I change to sweats and tennis shoes. Making sure the plastic key fob is in my pocket, I step into the night.

The slight breeze is cool on my hot face. It carries the hint of many dinners: curry, grilling meat, and is that pumpkin bread? I follow my nose to the dark hulks of houses rising from a subdivision across the street.

The hollow cavern opens in my chest. *Hello darkness, my old friend.*

I take off at a good pace, my heels hitting the sidewalk to the cadence of my heart. I wonder if anyone ever looks out their window to wonder why a young woman is haunting their neighborhood at night.

Haunting. A good term. I'm like a lonely ghost, on the outside of the life these houses contain.

I pass the picture window of a brick home, faces revealed in the blue-white television light: a mother, father and two little ones. A few houses later, a woman washes dishes. The light over the sink spills onto her hair, chunks of curls falling from a workday updo. A man steps behind her to wrap his arms around her waist. She leans her head against his, her smile pure contentment.

The cavern in my chest fills with an ancient longing. I don't envy her the man. This is much deeper and Neanderthal than that. It's knowing you're not alone when the wind howls and the dark presses in the windows. It's that someone chooses to stand beside you to face the night. It's the safety of fellowship. Chosen kinship.

I walk on. In the next house, an overhead light reveals a bedroom—a child's from the comic border around the top. I can't see the bed, but a woman with storybook in hand, sinks out of sight.

I fall to a walk, breathing hard. This is what I do. I don't want to—it hurts to do it, and I know it's not normal. Every time, I say it won't happen again. But then I find myself in places like this, haunting neighborhoods like a wistful ghost, taking in the dioramas of everyday family life.

I learned long ago, the distance from the sidewalk to the front door is the closest I'll ever get to this. It's not surprising, I guess. How do you know a good relationship if you've never seen one? I can't count the "boyfriends" Mom brought home. Some wanted to save her, some wanted to party with her. Some wanted to party with *me*. None stayed. I never got close enough to classmates to see their parents' marriages. Once they met my mother, their invitations to visit dried up like weeds in Vegas.

There was a time I still believed forever love possible. The kind of love I observe in these nighttime dioramas. But I'm a dismal "picker," and that college disaster almost took me down.

Like they say, know better, do better.

I know better.

Yet here I am, at the mercy of a need that won't be suppressed. It's a sharp, uncomfortable place, but it's strong.

I hate the crack in me that won't heal.

Chapter 2

*Life is like writing with a pen. You
can cross out your past but you can't
erase it.*

E.B. White

Sunday~

I don't remember waking, and I don't recognize the cracked ceiling above me. The room isn't completely dark, thanks to a hot sliver of light around the plastic blackout curtain. What time is it? I scrabble for my phone on the pressed board bedside table. Ten? How can that be? I haven't slept past seven since forever. But it was well past one when I got back from my run. The heavy perfume of cheap disinfectant and legions of cigarettes linger like ghosts from my past.

You never forget the smell of despair.

Dredged memories crawl like ants over the surface of my brain. I've got to get out of here. I sit up. I'm still wearing the clothes from last night because I only brought one other outfit.

I called the car rental company last night, they thought it could take two days to get another car up here. I guess I can't blame them for not maintaining a presence in this tiny burg. One more thing to deal with today.

Nellie was so tired last night she fell asleep in the tow truck. I step to the door that separates our rooms. I left it cracked last night, just in case . . .

"Nellie?" Her curtains are billowing in a breeze, and the sunlight pouring in makes me squint, but even so, I can see the room is empty. Her walker is MIA as well. "Oh hell." I hustle to the bathroom, pee, brush my teeth and run a brush through my hair. She's probably sitting outside, taking in the sun. I mean, how far can she go?

But when I step out, the only thing in the cracked asphalt parking lot is wind-blown trash.

If she's right, and there is reincarnation, Nellie is Houdini. I sigh and walk across the gravel lot to the road, then scan left and right. The old brick buildings of downtown are probably a half mile away. She couldn't have walked that far, could she? Surely, she wouldn't try to hitchhike. Wait, of course she would. She knows better, but that wouldn't count for much in Nellie Oliver's tie-dyed worldview.

This is a nightmare. It's like I stepped onto the plane in my neatly ordered reality and stepped off into bedlam. And my grandmother is the gatekeeper. I've got to find her, somehow wrangle a ride and get us to—

Beep . . . beep-beep!

An old, sun-burnt yellow Mustang top-down convertible with front-end damage barrels toward me. No one appears to be driving. But there's a walker sticking up from the back seat, and as it passes, I spot Nellie, in an eye-searing neon green polyester pantsuit behind the wheel. She's squinting between the steering wheel and the dash, smiling like a Cheshire cat on 'shrooms. "What the—"

There's a squeal of brakes, and the car does a donut, aiming right at me. I run for the ditch.

With one more screech of rubber, Nellie stops and cackles out the window at me. Her short white hair floats around her head in a gossamer fog. "Aw, have a little faith, Jack. I wouldn't run you over. Hop in!"

"Nellie Oliver. Where in God's name did you get this . . . thing? It's forty years old if it's a day, and you don't have a license. Please tell me you didn't steal it." The black leather interior is faded to charcoal with spider-web fissures, and the dash has a huge crack through the middle.

"I bought it. And I'll have you know that my license doesn't expire until my birthday next month."

A million questions all trying to get out at the same time make me sputter, "Where did you get the money?"

She winks at me. "You don't know everything, Jack."

"But as your guardian, I should. If you've got a bank account hidden somewhere . . ." I take a step to the car, but my shoe stays in the mud. I hop, pulling until it pops out. "Shit. Shit. Shit."

"Hey, I solved our transportation problem. I thought you'd be happy. Come, get in. We'll grab some breakfast."

Put myself at her mercy? Not. Happening. I grab the driver's door handle and jerk. It comes open with a screech of metal. "I'm driving. Scoot over." Nellie ate everything put before her last night, but I haven't eaten since I left Seattle—decades ago. I'm starving. And I've got to call my manager.

"Really, Nellie, where did you get the money for this?" I slide in and see it's a stick shift. Luckily, I taught myself to use one back when I had to retrieve Mom from the bars, back when we could afford a car.

"Well, if you must know," she tips her nose up and sniffs like a Nobb Hill socialite, "I read the Tarot."

Oh, for the love of—I check the mirrors, make a U-turn, and head for town.

"On the internet. For good bread, too."

"Sorry I asked."

"Hey, don't knock it. Many are seeking answers."

"You are taking money from fools, telling them what they want to hear."

"I am only channeling The Dude."

I'm going to let that go. Wait, no, I can't. If some shyster got his hooks into her . . . "The *Dude*?"

"He's my spirit guide. I read the cards, but he interprets them, based on what my client needs to know."

I now know how Alice felt, going down that rabbit hole. "This is not a real person, right?"

"He's real. He's not currently alive, but he's real."

Luckily, Wally's Diner keeps me from asking more questions. Massive mud-spattered trucks take up every space but one. I tuck in between them, a tattered Barbie car in a G.I. Joe world.

When I turn off the key, the engine lugs and lugs, wheezes, then with a jerky rattle, dies. "Nellie, I'm not sure this car will make it to Phoenix."

"You think I'd buy a car without checking under the hood?" She pats the cracked dash gently. "We old girls are in better shape than young folks give us credit for."

"How would you know if the engine is sound?" I'm starting to realize there's a lot I don't know about my grandmother.

"Easy taught me." She gives a teenager's theatrical sigh and flutters her eyelashes. "We kept that ancient VW running all the way across the U.S. God, the sex in the back of that van was incredible."

I rub my temples and try to unhear that. She must be delusional, believing her imaginary friend isn't.

She strokes the dash. "We have to name her. Any ideas?"

"Name a car? For what purpose?" I extract the walker, carry it to the passenger side, and open the door.

"You want her to run, don't you? A car this old needs to feel loved. What do you suggest?"

I've got to call Steph. "I don't care."

"That is a crappy name." She puts her liver-spotted hands on the frame and hauls herself up.

Was that a whimper? "Are you all right?" I grab her arm to steady her.

"I'm fine. Stop fussing." She swats my hand away. "This car needs a name befitting her status. How about Duchess?" Nellie leans on the walker and shuffles toward the curb.

"Whatever." This car is ending its life in a junkyard in Phoenix. If she wants to name it for the four hours it takes to get there, fine. I slam the door and follow.

She insists on sitting in the same booth in the back, which means we're walking at a funeral pace past a room full of rough working men. I shoot a glance to my muddy shoe. Yeah, like any eyes in the place are looking anywhere other than my butt.

Nellie orders eggs, pancakes, grits, toast, and prunes ("gotta keep things moving, you know"). I order a poached egg and cottage cheese. And coffee. I long for Seattle Elite, but even diner coffee is better than no coffee.

Nellie points overhead, where elevator music pours from dusty speakers. "I'll bet hearing that crap, Jerry is truly grateful to be dead."

It takes me a few seconds. "Oh, you mean the ice cream, rocker guy?"

She closes her eyes, and her wrinkles relax into a smile. "Jerry Garcia was a God at Woodstock."

I just stare, one eyebrow raised. "You're telling me you were at Woodstock."

"Hell, Jack, I'm on the album cover."

Finally, I catch her in a lie. I Google a photo of the cover and point. "I saw an article about that couple. They've been married for like fifty years."

Nellie leans in. "Not them." She points. "See the guy with the red bandana, sitting with his arms wrapped around his knees? That's Easy."

Wait, Easy was a real person? Or is she lying again? "Where are you?"

"I'm lying next to him, see?" She points.

"You mean that person, on their side, facing away from the camera and the photo cut the head off? I can't even be sure it's a woman."

"It's me." She shrugs. "Who else would be lying beside Easy?"

"How would I even know that's . . . oh never mind." If she's lying, she's good at it. Of course, she's had decades of practice.

"Gotta say though, even if Easy liked it, I'm not a fan of Jimi's Anthem. 'Bout burst my eardrums." She shakes her head, then looks up at me with the innocence of a child. "Can I ask you a favor, Jack?"

My stomach twists. I pocket my phone..

"I just want to see the Grand Canyon one more time and—"

"We've got to get you back. I have no doubt you've missed doctor visits, physical therapy—"

"Please?" She raises her hands in supplication.

Which is *not* working on me. Breakfast hasn't even begun, and the day is stretching ahead like peering down the wrong end of a telescope. "And I have to get back. I have an important show next weekend to get ready for." I glare at her. "And don't give me that pound-puppy look."

"Did I ever tell you? I worked a rafting expedition through the canyon." Her rheumy brown eyes get a faraway look. "You never forget that kind of beauty. I'd like see it once more before I die." Her bird-like shoulders rise on a heavy sigh. "I looked it up. It's only two hundred miles out of your way, and we have all day. You could be home by tonight. I've never asked you for anything. Please, Jack?"

Anger flash-boils my blood. She never gave me the one thing I wanted—the one thing I *needed*. I open my mouth to spew, but when I look across the table, the fragile face of my family looks back at me. If my mother had lived, her face would be a twenty-year younger version of Nellie's. Regardless, there's no denying genetics. This is my last living relative.

I left Vegas in a cloud of Greyhound diesel fumes more than a decade ago and thought I'd put the past behind me. I'm not a good liar, even to myself. If I had left the past in that Vegas bus station, Nellie wouldn't matter. The fact that I'm furious with her proves the past has followed me like a shadow, mostly unnoticed, but always there. Suddenly, my life seems like a great camouflage to cover the stuff underneath; like an exclusive neighborhood built on a landfill.

That's the problem with denial. You hide the truth from yourself, but deep down, you already know what you need to do. And the harder it is to do, the stronger the denial. The hollow place reopens in me. This woman is the last person to hold my history. The last person I'd want holding it, but it is what it is.

If I'm brave enough to ask the questions.

And to bear the answers.

What the hell. It's a four-hour diversion. But it won't be a free ride. "First." I tick points off on my fingers. "*If* we go, you get a half hour to stare over the side, then we're leaving."

Her smile brightens the booth.

"Second. You have to promise not to run away from the rehab facility, or Village Breeze, or anywhere, ever again."

Her smile dims and her mouth pulls to a grimace. She stares at the wall a few moments, but then nods.

"You have to promise. I have to hear you say it."

Her eyes dart around the room. She's looking for a chink—a weak spot, she can twist to break her promise. When she realizes my offer is airtight, her shoulders bow, and her eyes meet mine. "I won't run away again. I promise."

Freedom washes over me, rare as a fresh breeze in the desert. No more MIA phone calls. I can drop her off, knowing she'll be taken care of to the point of pampering. "And last, you stop calling me Jack." I drop a paper napkin in my lap. She cocks her head. "But that's what I always called you. Don't you remember?"

As if I could forget. When I realize I'm shredding the napkin, I force my fingers to still.

"Do you remember what you called me?"

"No."

"You called me, G'ma. Gee-ma. Remember?"

"No."

Her smug smile sees through my lie.

"Look, why don't you head to the car. I'll pay the bill, and I've got to call my manager."

"Okay." She totters off, pausing to talk to the truckers at the table by the door.

I hit speed dial, just as the men burst into uproarious laughter. I don't even want to know—

"Hello?"

Steph's voice brings a wave of homesickness for the old red brick building storefront, the white-framed windows are tall and curved at the top, the door recessed with the sign, *Heart's Note*, above in gold handwritten font. The glass shelves in the windows are staggered so the late afternoon sun flashes on cut glass bottles: clear, gold, amethyst and ruby. It's gorgeous. Special, yet not high-brow or intimidating. "I'm so sorry to bother you on Sunday, Steph."

"Jacqueline? Are you okay?"

I know why she's confused. I've been careful to keep our relationship strictly business, though she's extended a hand in friendship a few times. It would be so nice to say yes. To have someone to talk to, to confide in. But she's an employee. I've made it this far without friends, but good managers are impossible to replace when they leave. "I'm in Arizona, and if things continue the way they've been going, there's a slight chance I'll be late tomorrow. Could you open for me?"

"What the heck are you doing in Arizona?"

"Personal matter. I plan to be there tomorrow morning, but . . ."

"No worries. I'll open, and you can close."

"Great, thank you."

"Jacqueline? I was off on Friday. I'm wondering if you had a chance to try out the scent sample I left for you?"

Steph told me she'd been playing with scent combinations in her garage. I was flattered that she wanted to follow in my footsteps. "I did, and—"

"Great. Now, I've researched how to do this, and I can have it manufactured and sell it at Heart's Note on consignment, or I could sell you the formula. Your up-front outlay would be a lot more of course, because of the potential for it to go big."

I scramble for compliment crumbs, to lessen the sting. "Steph, I think it's a great first effort. Really, this stuff isn't easy and your scent is . . . different. But in my opinion, it tries too hard. The notes clash, all fighting for precedence instead of complementing each other and combining to a sum more than the parts. See what I mean?"

"Oh." Long pause. "I see."

"But you're young, and new at this. You should keep trying and I can offer tips, if you're interested." Nellie is still talking to the truckers. "Look, I've got to jump. I'm sorry to disrupt your day off."

"No problem. I'll see you Monday."

I hang up, worrying about the business. Most months, the bottom line is black, which I know is great for an indie startup, but there's nowhere near enough in my safety net account. And this trip sure isn't helping. I scribble my signature at the bottom of the charge slip for breakfast.

When you grow up where "drive-through" means visiting the dumpsters behind fast-food places, and even Goodwill back-to-school shopping is too pricey, money equals safety. There will never be enough money to fill that hole. I know that. But as long as I can add to the fund every week, it feels like a tiny win. Like I shoveled a bit more ground under my feet.

More laughter from the front table gets me moving.

Nellie says, "A gynecologist was fed up with his job, so he decided to switch careers. He enjoyed tinkering with engines, so he enrolled in a school for truck mechanics. For their final exam, they were to strip a truck engine and reassemble it in perfect working order.

"The gynecologist was amazed to find he scored 150%. He asked the instructor, '150%? How could I score that?'

"'Well,' replied the instructor, 'I gave you 50% for taking the engine apart. I gave you 50% for reassembling it perfectly.

You got the 50% bonus for doing it all through the exhaust pipe.'"

The men within five tables fall out laughing.

I take Nellie's elbow. "We've got to go, Nellie."

"Aw, does she have to?" A big Bluto-lookalike asks.

"Gotta go spread the love, dudes. Keep on trucking!" Nellie blows them a big old kiss and motors for the door.

The outside air feels cool on my hot cheeks. "I swear, Nellie you could make friends with a Honey Badger."

"Aw, they're just good ol' boys. Back in my day . . ."

"Come on. You want to see the canyon, right?"

Luckily she heads for the car, sparing me more sexual escapades. Those aren't the secrets I'm looking for.

Chapter 3

A person often meets his destiny
on the road he took to avoid it.
Jean de La Fontaine

I took a detour and am carrying a little plastic basket through the Rexall beside the diner. "This is ridiculous. That excuse for a car has air conditioning, doesn't it?" Nellie's insisting on riding with the top down, so I've got to get a head scarf, or my hair is going to turn to straw.

"Her name is Duchess." Nellie drops a bag of cheese puffs in the basket.

"Where do you put it all?" That's going to make a mess. I reach for baby wipes. "I fail to see why we can't be comfortable."

"Spring in the desert is very temperate. Don't you remember?"

I've tried very hard to forget. I put a jug of sunscreen in the basket. I don't plan to die of skin cancer.

She stops at a rack of sunglasses and tries on a pair. "These are so me." She turns. Two huge glittery silver stars frame her eyes and dwarf her saggy face.

"Ridiculous." I take an age-appropriate pair from the rack and hand them to her.

"You've gotta learn to live, Jack." She drops the star glasses in the basket and abandons the ones I chose on the shelf. "You worry too much."

"Well someone has to be the adult." I pick up a small Styrofoam cooler and a six-pack of water bottles.

"Why?" Her walker squeaks behind me to the checkout stand. "Didn't you have more fun before you took on all that responsibility?"

I'm sure she's referring to the business, not my mother. But the answer to both is the same. "I didn't have much choice, did I?" I meant to say that only in my head. Nellie totters down the aisle, wheels squeaking.

Maybe she didn't hear.

Back at the car, I get her settled, slather us both in sunscreen, tie on my white head scarf, and we blow out of town. The road is much less scary during the day, curving lazily through a forest of scrub pine. We pass the site of the deer encounter, recognizable by all the torn-up grass and the scarred tree.

Nellie yells over the sound of the wind. "I'm grateful that my meditation could save us."

Just like her to try to take credit. I shake my head like I can't hear.

Leo would love this. The sun plays over the wind-combed grass at the side of the road, forming rivers of buff, tan, gold, reminding me of his sculptures. I let the wind pull away the scrap of a regret. Neither Leo, nor his art are my concern, as of —was it only yesterday? Suddenly, Seattle seems a faraway planet, and I'm E.T., stranded in a strange land.

I'll be back in my world tonight. Back where the world makes sense because I built it that way.

The rustic scent of pine blows into my sinuses, bringing a spark of an idea. A clean, outdoor scent for men. Not like others on the market, obvious or in-your-face, but a subtle bass note . . .

Then the scent is gone, but a tentative wisp lingers. Here I am, in the middle of nowhere, in a car that was new before I was born, with my grandmother no less, and I'm getting cologne ideas.

If there were a God, he'd be laughing.

When we hit Highway 40, the road straightens. This is more the desert I remember. The dry air crawls into my sinuses and dust coats my throat. The wind blows hot and dry, and vegetation shrivels to patches of cactus and spiny plants. Everything here is hard, hardy and hurtful. I understand that—survival depends on shielding your soft parts. But I have too many memories of the hard parts to want to see the small, fragile beauty it holds.

I turn onto Highway 89, and mountains rise ahead of the car's hood, even as the ground around us falls into arroyos. Small ditches at first, deepening to mini canyons. Nellie shifts in her seat, as if sensing the canyon's nearness. She chatters like a squirrel on Red Bull, about vibrations, crystals and the healing energy of Mother Earth.

I shake my head like I can't hear, and turn in at Center Road, then at Village Loop Drive. "There's not much traffic."

Nellie cranes her neck to try to get a glimpse of the canyon. "The vultures don't show up until their chicks are out of school for the summer."

"Well, that's a little harsh." I slow at the large map of the Village. "Do you want to see the Visitor's Center?"

She looks at me like I suggested she run for congress. "Trinkets and T-shirts and plastic dinosaurs? I want to see the canyon."

"Well, that should be easy enough, it's what, a hundred miles long?"

"Two hundred seventy-seven miles long, up to eighteen miles wide and over a mile deep."

"How do you know that?" A horn beeps behind me and I step on the gas.

"My Jitterbug phone doesn't have internet, so you know I didn't Google it. I told you, I worked a rafting charter." She points right. "Take Yavapai Road."

The road winds, then dead-ends at the Visitor's Center.

"I thought you said—"

"Hang a Louie."

"A what?"

She gives me an eye roll and points left.

I turn onto a paved road about a car and a half wide. It ends at the Yavapai Point and Geology Museum.

"Park here." She points to the lot in front of the museum.

It takes minutes to get her out and up on four wheels. Or, more accurately, two wheels and two chartreuse tennis balls. I head for the building before I realize she's rolling the opposite way. I trot to catch up.

She speeds up a bit, aiming for a wide dirt path that leads to a clump of trees.

I follow, watching my footing for rocks. "We need to—" I bump into her bony back and stop. I close my eyes and pull a lungful of the breeze that washes up from the canyon. The Top Note is dry—I can't place the source, but it smells like hot sunshine. The Heart Note is the Pinyon pine I'm standing next to. But the Base Note . . . I pull in another breath, trying to capture the elusive fragrance. What is it? Not floral, not woody, not—

"Jack. Are you coming?"

Nellie has taken the two stone steps down to the lookout point and abandoned her walker to lean too far over the metal railing. Panic flares down my nerves and my feet almost tangle on the steps. "Stand back—you'll fall!"

The young couple embracing on the other side of the point stare, like *I'm* the strange one.

I reach Nellie's side, grasp her arm to pull her away, but then I look down. "Ohmygod."

The pipe barrier is the only thing between us and the abyss. My heart hammers out S-O-S, as I struggle to take in what my eyes are seeing. The color hits: striations of buff, tan, gold, burnt umber, and a delicate peach, broken by the dusty olive of scrub bushes and evergreens that somehow cling to vertical walls marching to the bottom in broken waves. The walls on the opposite side of the canyon look worn, like ancient battlements, the victims of God's siege.

And at the very bottom snakes the river, bordered by bands of thirsty green plants. The water is ocher from the mud that was a part of the walls, farther upriver. I pull out my phone and snap photos of the panorama.

Nellie sighs. "We ran from Lee's Ferry to Lake Mead. This was one of my favorite places." Her hands are like liver-spotted claws, clenching the pipe. She makes no indication she feels me tugging, and she's not letting go. The yearning look on her face makes me ache. After all, I know that feeling well.

For just a moment, I can almost imagine the woman she was back then. I wonder if she's telling the truth about being a guide. If so, it must have been amazing. I release her arm.

"Back then, they only gave out a few dozen raft licenses a year. The canyon was pristine; you even had to pack out your poop. But damn, what a great time. I took a backpack rod with me, because one of my jobs was to catch fish to feed the customers. Those trout had never seen a lure—maybe not even a human."

"You? Killed a fish?" Nellie is proud of her pacifist status. Though I've noticed it doesn't stop her from chowing down a burger.

"Of course. There's no sin in killing to survive. What I could catch was the only non-freeze-dried food we had."

I don't point out that if they had freeze-dried food, survival was not at stake. I close my eyes to better focus and take in a breath. What is that Base Note? I know I've smelled it be—

"Remember the day when we discovered your gift, Jack?" She's watching me with a fond smile, and it conjures a memory.

When I was young, I believed my G'ma was magic—a sister to Glinda the Good Witch. She even looked like her: dancing eyes, perfect skin and blonde hair that gave a halo-like aura. But that's just a nine-year-old's remembrance.

She breezed in one summer day, showering us with laughter, gifts and kisses. And she did have magic, because she brought the happy back to Mom's face when I'd forgotten what that looked like.

G'ma made food, put it in a bag, and drove us out for a picnic. She drove until the desert gave way to mountains, and we went high into them, then stopped and pulled off the road at a meadow rimmed with evergreens and covered in tall grass, a stream running through it.

We ate, listening to the water talking to the rocks it tumbled over. The sun was warm, the food tasted amazing . . . but what I remember best were the smells. I picked flowers and brought them to G'ma to identify. Their names were as pretty as their scents: Queen Anne's Lace, Alyssum, Sweet Pea, Wild Mint.

She taught me to weave them into a circlet crown, and I played at pairing them until I had a smell I liked best, a combination that magically became something all on its own.

I presented it to G'ma and she made a big deal of it, wearing it the rest of the day. Her attention and approval made me feel the center of the Universe.

And the next day when I woke, she was gone, my wilting crown left behind on the Formica table in the kitchen. It wasn't the only time she left without warning, but it was the one that hurt the most. After that, I learned not to trust magic.

The sweet memory curls at the edges, burning like old celluloid film. "I remember." I pull my phone. "We leave in fifteen minutes."

Her wrinkles cave in on themselves before she turns back to the view.

She's hurt? A coal of old anger flares. "I remember it well. You came in, made things better for a couple of days, and left. You left us. You left *me.* After seeing what shape Mom was in, how could you do that?" The old hurt comes out on the hiss of a snake.

"You may have a fancy degree Jack, but you don't know everything." Her skeletal hands tighten on the railing, the tendons stretched tight.

I warn myself not to ask, but the cold flames are licking the inside of my skin. I grasp her upper arm and turn her to face me. "Then tell me. Because I've tried for years to understand how you could walk out and leave a child with a hopeless alcoholic."

"There are many worse things than that, Jack." She looks up at me, and it's as if a cover has been drawn from over a bottomless well of pain. She turns away.

Wait. What? "What don't I know?" Maybe, if I could understand the labyrinth of family dynamics, I can stop carrying bitterness around in a kid-sized backpack.

I lighten my touch on her arm. "I need to know. Please tell me."

"Maybe, sometime." She gazes down at the river. "This will be my last time to commune with this amazing place."

There's a bong in my chest, like the vibration of a large bell tolling. It sends reverberations through me. "Why, are you sick?"

I see half her sad smile in profile. "Not that I know of. But I promised not to run away again, so unless you're going to bring me out here again sometime . . ." She glances at me, her sad smile still in place. "I didn't think so." She heaves a bone-deep sigh. "I'm ready." Though she has minutes left, she turns from the view and doesn't look back. She almost stumbles on the second stair, and I catch her shoulders. Her back is hunched, it seems more than when we came, and she's not rolling fast enough for the wheels to squeak.

She may be trying to manipulate me, but it'd take a harder woman than I not to have sympathy. When I get her settled into the car, she puts her head back and closes her eyes.

"Are you all right?"

"Sure." She dons the stupid glitter-glasses.

"Do you need some water? I have some in the back." She looks spent. Is this side trip too much for her?

"Stop fussing. I'm fine."

Nevertheless, I stop on my way around the car and pull two water bottles out of the Styrofoam cooler. I get back into the car and realize there are no cup holders. Did they not drink back then? I squeeze the bottles between the seats. It's not worth the put-the-top-up argument, so I start the car and pull out. The sun is warm on my shoulders, and the breeze is fresh and desert-scented.

I take the more direct route, down Highway 64. A half hour later, I steal a glance over. Nellie is sleeping, head lolling, mouth open, and if possible, she looks older—like a wrinkled skull in Hollywood sunglasses. Alarm zips down my spine and I glance down to be sure her chest is moving. Eighty-four is old to begin with, but she has extra mileage. Who knows how much longer she has? The road is straight, and I drive on autopilot, following my rabbit-hole-thoughts.

Where did she go, all those times she left me? I've never looked past the *why* before. Did she have a home? Did she wander the desert all alone? I realize with a start that the thoughts I've had all these years are a child's, which are inherently selfish. I know almost nothing of my grandmother's life.

Like it or not, she's my only living relative. The only one who can tell me what my mother's life was like, growing up. The kind of things that everyone wants to know when they're old enough to realize their parents are people too. Maybe those answers will help me answer questions about myself . . . Or maybe not, but at least I'd know why my grandmother acted like she loved me, then proved she didn't. Because after a while when you eliminate all other possibilities, you come to know the reason had to be *you.*

I still don't know if I can stand the answers, but when you finally get to the end of indecision, there's really only one way left—forward. An idea gathers like fog in my brain, clouding thoughts of anything else.

Nellie comes awake with a snort when I slow at an intersection. "Route 66. Oh, how I love this road . . . so many memories."

"You're mistaken. This is Highway 40."

"They're the same road through here. See the sign?"

Sure enough, both road signs are on the crooked post to our right. And past it, a sign for the town of Williams, one mile. "Are you hungry?"

"Does Jupiter align with Mars?"

"How should I know?"

She snaps her fingers. "Jack, you gotta get with it, girl. Hang a Ralph."

Since left is Louie, I take the other choice. We go under a wrought iron sign that spans the road, declaring the town founded in 1881. Old fashioned buildings pop up on either side, looking like we've taken a turn back to the '50s . . . only shabbier. Every other one is a souvenir shop featuring the Grand Canyon, old movie stars or Route 66.

Nellie's head swivels, taking everything in. "This place was hopping back in the day. More bars per block than almost anywhere."

I pull up in front of a diner with Betty Boop on the sign and shut down the engine. I pull my phone to see a missed call. "I have to check this. Can you get us a table?"

"I'm old, but I'm capable." But she hardly has the strength to push open the heavy car door.

"Wait. I'll help." I scramble out of the low seat and reach for her walker.

She leans against the seat and closes her eyes. "The last time I was here, I was wearing micro minis and tube tops. Now look at me."

I push the door open all the way, wedge the walker as close as I can and steady it.

Her hand closes over mine. "Jack, I know you have priorities. But don't leave living until it's too late. You're young. You're vibrant. You have hormones." She squints up at me. "You think you have forever, but you don't." She squeezes my hand. "Have some *fun* along the way."

Easy for her to say. I don't have someone who'll step in, should I fail. "Come on, up you go." I put a hand under her elbow to help her, and soon she's motoring for the door. She looks a bit stronger than she did at the canyon. "Order me some iced tea, will you?"

A man with a handlebar mustache comes out, tips his cowboy hat, and holds the door for her.

I pull my phone, wipe the car door with a tissue, then lean against it and dial.

"Thank you for calling me back on a Sunday, Ms. Oliver. This is Scott Rodgers from the Perfumers Trade Association."

The Vice President and organizer for the Ultimate Beauty Show? What could he want with me? If you're an indie, the Perfumers Association is Fort Knox. They allow you "Associate Membership," but that's it. Get a booth at the show? Even if I could afford it (I can't) that's reserved for full members. My plan is to walk the show handing out samples and business cards.

Heart bashing my ribs, I swallow and try to pull off nonchalant. "Yes Mr. Rodgers, what can I do for you?"

"Well, I've heard good things about Heart's Note, and I have a late opening in our workshop schedule. I wondered if you'd be interested in giving an hour talk on how to do a successful startup?"

Holy frankincense. That could make a huge—

"I'm sorry, the budget won't allow you compensation, but if you do a good job, we may be offering you full membership. Hit it out of the park, and I'd be happy to introduce you to several buyers from chain stores. What do you say?"

I'm proud of my storefront, and the progress we've made, but hand-selling perfume a bottle at a time will always be precarious. Introductions to big chain buyers is worth more than any sum he could name. "I'd be honored, Mr. Rodgers."

"Great. I have your email from the Association rolls. I'll send you all the details."

"Thank you for the opportunity, sir. You won't be sorry."

"I wouldn't have called you if I thought I would. Good day, Ms. Oliver."

The line goes dead. I can overlook his arrogance, because he can help me put Heart's Note on the map. Shivery sparkles shoot down my spine and my feet do a tiny happy dance on the pavement. We're going to be big-time, I can feel it. I consider for a few moments about the idea I had on the drive, then hit speed dial.

Steph answers, "Let me guess. You're not going to make it in Monday."

"You're not only the best manager in the world, you're clairvoyant. There's been a change of plans. I'm driving to Vegas. I'll need you to send the samples to my room at Caesars Palace."

"Ookay . . ."

She's confused, but I'm not spilling family baggage at her door. I tell her about my last phone call, instead.

"That's incredible. What an opportunity."

"I know, right? Could you include our brochures and a box of my business cards? I'll work on the presentation on the way."

"You got it. If you think of anything else today, let me know. I'll ship it all out tomorrow morning."

"Great, and Steph? Thanks for being someone I can depend on."

"Remember that when my next review comes up."

I smile. "I know you won't let me forget." I sign off and call Caesars Palace. I booked the room weeks ago, but I need to let them know to expect a box.

Now that I've made the decision and have accepted the road I'll take, I step onto the curb and walk to the diner. My other problem sits on a stool at the soda fountain, swinging her feet and eating a massive banana split.

I try not to do the math on how much this trip is eating into my safety net, and perch on the stool beside Nellie. At least I'm saving on a plane ticket, but this road trip will cost more by the time we're done. And my idea is starting to stink like dog poop in the Vegas sun. What was I thinking?

"Here." Nellie hands me an extra spoon.

I eye the melting ice cream. "That would go straight to my hips."

"Jack, I keep telling you, you have to live a little. Maybe if you had some fun, your aura would lighten up." She waves the spoon. "Besides, you could use a little padding." She winks. "Men like a little more cushion for the pushin'."

"Oh my God, Nellie." Face burning, I glance around to be sure no one heard that.

"Why? Are you gay?"

"No! And that is a totally inappropriate question."

"It's fine if you are. I was more the girl side of bi myself for a decade or so."

I choke on my tea.

"I mean, who knows better how to please a woman than—"

"Stop. Just stop." I wheeze.

"Honey, you gotta remember, mine was the free love generation."

I rub my forehead.

Her white, scraggly brows come together. "Do you have a headache?"

"Yes." The biggest one is sitting right next to me. "Among other things."

"Why didn't you say so? Where does it hurt?"

"Right between my eyes."

She spins to her walker and roots in a small, buckskin beaded bag.

"I'm not ingesting anything you have in that filthy thing."

"You don't have to." She spins back and in her hand is a small pot the size of a lip gloss container. "You have a Pitta headache. It's due to an imbalance in your stomach and intestines, brought on by stress."

"Imagine that," I mutter.

She screws off the lid.

The exotic fragrance is unmistakable. "That's sandalwood."

Her face brightens. "You still got it, Jack."

"Stop calling me that."

She dabs the tip of her thumb in the powder. "Here, lean over."

Against my better judgment, I do. She pushes her thumb between my eyes, hard.

I sit up. "What are you doing?"

She rolls her eyes. "Okay, you do it. You press down for three to five minutes, and your pain will be gone."

It's going to look stupid, but surely a little sandalwood and pressure can't hurt me.

"For the next week, no dairy. You need to eat cool foods: cucumbers and dates and nuts for protein."

"When did you become a doctor?" I press harder and relish the brush of cool air on the back of my neck.

"I'm not. I'm a shaman." She kicks her feet like a little girl.

I knew better than to ask. I sip tea, keep the pressure on, and watch in amazement while she devours the remainder of her banana split, wishing I'd inherited her metabolism.

"Okay, you can let go now. How do you feel?"

I use my napkin to wipe off extra powder. "Odd. The headache is gone."

She smiles. "Tonight, I'll rub coconut oil on your feet. You'll sleep like a baby."

No way I'm letting her touch my feet, but I do feel better. "Thank you."

She shrugs. "It's what healers do."

"I have a proposal for you." I study her for a moment. "What do you say to a short road trip? I'll drive you home, but I need to make a stop over the weekend in Vegas."

She claps her hands with glee. "Oh Jack, you've just made me so happy."

"Don't get all crazy. It's only a few days reprieve, and it's going to cost you."

She squints at me like I'm a vacuum cleaner salesman on her front porch. "What do I have that you could possibly want?"

"Your memories. You are all I have of family, and there's so much I don't know."

She tips her head, considering. "I'll make you a deal, Jack. A memory of mine for a memory of yours."

My spine stiffens. "If you'd wanted to know mine, you could have been there for them."

The anguish I saw at the canyon flashes across her face. "I wanted to. I couldn't. Please, Jack?"

I'm getting the short end of this negotiation. I'm taking her, on my dime and I'm only getting a tit for tat memory.

Except her memories are more important to me, and she's not going to like mine, so maybe it's not so uneven after all. "Ooookay."

Her smile is bright as the afternoon sun blazing through the glass door. She studies the paper placemat, a cartoony map of the area. "Can we follow Route 66? There's so much along it I'd like to see again."

I glance at the map. It looks like the edge of nowhere. "What's out there?"

"Only Everything. You'll see." She touches my arm. "You have no idea what a gift this is for me. Thank you."

I tighten my chest muscles, to squeeze out the soft spot on my heart. She only looks like Glinda's grandmother. "I have to be in Vegas for a show next weekend, and it makes no sense to fly home, then back, when we're less than a hundred fifty miles away."

Her eyebrows shoot up. "And we have five days to get there?"

"Yes." If I were a believer, I'd think the Universe set me on this road, bumping me every time I tried to turn off.

Her canny squint makes my stomach jump. "So, you don't care where we go, as long as we're in Vegas by Friday?"

I remind myself I'm getting something out of this, too, if she doesn't tip me into insanity first. Besides, Nellie is right about one thing: this will doubtless be the last chance she has to visit the sites of her wild youth. "That's right."

She squees like a preteen at a Bieber concert, then drops her head to study the map.

I just hope she keeps her delusions and sexual escapades to herself.

Chapter 4

It isn't what we don't know that
gives us trouble.
It's what we know that ain't so.
Will Rogers

I pay for the banana split and my iced tea, and we walk out into the smell of heat, dust and relentless sunshine. I pull my sunglasses from my purse. I'm more used to soft-cotton-overcast—nocturnal compared to the searing spotlight overhead. Nellie puts on her Hollywood pair.

I glance up and down the street. "First thing, we need to buy some clothes. I only brought one change, and you had to have run through the few in the pillowcase."

She veers left. "Oh, I'll bet I can find some groovy stuff here."

"Please God, no tube tops," I mutter.

"Not for me. But you'd look adorable. Wonder if they have any with sequins?"

I'll just bet they do. This town is more hooker than Hermes. Nellie stops at the souvenir shop beside the diner. I push the door open, and a little brass bell jangles against the glass door. Every available surface is jumbled with junk. Above, neon poster board signs declare:

Pre-summer Sale!

Last Route 66 souvenirs until the next shop!

YES – *we have* ***ELVIS!***

I step deeper into the explosion of the trite, tawdry, and tasteless, wondering how I'll ever find anything to wear here.

"Oh, look, Jack."

I turn at Nellie's awed tone.

She's standing in front of a display of lava lamps, each belching a different color goo. "You haven't lived until you've spent an hour in front of one of these, tripping and listening to the Revolver album."

"I'll take your word for it." They're cheap enough. "Do you want one?"

She looks at me like I don't get it. Which, of course, I don't. "I learned a long time ago not to own more than I can carry. That crap ends up owning you, Jack. Trust me on this." She squeaks off down the aisle.

Spare and clean, there's one thing we have in common. Of course, mine came from growing up in filth and chaos. Nellie probably ran away from a nice suburban neighborhood with picket fences and iced tea served on the porch on warm evenings. Wait, where *did* she grow up? I suddenly realize two things at the same moment—that I know very little about my grandmother, and I'm not sure I want to know more.

"We hit the motherlode!"

A table in the back is covered in tie-dye. T-shirts, shorts, even leggings, in a jumbled mess of colors and sizes.

"And it's on sale!" Nellie turns to me, the glittery stars catching the light, her face a wrinkled picture of delight. "What size do you wear, Jack?"

I take a step back. "I'm not wearing that."

"Well, look around then. I saw some T-shirts with dogs playing poker on them, over there." She points.

"Very funny." I walk away but it takes me all of two minutes to know that there's nothing the least bit better than the tie-dye table. Don't get me wrong, I can thrift shop with the best, but—

"Jack, hey, Jack!" Nellie's voice comes from the plywood cubby in the back with a bilious green shower curtain pulled across it. She shoves the curtain aside with a rattle of hooks. "What do you think?"

She's in an eye-searing yellow T-shirt, tied up to her bony waist on one side, exposing matching tie-dyed tights that sag like the skin on a pachyderm.

"Why are you so big on tie-dye?"

"When you get as old as me, you kinda like wearing things that make you feel good. Besides, all styles come back around, right? I'm just ahead of my time!" She cackles.

"Seriously? Is your whole goal in life to be noticed?"

A wince flickers on and off her face, lightning fast. Maybe some of my darts *do* hit home.

"My goal in life is to be happy." She raises one sparse eyebrow. "Isn't it yours?"

"Touché."

She turns to look at herself in the cheap mirror in the "dressing room." "Well, I like it. I'm buying it, and I'm wearing it out of here." She pulls up her walker and rolls on, leaving me to pick up her discarded clothes. "You don't even have a T-shirt yet, Jack."

"I haven't seen anything I would wear."

"We could try somewhere else, but these places are usually owned by the same person, so the stock will be the same."

Why didn't I just fly her home? At least I could find clothes in Palm Springs. "Oh, all right, hang on." I march to the psychedelic section and pull out the most sedate navy-blue shirt I can find in my size. When I pull it out, I see a glimpse of black material underneath. I pull out a pair of plain black leggings. And they're my size. "There may be a God after all."

"There are many." Nellie puts her nose in the air and cruises by. "Now, footwear."

"You have your high tops. I have these."

She looks down at my taupe heels. "Oh, they won't do. This is the desert. You need sandals. Follow me."

Knowing the odds of finding anything made of leather here are as likely as finding a brand name that wasn't manufactured in Taiwan, I follow anyway.

Nellie stops at a wire bin overflowing with rubber flip flops. "We're in luck." She claws through the pile, looking for the match for the yellow daisy adorned hot pink one in her hand. "Come on, Jack, dig in."

I sigh, soothing myself with the fact that I'll never run into anyone I know here. I dredge up a blue pair with a red plastic rose in my size. I tear off the roses, slip out of my shoes, and—

"Jack, there's hope for you yet." Nellie points at my feet and winks. "Your nails have clear polish, but hidden away, there's whimsy."

I look down. My face heats. My toes are a delicate shell pink, with a red hibiscus on the big toes. "The pedicurist did it while I was reading, and I didn't have time for her to do it over."

"I think it's the tits."

I shoot a look around. "No, those are toes, and please don't refer to my—"

She snaps her fingers in front of my nose. "You gotta get with it, girl." Then turns and rolls for the check stand, leaving me to gather her purchases along with what dignity I have left. I pay for everything, and we leave.

Nellie looks up at me. "Did you mean it? I can decide what's next?"

"Where we go, yes. Not necessarily what we do." God knows what we'd end up doing if I gave Nellie the lead.

She smiles. "Great. I want to spend the night here."

"I'm not sure there's—"

"There's a hotel right there." Nellie points down the street.

It looks like a motor lodge from the '60s. I can only hope it's not original. The neon sign out front reads: *Hot as Hell Motel.* I frown down at her. "Seriously?"

"Where's your sense of humor, girl?" She rolls on.

As I suspected, the ambiance of the place is original. I get us adjoining rooms complete with identical metal keys on neon plastic tags. You may not be able to smoke in the rooms now, but stale funk of long dead cigarettes oozes from the walls and carpet. I drop the bags on the bed. "Do you want to take a nap?"

"Nah, let's hit the bar."

I raise an eyebrow and she shrugs. "Like Jimmy says, 'It's Five O'clock Somewhere.'"

"Is he a friend of yours from the retirement home?"

She shakes her head. "Never mind. There used to be a great place, two doors down. Let's check it out."

I glance to the alarm clock on the nightstand. I'll go, have a soda and keep my eye on her.

The *Patron* is a small adobe structure with tables out front. There's no air conditioning; fans are moving sluggish air in the dark interior.

"We want to go out back." Nellie says to the young waitress.

She leads us through a door to a dirt area shaded by dusty trees and the smell of sage. Small tables are surrounded by a twisted grape stake fence. We are the only ones here.

Nellie orders a pitcher of Sangria, and I order a soda. When they come, she pours, then raises her glass. "To peace in our lifetimes. And barring that, another piece in mine."

"Nellie Oliver, I am not drinking to that."

"Suit yourself." She drinks, then smacks her lips.

There is fruit floating in the red-purple concoction. "That looks good."

"Want some?" She pushes the pitcher to me.

"You know I don't drink." But it looks so refreshing. "Can I have the fruit?"

"Knock yourself out."

I sip my soda and eat the tidbits of fruit. I have no small talk, so the silence stretches like spandex. Might as well ask what I want to know. "That man that you say you traveled with in the minibus. Is he my mother's father?"

"What?" She rears back in her seat. "No. Easy and I came through here in '61. He was long gone by the time I got pregnant."

I try to wrap my brain around the fact that G'ma's imaginary friend was a real flesh-and-blood person. I shake my head to refocus. "Then who was Mom's father?"

She looks up at the spindly tendrils from a bush that hang over the fence. The lilac-blue flowers are beautiful. "These are the Sophora secundiflora, the Texas Mountain Laurel. The natives used the beans in ceremonies. The leaves help stomach

ailments and earaches. But you have to be very careful, because
—"

"So, you're not going to tell me who my grandfather is."

"A memory for a memory, remember? You want to tell me one?"

I shake my head.

"Then have some more of this fruit. Did you know that a Western with Frankie Avalon was filmed in this town?"

The deep throated growl of big bikes pulling up outside drowns out whatever I was going to say next, and in a few minutes, the waitress comes through the door holding aloft two pitchers of beer, four biker dudes trailing. She seats them at a table across the small yard, but they're close enough that I can smell motor oil drifting off their leathers. The biggest, a sweat-stained bandana around his forehead, pours a mug of beer and raises it in a ham-hock fist to us. "Ladies."

Nellie raises her glass. "Dudes! Did you ride in from Oatman?"

What is she doing? They've probably seen prison time. I glare while trying to find her foot with mine under the table to get her attention.

The one in a black leather vest displaying massive hairy arms says, "Nah. Came up from Prescott."

"That's cool." Nellie settles in for a chat, and I finally find her foot and tap it with mine.

When I have her attention, I give my head a slight shake and mouth, "Don't."

The one with his back to us in a, "If you can read this, the bitch fell off" T-shirt, turns. "We'da gone to Oatman, but I've got a big case tomorrow, and LeRoy here is buried in tax returns."

Nellie gives me a "so there" smile. "Yeah, workin' for the man is a bitch, huh?"

"Can't say that. I've got my own company." Mr. Bandana says. "But my boss is an asshole."

They laugh, then thankfully fall into conversation amongst themselves.

"Nellie, they could have been gang members." I whisper-hiss across the table.

"Nah." She pours more Sangria in her glass and using a spoon, nabs more fruit and slides it onto my plate. "Do you have any idea what a Harley costs nowadays? Besides, those are Ariat Bison leather boots," she nods at Bandana Man's feet. "$600 a pop."

The sun is warm on my shoulders, not too hot, just perfect. The scent of the drooping Mountain Laurel branches fills my head. I'm suddenly and inexplicably happy to be right here, right now. "This is nice."

"Told you. See what happens when you don't plan every minute of every day?"

I have no intention of doing this often, but just for now . . . My muscles are slack, my mind has gentled, and my stomach is cool and quiet.

From the speakers comes a blast from the past: *Under the Boardwalk.*

Across the table, Nellie smiles. "Remember?"

I have to smile back. She taught me to dance on the ratty shag rug in our living room to this song.

"Come on." She tips her head to the open area. "Let's dance."

"Yeah, right." But when she stands, my peace is shattered. "Wait, I'm not getting up in front of—" I shoot a look to the bikers.

"Oh come on, Jack. No one in your little circle will know."

"No!" Just let me melt into the dirt under my feet.

Mr. Bandana stands and walks over, hand out. "May I have this dance, Miss?"

Nellie giggles like a girl at her first dance. "I'd be delighted."

They step to the middle of the patio. He spins her, and they begin the steps she taught me so long ago. Step, step, slide, turn, dip, step, step . . .

It should look ridiculous. He's six-feet-four and built like a refrigerator, she's a five-foot-nothing fragile octogenarian. But it's not. They move like they've been dancing together forever. He handles her as if she's made of glass.

I realize my foot is tapping. And I'm smiling.

When it's over, he leads her back to our table. Nellie looks up at him. "You dance like a dream."

"My mom taught me." He bends over and kisses the back of her hand. "Thank you. That was special." He walks back to his table to the catcalls of his friends.

Nellie is glowing.

"You looked wonderful out there. Kinda made me wish I'd taken you up on it."

"Well, come on, girlfriend." She stands.

"No, no. I think we've had enough excitement for one day. Let's head back to the hotel."

My shoulder clips the doorframe on the way out. The sun is setting in a blaze of golden orange. "Look Nellie. Isn't it pretty?" The sun must have really taken it out of me today. I feel muzzy and a bit off kilter.

Nellie watches me over her shoulder. "You've got a buzz on, Jack."

"I most certainly do not. I had soda, remember?"

"The fruit absorbs the alcohol; it's deadly."

I narrow my eyes. "And of course, you failed to tell me. You sneaky little—"

She shrugs. "Don't you feel better? Like you fit better in your skin?"

"I feel—" A wisp of a scent twines with the base note of asphalt and gasoline. Not sage, not mesquite . . . it's a bit more floral, but not much. "What *is* that scent?" I step into the road to align the sunset with the converging parallel lines of the road. It's beautiful. I pull out my phone and snap a few photos.

"Come on, Jack, you're holding up traffic."

"Oh, excuse me." I say to the waiting car, then follow Nellie's winding trail back to the hotel. My mind is unfocused, my stomach has cooled, and my muscles are slack on my bones. "This is kinda nice."

"See what happens when you fluff out your panties a little?"

I make a sound, then slap my hand over my mouth when I realize it's close to a giggle.

"We should get some dinner."

She stops at her door. "There's some cheese doodles in my room. Come on over."

I stifle a yawn. "I'm going to take a short nap. Then we'll go to dinner."

Sometime later, I fight my way out of a nightmare of Vegas and open my eyes to darkness. The smell of the room's desperation has settled into my sinuses, into my mind, sending me into a panic until I remember what year it is. The red numerals on the alarm clock: 1:00. Wow, some nap. I flip on the bedside lamp, sit up, put on my shoes and walk to the door in the wall to Nellie's room. The kiddie lamp is dim, but from the sodium lights streaming in the open window, I see she's not here.

The dragon in my stomach breathes fire. "Shit, Nellie," I mutter, stepping out to the parking lot. "What now?" This is beginning to feel like my past—every time I turn around, she's gone. I step into the night. No walker, no Nellie. I follow the breezeway beside her room to the back of the hotel.

The full moon reveals Nellie, sitting in a flaking paint metal lawn chair beside a broken birdbath.

"What are you doing out here in the middle of the night?"

"Can't sleep."

An orange coal floats like a firefly in the dark, and the smell of pot hangs in the still air.

"That is not legal."

"It will be in January."

"January is nine months away."

"Trust me, Jack. They are not going to arrest an eighty-four-year-old woman for toking a doob." She pats the arm of the flaking chair beside her. "Come, sit."

It's useless to argue. Besides, this is tame compared to some of the stunts she's pulled. "Why can't you sleep?" I brush off paint flakes and sink into the chair

"There'll be time enough for that when I'm dead."

Nellie's always been relentlessly cheerful. A thread of melancholy in her voice sends alarm jangling down my nerves. "What is it?"

She takes another hit and passes me the joint. I wave it away.

We sit until cicadas start their rattling thrum in the brush.

"Today, you asked where I grew up."

I'm afraid if I say anything, the spell will be broken so I nod and settle in to wait.

"My father was an Okie sharecropper when the dust bowl hit. They had no money, but it didn't stop the babies coming. I was number six, in '32, and my brother Joshua was last, six years later. It was bad, and fixin' to get worse."

Nellie isn't known for truthfulness, and I minored in history. "But things were getting better. The dust bowl was over in '36, and the depression ended in '39, with WWII. The economy improved."

"So smart." She takes a hit of the joint, squinting through the smoke at me. "You gonna listen to a history book, or somebody who was there?"

1942~

By 1934, we'd made it through three dust bowl years, thanks to a deep well, and Daddy building a mesh fence around Momma's truck garden to keep out some of the blowing sand. Everyone hauled water to the garden every day, except me and Joshua. We were too little to lift a bucket.

Momma put me in charge of her huge flock of chickens. I hate chickens—stupidest things on the planet. I still get satisfaction, every time I eat one. The danged things saw me comin' with an apronful of feed and charged, pecking at my legs and feet. I'd drop my apron and run. Scared the bejeezus out of me.

But the store traded Momma for eggs, which bought gasoline, and in the winter, shoes so the older ones didn't walk to school barefoot in the snow.

By the fourth year, the sky only rained sand, and when the well dried up, we were done. Even terrorist chickens need water.

Daddy kept that old Ford truck running all the way to Oklahoma City, us kids in the back, perched on everything we owned. He was good with his hands and mechanical things, but most farmers had flocked to the city earlier, taking what jobs there were. He worked a day here and there, but there was nothing steady to be had. The older kids quit school to do odd jobs and, I expect, stole from street vendors. Somehow, they all kept us from starving.

When America went to war, Daddy was one of the first to sign up, figuring he'd have money to send home. Momma told him it was more important to keep the family together, but Daddy said his people came from England, so in a way, he *was* helping family. He kissed her at the station, told us to be good, and stepped onto a train.

After he left, Momma got a job in a chicken processing plant (more damned chickens). We lived in what I know now was a tenement. It was smelly and drafty, but I thought it was fun, with lots of kids running around. Not that I didn't have responsibilities. Momma was exhausted by the time she got home after dark every day. I was only nine, but I kept house, watched my little brother, and boiled whatever was brought home for dinner.

One evening there was a knock at the door. Momma opened it to a man in a green wool uniform with a hat tucked under his arm. He said Daddy died in a place called Bataan.

Funny, I always thought Momma was the strong one, barking orders, keeping us in line. Daddy was the quiet one, and sweet. But that night, when her knees hit the floor, there was a loud crack, like when a dried bone breaks. It was the sound of our family splintering. Turns out, Daddy was the marrow that held the family together—kept it alive.

Momma still went to work every day, but she was like one of those wind-up toys, jerky and aimless. She'd speak only when spoken to and gave one-word answers. But it was her eyes that spooked me—those fake Momma-eyes—empty and dead. She hadn't given up when we left the barren, sand covered farm, or when she saw the narrow, one bedroom "apartment" that we could barely afford.

I hadn't known there was worse than giving up. It was like she was already dead, but she didn't know to lie down yet. We treated her like one of her eggs, careful not to be loud, or happy, for fear she'd look around and realize she *could* lie down. Then where would we be?

One day, months later, she came home and sat us all down, saying she'd gotten a letter from her mother. We were moving to Minneapolis. Arthritis put Grannie in a wheelchair, and she needed help.

We looked at each other, surprised at the flow of words as much as the news. We'd never met our Grannie, but crippled or no, maybe she could take charge and put a little life back into our family.

I never got the chance to find out, because the day before we were to move, Momma packed up me and Joshua, and drove us in a borrowed car out to where the city gave way to the country. There was a big old brick building with a dingy sign that read: *Children of Charity Orphanage.*

She shut off the car and we stared through the windshield while she told us that Granny didn't have room for everyone. The older children could work to support the household, but we were too little. I told her I'd do the cleaning and take care of Joshua, just like I always had, but she just shook her head. I could see it was no use arguing. Joshua cried, and I admit I did some, too.

When she turned to us, for the first time since Daddy died, I saw a glimpse of my old Momma. There were tears in her eyes and her hand shook when she took mine and pressed something into it. "My Saint Anthony medal. He's the patron Saint of travelers. He will keep you safe."

I didn't know how a chunk of steel could take over her job of keeping us safe, but I stared at the silver circle of a man carrying a child on his back while she explained that she had no choice. We were to be good, and she swore that someday we'd see her coming back down the road to get us.

Not even Joshua believed that one.

ele

When Nellie falls silent, I shift in my chair, thoughts shooting through my brain too fast to catch. My grandmother lies, but this story has the hefty weight of truth. Besides, could she make this up? To what purpose? I can't afford to suspend disbelief around Nellie, but for now, I believe. "So, did she?"

The words break her spell. She turns to me. "What?"

"Did she ever come back for you and your brother?"

"That was the last I saw of her, and the rest of my family, to this day."

God, how horrible. "You mean when you were grown, you never tried to find them?"

She looks out into the trash-littered weeds and shrugs. "Why would I? Their path was different than mine."

My grandmother is always sunny. How selfish was I to never look beneath it? I'm aching for those kids, for that poor woman, having to make an impossible choice, then living with it for the rest of her life . . . for my grandmother. "What was the orphanage like? Where is Joshua now?"

Nellie heaves a heavy sigh. "Another time. I'm tired. Will you help me?"

Her voice wavers, and in the two days—God, could it have only been two—since I've been with her, she's never seemed weak, or asked for help. I jump to my feet. "Of course." I help her stand, and holding an elbow, lead her through the breezeway to open the door to her room. "You should have taken the walker. If you had fallen out there . . ." I wait for her to snap not to fuss over her, but she says nothing.

I turn down the covers while she sits at the bottom of the bed, taking off clothes. She pulls a hot pink T-shirt out of her bag that reads: *Sexy AF.* "You owe me a memory now, you know."

"Tomorrow." Maybe she'll forget. I help her into bed. Her pallor is ghostly in the light of the bedside lamp. My hand strays to touch her cool forehead and trail down her cheek. "Are you okay now?" Unexpected tenderness slips out with the words. No matter what she did later, Nellie was once young, and abandoned. Someone may be able to turn away from the old pain etched into her face, but that person is harder than me.

"Yes. Goodnight, Jack."

I reach to turn off the lamp, but her hand stops me.

"Leave it."

"Okay. Sleep well." I stand, walk to the window and grab the crank.

"Don't close that!" Her words are fast and urgent.

We're on the ground floor. It's not safe. But I'm not upsetting her more. "Good night." I walk through the door between our rooms, leaving it wide so I can hear if she calls in the night. Or if someone climbs in the window.

I take my time getting ready for bed, but I know after I lie down, my wind-tossed emotions won't allow me to sleep. I've always thought of myself as an honorary orphan, since I had no Dad, and Mom was . . . Mom. But Nellie was *abandoned*. The melancholy lodged in my chest burns like a swallowed ice cube. But then I realize what that means. She must have known *exactly* how I felt when she walked away from Mom and me.

Aloneness settles over me like a weighted blanket. I feel like the only person awake on the planet. I check my phone. It's past two. Too late to call Leo, even if I hadn't told him we were through.

We met at a showing at the Momentum Gallery, one of Seattle's most prestigious. Leo is a metal artist. A good one. He uses small leaves of steel to capture nature; animals, mostly. On display was a six-foot-tall draft horse in traces, captured mid-pull. The lights on chrome created the illusion of movement, and I could feel the animal's straining in my chest. On the wall, a tree bent in gale force winds, shedding a trail of yellow and gold metal leaves. He is so talented. He's also intense, unpredictable and untamed as an animal in the wild—a cheetah maybe, or a panther. His messy loft doubles as his workshop, and it smells of acetylene, stale Indian food, and our lovemaking. I'm uncomfortable there. Yet I find my mind wandering to striped sunlight on messy Sunday morning sheets and lazy breakfasts spent discussing the Op Ed pages of the paper.

But I know what happens next. He'd want things. Close, know-you-down-to-your-soul things. Things I want so bad that the ever-present hollow in my chest expands, squeezing my lungs, making it hard to catch my breath.

I've tried before. I let go my precarious handhold on a vertical cliff to reach for another's. I barely survived the fall. The memory of the pain, the shame, was a powerful lesson. It's like once I've touched a red-hot stove, my instincts won't allow me to touch it again, no matter how I long to.

I have no right to call. Even though he said we'd stay friends, it's selfish, and I know it. I dial anyway.

"Hello?" There are no sleepy edges to his voice.

"Are you working?"

"Hello Jack. You know I get my best ideas at night."

His warm tone flows over me, and I lay back, picturing him in his loft, working on . . . "What are you working on?"

"I'm making a life-sized man in full armor, made of small leaves of many shades of green. I'm calling it, Twenty-first Century Man."

"But leaves as armor? That's not much protection."

"See? You get it. Now, tell me what's happening with you. Are you home?"

"No. Through the most messed up series of events, I'm on a road trip with my grandmother."

"I didn't know you had a grandmother."

Of course not. I never let anyone in that far. "I don't. I mean I didn't. No, I mean—"

"Sounds like you've worked yourself into a corner, Jack."

At his deep chuckle, a picture flashes of us late at night, talking in bed. A flush of heat spreads across my chest. Maybe it's the dark, or the memory but for some reason, I tell him an abbreviated version of the past days' journey, right up to what brought me to this cheap hotel in the desert.

The last thing I remember is his deep, soft voice flowing over me in the dark.

Chapter 5

Be kind, for everyone you meet is
fighting a hard battle.

Plato

Monday~

The next morning I wake more refreshed than since I left Seattle. But I'm having late-night phone call regrets. I take my phone from the pressboard nightstand.

Me: Sorry to disturb your work last night.

Leo: I'm glad you did. I told you to call anytime.

Me: But then I fell asleep while you were talking. It was rude.

Leo: You were relaxed and knew you were safe with me. Not complaining.

Me: Well, thanks for understanding. Have a good day.

Leo: You too. No pressure, but I'm looking forward to another installment of your trip.

I click out. I was selfish last night, taking what isn't mine. We're not dating any longer, and it sends conflicting messages.

It's too early to call work, so I pee, then make myself check social media.

Looks like Jacqueline Oliver from Heart's Note is giving a workshop. Should be a steaming pile. #UltBeautyShow

Why ask an amateur like Oliver to do a professional's job? #Wannabe #UltBeautyShow

What the heck? My stomach burns. I check the profile, but it's generic and probably fake. It sounds like a full member, but surely they have better things to do than trash an indie. I'm a bit surprised Heart's Note hit someone's radar. A tweet won't make a difference, but a new business sure doesn't need any bad press.

I close out and shut my laptop and tiptoe to the open door between our rooms.

Nellie is sitting at the desk, playing cards. Except she's not. She's staring intently at the cards on the table, her raised but unmoving hand holds another. I can see enough to know this is not an ordinary deck.

"Good morning."

She starts, then sweeps the cards to her and shuffles them. "Hello, Jack. I've been waiting for you. Come, sit."

I glance down at my bare legs and sans bra T-shirt. "I'm not dressed."

"I won't call the fashion police, promise." She pats the card-table chair beside her.

"What are you doing?" I step to her and sit.

"I want to do a reading for you."

I recognize the tarot deck from a commercial I saw on TV once. Nope. No crazy before caffeine. "I'm good, thanks." I push back the chair. "We need to eat breakfast and get on the road."

"We have all of sixty-five miles to go today." She rolls her eyes and keeps shuffling. "I'll do a three-card reading. It won't take long."

I shake my head.

"Oh come on, Jack. If you don't believe in it, how can it hurt?"

Trapped by Nellie's logic? I lost normal down the road somewhere. I settle on the edge of the chair. "Oh, fine then."

"The Dude is going to help me."

"What Dude?"

"My spirit guide. I told you about him. He's leaning on the doorjamb right behind you."

I can't help it. I sneak a look over my shoulder. Nothing, of course.

"He's saying that you don't need to believe for the reading to be true."

"Thanks, Dude."

Droll rolls off my grandmother like rain down a window. She lays the cards on the table. "Cut them once."

I do.

She points to the second stack. "Now, one more time."

Once I do that, she gathers the cards and fans them in front of me. "Choose three cards, then lay them face down on the table."

Pick a card, any card . . . says the sideshow barker's voice in my head. I'll give her ten minutes, then I'm getting in the shower.

I lay three cards on the table, and she puts down the rest, shoots me a meaningful look that I don't know the meaning of, then touches the first one. "This card will tell you something about your past."

"I already know that."

"It can reveal what you learned from your past."

I know that too, but pointing it out will extend the foolishness, so I let it go.

She flips the card. The picture looks Egyptian, with Sphinxes crouched below a guy in a golden bucket. The title at the bottom is *The Chariot.*

"It's upside down." I reach for it, but she pushes my hand away.

"That's called reversed. And it changes the meaning."

"Which is?"

"Upright, it's a strong symbol of perseverance. Being one hundred percent in control. In this position, it means that in your past you felt out of control. Defeated."

My turn for an eye roll. "You think?"

She taps the card with a fingernail. "Tell me one of your memories from back then."

"It's too early in the day for—"

"You owe me one, remember? You're not going to renege on our deal, are you?"

I squirm, my thighs sticking to the plastic chair. I want to leave the past buried, where it belongs. I made a bad deal after all.

She puts a hand on my bare leg, and I jump. "Just a quick one. The first one that comes to your mind."

She's not going to like it, but she asked for it. "In the third grade I was invited to a classmate's birthday party. I wasn't special; she invited the whole class." The wall has become a movie screen, and my memory is the feature film. "She lived in a real house, with a yard and a dog, and a bedroom all to herself. Her mom was pretty and young and . . . anyway, we played games in the big back yard that was covered in grass so green it almost hurt to look at it. We ate pizza and cake. It was so fun."

Nellie's soft smile ignites a spark of anger that shoots through me, fast and hot. "Things were winding down, and parents were showing up to take their kids home. The grown-ups were standing on the patio chatting when Mom came around the corner of the house. 'Well, isn't this sweet?' She said, too loud. Her dress was tight and shiny, and her hair was all a mess, her lipstick smeared.

"She'd been drinking. My stomach went jittery.

"The other women turned to her, their eyes went all big. Mom's spiky heels dug in the grass as she wobbled her way to the patio. 'Which one of you is Ms. Rayburn?'

"The birthday girl's mom stepped forward. 'I am. And you are?'

"Mom turned and pointed to me. 'I'm Jacqueline's mom. Hi Baby!' She waved, all big and loud. 'You having fun?'

"The other mothers called to their kids, saying it was time to go. I trudged to the patio, my guts slick with grease and getting hotter by the second.

"Mom leaned in, 'Thanks for inviting her.'

"Mrs. Rayburn leaned back, lips peeling from her teeth in something that was probably supposed to look like a smile but wasn't. 'Happy to have her.' There was a tiny emphasis on the *her*.

"Mom's face went tight. 'Sorry to be late, but I had to work.' She raised her arms, waving at the house, the yard, the neighborhood. 'Some of us little people do that, you know.' She said in a fakey-syrupy voice.

"'Mom. Let's go.' I grabbed her hand, desperate to get out before something bad happened. I didn't pull, but she was unsteady to begin with. She swayed and one of her spike heels stuck between the patio bricks. Over she went. She hit hard on her hands and knees, her dress sliding up to her tiny red silky underwear. 'Goddam it, Jacqueline, now look what you did!'

"Everyone froze in shock-filled silence, except for the indrawn breaths.

"Mom flipped over and tried to stand, but she was like a turtle on her back, all scraped knees, elbows and underwear. After what seemed like forever, one of the women helped her up.

"My head buzzed like there were bees in it. I stood, sick and mortified, hoping it wouldn't happen . . . but it did. I threw up pizza, soda and cake all over the patio, and several ladies' shoes." I look away, breaking the newsreel on the wall. "Needless to say, that was the last house I was invited to."

Nellie's eyes fill with empathy. "Thank you for sharing that."

My stomach is queasy, just recalling it. "Oh, hang around. I've got a million of 'em."

"The Dude says that your past built your strengths you rely on today."

"Well, lucky me then, huh?"

"Which brings us to the 'present' card." She flips the second.

Even upside down, the card is scary. A black and white drawing of a skeleton on a skeletal horse, waving a scythe, jaw open in a scream. As if I couldn't figure it out, DEATH is in heavy print at the bottom. "Well, that can't be good."

Nellie grins at me. "The Death card is wonderful. Very powerful. Reversed in the present position, it stands for immobility, slow changes, a narrow escape. In a word, you're stuck, Hon."

No shit, Nellie.

"The Dude says that all you need to do to be free is to let go and move to the brighter future that's just waiting for you."

Sure, because letting go is the reverse position of my super-power.

She puts her hand on the last card. "This is your future." She flips it over.

It's a hand coming out of a cloud, holding a stick. Below it, "Ace of Wands," in script. I have no idea what that means, but at least it's upright.

"Ahhhhh." Nellie says, in a doctor reading-test-results voice.

"What? What does it mean?"

Her eyes sparkle. "For a non-believer, you're awfully interested."

My cheeks heat. "Just trying to get this over with. I want a shower."

"This is a perfect card for your future, Jack. The Ace of Wands is a card of creativity. You will be daring and brave and take risks. It shows that now is the time for passion. A time to trust your potential and go for what you want."

My heart rises on a cloud of hope, until I remember this is Nellie, and nothing Nellie says can be trusted. I push out of my chair. "I'll see you in fifteen, and we'll find some breakfast."

I walk away from her know-it-all grin.

Twenty minutes later, I'm ready. When you only have three changes of clothes, it simplifies things. I slather moisturizer everywhere. Arizona makes me feel like a grape in a dehydrator. "We need to get a few more changes of clothes . . ." I step into Nellie's room.

She's dressed and sitting at the end of the bed, bag of clothes at her feet, shoulders slumped, staring at the floor.

Seeing my irrepressible grandmother . . . repressed shoots a bolt of worry to my stomach. I take two steps and sit on the bed.

This rouses her. She looks up, a smile on her face. "I'm ready."

I put a hand over her gnarly, spotted one. "You're sad. Won't you tell me why?"

She shakes her head. "It does no good to dwell on what is gone. You learn the lesson then move on."

The truth slips around my misgivings and out of my mouth. "But it would help me to know." I'm willing to risk opening myself to Nellie if it means filling the holes in my past. "I know it's selfish but it matters a lot to me. Please? What happened after your mother left you at the orphanage?"

She sits long enough that I think she's going to refuse. Then she starts talking in a faraway voice; as if she's telling me *from* that place, so long ago.

1942~

When there was nothing but a shimmer of dust where Momma's car had been, we turned to The Children of Charity Orphanage; a large, old, drafty Victorian. Joshua said it looked angry, scowling down on us with dark windows, rotting boards and flaking paint. I thought it just looked tired. I took his hand and told him not to worry; I'd never leave him. Then we trudged up the steps.

They had to take us in—Momma was long gone. I know it sounds horrible, Momma leaving us, but it was far from rare back then. Parents didn't want to give up their kids, but when the only other alternative is watching them starve, who wouldn't have chosen the same?

The system wasn't set up to handle the volume of young bodies. There weren't enough beds, enough matrons, enough food . . . enough anything.

A harried woman took us through the front hall and back to a dorm room. They were all dorm rooms really, with some cots, a few bunkbeds, but mostly straw pallets on the floor. There weren't any empty ones, so they gave us some straw and burlap bags, and I made them up for Joshua and me, butted up against each other. She gave us each a half a blanket; holey, scratchy smelly things that must have been army surplus from the first World War.

It was bedlam. Kids ran around, chasing each other, yelling, crying, huddling in corners, staring out windows. Some of the older girls tried to help, but they too were overwhelmed. Joshua and I watched from the musty straw bed.

A ringing bell announced dinner and everyone ran to line up in front of a Dutch door to the kitchen, where a fat, sweaty woman in a gray stained apron spooned soup into bowls. Another handed them out with a spoon each. We got in the long, jostling line and eventually made our way to the front. The soup was almost clear, with an oily film, and a few small bits of cabbage and carrots floating in it.

We took them to our pallet and when Joshua finished his, I gave him half of mine. He was small for his age, and prone to croup, especially in winter. I wanted to build him up, because I knew the place would be cold in a month or two. I always considered him more my baby than Momma's, anyway. I made a silent vow to keep him safe, and that we'd leave this place together someday soon.

Breakfast was oatmeal. I don't know if the cook considered the mealworms protein, but we ate it, wigglers and all. It was better than the pain of an empty belly.

I thought about taking Joshua and leaving in the middle of the night, but where would we go? At ten, I couldn't pass for old enough to get a job, and winter was coming. So we learned to negotiate the place—how to stay away from the bullies and the thieves. We even made friends with a few. Some of the older girls helped with the little ones, and I did, too. There was no school; the matrons had their hands full just corralling and feeding us. The days ran together, and before I knew it, there was snow on the ground.

They tried to keep the temperature livable inside, but the old windows leaked cold air, and when the winds howled, the drafts at floor level were more like frigid breezes. I wrapped myself around Joshua at night, and learned to sleep through his shivering, and my own.

The kids on cots fared better, but it was jungle-rule and the bullies were the top of the food chain. I fought them and lost. I kept trying, especially after Joshua developed a barking cough with a fever—croup. I was desperate and tried again to commandeer a bed, but they knew I was coming and ganged up on me. Bruised and scraped, I kept trying until I finally won him a place by the radiator during the day. I gave him most of my food, but he got worse. He wasn't alone; we all learned to sleep through coughing all night. There were no doctors, no medicine.

Christmas came and went, with only seconds at dinner to mark the day. Joshua weakened. His fever warmed me at night. I went to the matrons, telling them I'd do anything: clean the outhouse, sweep the ashes, carry water—if only they'd bring a doctor. They were sorry but told me nothing could be done. There was no money for doctors.

I don't know the date, but I know it was in February the day I woke to find that Joshua didn't. They buried him in the cemetery on the grounds, and his wasn't the only fresh grave.

We wouldn't be walking out of there together. I'd failed in my vow to keep him safe.

When Nellie trails off, I sit for a minute, waiting to see if she'll go on while she studies the worn green carpet. I have so many questions, but don't want to force her back to her memories by asking them. I can see what visiting them cost her. She looks shrunken—frailer than she was.

Ten years old and blaming herself for something she had no control over. "Many people failed your brother, but you weren't among them." I swipe a tear for that little girl, and even younger little boy. "You know his death wasn't your fault, don't you?"

"Yes. But understanding and knowing are two different things, aren't they?" Her eyes are haunted.

"Yup." Like knowing as a child you're not responsible for your mother but taking care of her anyway, because someone had to. And I ultimately failed, just as Nellie did. My grandmother and I have more in common than I could have imagined a week ago.

I put an arm around her bony shoulders and squeeze. "Thank you for telling me. Now, are you ready for some breakfast?" I try to put some lilt in my tone, but lead-weight of the past weighs it down.

"That would be groovy." Her standard, all-in smile is firmly in place.

Before today, I never wondered if that grin was fake.

Chapter 6

One more day, one more time
One more sunset, maybe I'd be
satisfied
But then again, I know what it would
do
Leave me wishing still, for one more
day with you.
Diamond Rio

I have to admit, the road to Seligman is beautiful. Green hills and rust colored plateaus circle grassland studded with scruffy brush that aren't as pretty as the names Nellie told me: Pointleaf Manzanita, Fourwing Saltbrush, Desert Broom and Beebrush.

"How do you know all the names?" I yell over the wind, since Nellie still insists on keeping the top down.

"I've lived out here all my life." She turns to me, the glitter on her silly sunglasses flashing. "I'll bet you know the plants in Washington."

Um, no. But I'm beginning to think that if I did, my life would be richer. I need to try stepping out of my work/home/work routine. Jitters shoot through me, making my fingers dance on the steering wheel. It's one thing to know I should make changes, it's another to actually make them. Routine, hard work and discipline are what saved me. Black and white is my comfort zone—the true north I steer by. The place in-between makes my stomach burn. I don't do gray.

"Why don't you let me drive?" Nellie waves a spindly arm making her bracelets rattle. "There's no one out here."

We haven't seen another car since we left Williams. What harm can it do? But I'll have to be careful. Softening around my grandmother isn't wise. I pull off the road and when I brake, dust rolls over us. "Why you insist on keeping the top —" A scent fills my senses and I'm out the door in a second, following my nose before I remember that I'll need my phone to take photos. I go back and snatch it from my purse. "Do you smell that?"

The car door squeals, and she climbs out and limps the few steps to me. "Yep."

I snap a photo of the landscape. "Do you know what it's coming from?"

"Nope." There's a twinkle in her eye. "But let's find out."

"You sure can't take your walker out there. You stay in the car." I tip my chin to the flat grass covered plain.

"I'm not made of glass. Let's go."

I sigh. She's not going to listen to reason. "If you break something, you're going to be sorry."

She walks into the knee-high grass.

"Wait." I offer my arm, and she takes it, leaning into me.

She looks down. "Mind your feet. Flip flops aren't appropriate in rattlesnake country."

My heart triphammers and I freeze. "You're making that up."

"Nope. But don't worry, rattlers give you plenty of warning. You smell, I'll watch. I think it's coming from over there." She points.

I inhale. It's a violet-tinged scent, but has an earthy base note . . . Sage, maybe? My nose leads me to a squat, twisty-branched tree. I shoo a bee away to smell the small, pink and variegated purple ruffled bloom. That's the delicate violet scent. "Do you know what this is?"

Nellie squints up at the tree. "Ah, desert willow. I guess I've never seen one blooming before." She fingers a flower. "Beautiful."

"It is." I snap photos, and pull a few flowers to press in a book, to remind me of the scent. "But there's more." I look around. "I'm smelling sage."

"Well that one's easy." She points to a plant with dusty leaves with tiny lavender flowers. "Texas Sage."

"But we're in Arizona." I snap more photos.

"Plants don't recognize human-created boundaries, Jack."

Duh. My mind is whirring. "But there's something else. I'm smelling a hint of honey." I take a few steps.

"Wait for me, Jack. I'm your snake scout, remember."

I retrace my steps and take her arm. "Sorry."

"You're like a scent-hound. Everything goes out of your head when a smell hits."

"Thanks for the flattering simile." I grumble, but inside, happiness bubbles like champagne. It feels so damned *good* to be out in nature, using my nose again.

Nellie's twinkling smile tells me she knows. "Told you. You just needed to remember your first love."

I can't help but smile back—this reminds me so much of our first time, in that mountain meadow. "Come on, G'ma. Let's find that honey."

"Now *there's* my Jack. I knew she was still in there somewhere." She chortles, taking limping steps.

When I realize I just called her by her old nickname, for some stupid reason, tears rush to my eyes. "Don't let it go to your head." I blink them back.

The honey turns out to be from what Nellie calls Brownfoot, a terrible name for a pretty plant with pinkish purple flowers. I snap more photos and pilfer a few blooms.

When I turn, Nellie is standing eyes closed, head thrown back, arms outstretched, chanting. "What are you doing?"

"Thanking the God of the Sun."

I glance around. "Better send one out to the snake God, too. Ask him to keep his minions away for five more minutes." I take one of her outstretched hands. "Let's not push our luck."

I lead her back to the car and help her into the driver's seat. After hearing her horrible childhood memories, it makes me feel good, doing something that makes her smile.

But I can't afford to trust her.

"Hang onto your butt, sista, we're outta here!" Nellie twists the key and the beast starts with a rattling roar. She shifts straight to second, floors it, lets out the clutch, and it spits gravel. When the car hits asphalt, it shimmies, the tires squealing for purchase. She slams it to third.

"Slow the hell down, Nellie!"

"Go Duchess you old broad!" She raises both fists in the air, "Woo hoo!"

I grab the wheel. "If we live through this, you are *not* driving again!"

"Ah you gotta let your tits flap in the breeze every once in a while, Jack." But her foot lightens on the gas.

We're about a mile down the road when steam puffs from under the hood.

"Uh oh." Nellie downshifts, letting it coast until we bump off road. Dust boils up when we stop. She shuts it down.

I spit grit and scan the empty road ahead and behind us. "Dammit Nellie, it was that burnout you did. I just know it."

"Hey, I was channeling Steve McQueen there for a minute. Hold the drama. I may be able to fix it."

"Oh yeah, probably." I pull my cell. "I have zero bars and we haven't seen a car in a half hour." I glance at the spiny brush, and all that sand. "We could die out here, you know."

She rolls her eyes. "Have a little faith, Jack." She tries to open the door, but it's stuck.

Not likely. I crawl out of my side, walk around and wrestle her door open.

Using the car for support, she walks to the front and when she pops the hood, steam billows out.

"Be careful you don't burn yourself." I hustle over.

"Give me some credit, Jack." She ducks her head in.

I scan the road, but it's as empty as the landscape. We could be in real trouble here. We're miles from anywhere on a map.

"Oh, I see the problem. Fan belt's busted."

"Crap. Wait, what does that mean?"

She squints up at me. "You don't know what a fan belt is? Where have you been all your life?"

"Within cell range of Triple A, thank you very much."

"Grab some of those bottles of water and let me think a minute."

I walk to the trunk and pull three plastic bottles from our stash. I hope she doesn't need more, or we could die of thirst out here. I slam the trunk and walk to the front.

"You have pantyhose, right?"

"What in the world—"

"When you picked me up in Show Low, you were wearing hose. Were they pantyhose, or garter belt?"

"I beg your pardon. I hardly think this is a time to discuss my taste in underwear."

"We could have a discussion about it, but if we do, we'll be out here longer. Just tell me."

"Pantyhose."

"Good. Get 'em. But I'll need your help."

I don't waste more time asking. I make another trip to the trunk and return with the goods. "What are you going to do?"

"Lucky for us, the Duchess is mature enough not to have serpentine belts. We'd be screwed." She pats the grill, then holds out her hand for my nylons.

"Okay, what do I need to do?"

It takes grunting and a bunch of swear words, but in twenty minutes, my pantyhose have been knotted together and taken the place a fan belt. I pour the last of our water into the radiator. "If this doesn't work, we could die of thirst out here."

"Not hardly." G'ma points. "The desert willow needs a water table to survive. We'd have to dig, but there's water." She drops the hood and slaps her palms together.

I've got to admit, Nellie knows things. Pitta headaches, car maintenance, desert botanist, diviner of the tarot . . . I've got to admit, I'm a little in awe of her. If I were alone, I'd be wailing at the injustice of it all, weaving around, phone in the air, trying to get a signal.

"Now let's fire up this old bitch and see if she can make it to a town."

"How long will the pantyhose last?"

"Depends if you bought an expensive brand." She peers up at me. "Didn't think so. Hey, at least we'll be closer, right?" She feels her way to the driver's side.

I trot to grab the door. "No way. I'm driving. It's your Fast & Furiousing that got us in this mess."

"And it's my MacGyvering that got us out." She puts her nose in the air, drops in and scoots to the passenger side.

"You know MacGyver?"

She shakes her head. "One thing old fart warehouses are good for is catching up on old TV shows." She raises an eyebrow. "Nothing else to do."

"Let's not go there." I depress the clutch. "Pray to the God of Mustangs or whatever."

Nellie closes her eyes, and I fire the engine. It starts. "Well, I've gotta hand it to you Nellie, I'm impressed. You're a wonder."

"'Bout time us old girls got some respect, eh, Duchess?" She pats the dash. "Now hit it, before your pantyhose get the chance to heat up for the first time."

"I'm ignoring that." I check the mirror, because it would be my luck to pull out when the only other car on this God-forsaken road came by.

Thirty minutes later we pull into the dusty desert town of Seligman. I drop the car off at the first gas station with a mechanic we come to. The guy says he's got the belt (miracle) and can get to it in an hour.

"We still need a few more clothes to get us to Vegas, so let's do that while we're waiting." At least it's not far to walk. I grab Nellie's walker from the back of the car.

The two block "Historic District" is studded with tourist-trap shops in old buildings.

"Easy, will you look at this place?" Nellie waves at the old buildings lining the street. "Damned vultures." Her mouth turns down. "What was wrong with the businesses that used to be here?" She points to a wooden façade on a brick building. "That was the Sundries Building. They kept the name but stuffed it with tourist-magnet crap." She points straight ahead. "They tore down the train depot. Used to be a Harvey House."

"Seriously?"

"Yep. This was a railroad town. But the railroad died, and all the young people want I-40, because they're in a danged hurry all the time." She glares at me. "Then they used Seligman as a blueprint for that cartoon, about the abandoned cars." She makes a sound deep in her throat. "Ruined the place, Easy. Just look at it."

It doesn't look much different to me than Williams: tawdry, tacky, and tired. But I'm not saying that when she's in a mood. "I guess they figured it was better than the town dying."

"Humph. A ghost town would be better."

The sundries store has no better collection than Williams, but we pick up a couple T-shirts with a Route 66 road sign on them.

"We need hats." She rolls down the aisle away from me.

"I don't."

She sighs. "This is the desert, Jack. The sunscreen isn't going to keep your scalp from burning, you know."

That makes sense, I guess. We find some surprisingly cute off-white Panama hats—if you ignore the hatbands with the obligatory Route 66 emblem. I choose a black band, Nellie, true to form, chooses Pepto-Bismol pink.

Luckily the mechanic is done when we return, so we gather the car and are rolling out of town when a bright red brick building appears on the right. A sign proclaims it, "The Roadkill Café—you kill it, we grill it." I slow. My stomach growls. "You want something to eat?"

"I'm surprised at you, Jack. Two days ago, you wouldn't have put a foot inside a place like this."

I pull into the parking lot. "It's a small step above the possibility of starvation."

"Cool beans." She rubs her hands together. "I wonder if they have a fudge brownie caramel sundae?"

"They might." Won't hurt to put some padding on her bones. "Let's check it out."

We walk past the inevitable gift shop and the pool table to a dining area set up with small tables. I sit with my back to the stuffed animal heads on the wall, but that puts me facing a dusty stuffed coyote with a bird in its mouth. Nasty, but I'm hungry enough to be a bit envious of his last meal.

The menu has gross but funny entrees: Flat Cats (pancakes), Armadillo on the Half-shell (breakfast burrito) and Guess that Mess (breakfast skillet). I order two eggs scrambled, and dry toast. Nellie settles on Turtle Innards—a three-scoop sundae with raspberry, caramel, and chocolate syrup.

At ten-thirty in the morning there are few diners, and none next to our table, so I decide to ask. "You know, I did some research online a few years back. There are tons of Olivers, but I can't find a line that traces anywhere close to us."

She fidgets with her glass of water. "That's because Oliver isn't my given name."

"What?" When diners heads come up, I lower my voice. "You mean to tell me that my last name isn't Oliver? What, do you have aliases? Are you a spy or something?" I thought being a virtual orphan was bad. This makes me feel like I don't even exist. Or that my existence is a sham I didn't know I was part of.

"Don't be silly, of course not. It's legal." But she doesn't look up.

"I'm entitled to an explanation." I push the words through my clamped jaw.

Her face is sad—a decades-long kind of sad. "Oh Jack, haven't you learned that what you're entitled to has little to do with reality?"

But her sad doesn't douse my outrage. "Seems I should have. I've had ample opportunity."

As usual, my sarcasm doesn't seem to touch her. "I'll try to explain. But down the road a piece."

"I want to know now."

"You also should have learned that what you want doesn't influence reality." Her face is closed, but relaxed. The words may spark my anger, but not hers.

Lessons in reality from a woman who sees spirit guides? This is too much. "Am I allowed to know my real name, oh bearer of all knowledge?" I twist the paper napkin in my lap.

"My parents were Rose and Walt Collins."

"My name is Jacqueline Collins? I share a name with a sleazy Hollywood romance author? That's just cruel. Why would you let my mother name me Jacqueline?" I pause while the waitress delivers our food. When she walks away, I lean in and hiss, "Why am I just learning this now?"

A spoonful of glop poised on the way to her mouth, Nellie looks into my eyes for the first time. "Not everything is about you, Jack." She takes in the ice cream and closes her eyes in bliss.

"Oh, I see. The last name I've used my whole life isn't mine, but it's not about me." I know I sound like a petulant teen, but frankly, I *feel* like one.

She shrugs. "When would I have told you? Before these past days, when's the last time I've seen you?"

The dart hits home, popping a pocket of old bitterness. I'm so *pissed*, but if I speak now, I'm going to vent my frustration, Nellie will clam up and I'll never know what other land mines

lie in my past. I straighten, close my eyes and take deep breaths
to try to calm down.

"That's right, Jack. Find your center. Let your inner peace
flow over you."

I chew anger with my eggs, and swallow, hoping both will
stay down. Why did I ever think this was going to work?

I'm not going to be the first to break the silence. The only
thing I want to hear from her is a reasonable explanation. Yeah,
like "reasonable" and Nellie Oliver—Collins—have ever been
used in the same sentence. I bolt my breakfast, pay, get her in
the car, and head out to the nothingness of Route 66. The
warm wind pulls at my head scarf. Next stop, I'm putting up
the top, no matter what she says. She may have bought this
disreputable bucket, but I'm in control, dammit.

When I decided to explore the holes in my past, I didn't
realize they would be studded with Punji stakes. If I'd known,
would I have embarked on this crazy trip? Doesn't matter. I'm
in it now, and it's starting to feel like Groundhog Day. Only
hotter, drier, grittier.

"Slow down."

"For what?" I snap, but I take my foot off the accelerator.

"It's right along here somewhere."

"*What* is?"

"The reason I changed my last name. Here. Turn here." She
points to a dirt trail that leads into the desert.

I slow to take the turn. The path is two dusty tire tracks,
wandering off to nothing. "I doubt there's a cell tower within
ten miles. If we get a flat out here, we'll be stuck for sure."

"Don't I know it. You can stop now."

I park at a bare space in the brush, just big enough to turn
the car around. I turn off the engine, praying it will start again.

We're well off a road where not many people travel, in a desert filled with snakes and God knows what.

We sit, listening to the wind rattling through the sage. I finally glance over to see Nellie swipe a tear.

She's staring at the bare dirt of the clearing. "Have you ever loved someone? I mean a best-friend-forever-adoring-soul-mate kind of love?"

The truth pops out. "No."

Another tear slips into a cheek wrinkle, but she gives me a wan smile. "I hope someday you allow yourself to experience that." She looks out over the landscape. "I know it's frustrating for you. I'm telling you everything in fits and starts and out of order, but some things take time to find the words for." Her voice drops to a raspy whisper, "And some things, there *are* no words for."

Her tone sends a shiver zipping down my spine, raising the hair on my arms, despite the heat. What could be worse than what she's already told me? "Wait. Are you saying that you've never talked about your past? Ever, with anyone?"

She shakes her head. It's a sad shake.

"Surely you have had friends along the way." I don't want to know if all the years I ignored my grandmother, she was alone.

"Of course I did. Friends, teachers, students, and other seekers like me. Hundreds of them."

"Then why—"

"None of them needed my past to help them find their way." She looks at me with faded, wise eyes. "You do."

I get a hit of gratitude, followed by the slice of irritation that she thinks I need her.

But of course, I do.

1962~

His real name wasn't Easy of course, but on the commune, everyone had a made-up name. Mine was Blue.

The others saw him as shy, serious, brooding. But to me, he was special from the start. His stories aren't mine to tell, but I'll just say that we'd both come from hard times and unkind people. We recognized the scars in each other that were invisible to everyone else. We came together like heat-seeking missiles, lighting up the sky. There was no need to fake anything; we got each other on a cellular level. We sustained each other.

He became my alpha and omega. I'm not being dramatic. I'm just telling you, so you understand what came later.

I suppose if we'd been more social, we'd have fit in better on the commune, but the others seemed so silly. Talking about peace, saving Mother Earth and fighting the "establishment," but never doing a thing that would make that happen.

After six months or so, we realized we'd be better off alone, so we took off in his VW camper-van. We spent our days driving The Mother Road, our nights getting high and making love under the stars. That was the closest I've come to Nirvana on this plane.

But after a few months, Easy was falling into what I called his black funk. He'd stare at nothing for hours on end, not responding no matter what I tried. All I could do was drive on, until he came out of it. Sometimes they lasted hours, at worst, days. I'd seen them on the commune but he'd been better since we struck out on our own. But they were back. Scared me spitless.

We were in Albuquerque when he told me he had something to take care of. He dropped me at a grocery store with money, and said he'd be back in an hour or so.

He returned with a secret. See, up til then, we'd known *all* each other's secrets. But he refused to talk about this one. I was hurt, and it pulled us a little apart. We traveled on, and I tried to forget about it.

It seems odd to me now that I never wondered where Easy's money came from. He just always seemed to have it. We must have traveled the western route of 66 three or four times. There were other roads of course, but we claimed this one as ours. If we enjoyed a place, we'd stay a few days, looking up the history and local plants in small town libraries.

May twenty-first, nineteen sixty-three we came here, to this place. It was a day like any other, as this place is like any other. Easy was relaxed and happy, so I was too. We set about making camp, laughing and chatting. I cooked, and when the sun went down, Easy lit a fire and we pulled our camp chairs around it. A typical day.

We had one unshakable rule. If one chose hallucinogens any given night, the other smoked only pot, to be able to help in case of a bad trip. Because of our pasts, bad trips were worse for us. Not that we'd had many—not enough to stop tripping, anyway.

Easy had scored some Mescaline in town, and I was dying to try it. I figured that since the natives used Peyote in their ceremonies, I might have a vision. I had a vision all right. I was out of it for four hours, staring at the Milky Way, looking for the meaning in God, and his meaning, in me. It was spectacular.

When I came to myself, Easy was slumped in his chair across from me, asleep. But when I built up the fire enough to see . . . he wasn't asleep. He was gone, an empty orange plastic bottle of downers at his feet. I tried mouth-to-mouth for the longest time, but he was gone.

I lost it. I screamed at God until I had no voice. *Why?*

When I became aware again, the fire had burned down. I went into the van, where I found the answer to my question. A note in Easy's handwriting, and a thick envelope.

I've tried to forget what it said, but I can see it when I close my eyes:

Blue,

I know you won't forgive me for leaving you. I'd like to say I don't have a choice, but suicide proves me a liar, so I'll just say it: I'm not strong enough to stay with you. Know that nothing you could have done would have changed this. You are the one shining light in all my life. You know that, just as you know that love is too weak a word for what we've shared.

But the dark has come for me, as I've always known it would. I can't fight it any longer. You have always been the stronger part of us; I know you'll fight on.

I hope to see you again—in the whatever-comes-next. In the meantime, you must keep healing, growing, and loving for us both from now on.

You'll hate me even more for what's in the envelope—my only secret. It won't make things okay, because only you have that power, but at least you won't have to wear stolen shoes, ever again.

Please forgive the one who loves you still, and always,

Reginald Oliver Strathmore IV

Always, your Easy

Chapter 7

You're going to be fine.
You're from a long line of lunatics.
Unknown

Nellie falls silent, and I couldn't speak if I wanted to. Easy not only existed but meant so much that she carries him with her still, talking to him every day. I try to imagine that kind of loss, and realize I have no reference point to do so. I've never experienced a love like that. Never let anyone matter that much. Never *needed* anyone for my existence. Trusting someone with your *soul*? Just the thought shoots red tracers of terror into my bloodstream. My way is better. Safer. How could Nellie have survived that soul-rending grief? I swipe a tear. I don't want to take her back there, but I have to know. "What was in the envelope?"

"His legal will." She pulls a tissue from the glove box and blows her nose. "He left me three point two million."

My jaw unhinges. "Dollars?"

"His family was old money San Francisco." She turns to me. "It's all gone now. But it allowed me to live free all these years." She sniffs. "I'd rather been penniless and had him."

I believe her down to my gut. No one could make up a story like this and the anguish on her face can't be faked. "I'm so sorry, G'ma." I reach to put my hand over hers on the seat, wishing I could do more to ease the old pain in her eyes.

She gives me a watery smile. "Thank you, Darlin'." She pats my hand, pushes open the door, and before I can scramble out, stands, and lifts her hands to the sky to chant.

Who am I to disturb a prayer? I sit, determined to stay for hours if that's what it takes. Her level of grief demands it.

After a few minutes she kisses her fingers and carefully bends to touch the dirt. Then she turns and hobbles to the car. "Now, let's blow this sad, sad place, and see what the Universe has for us down the road."

I let out a grateful breath when the car starts on the second crank, and I drive back to the "Mother Road." A few miles farther on, there's a faded billboard that announces the "Grand Canyon Caverns." That would be fun to see, and a tourist moment might be a way to bring the sparkle back to Nellie's eye.

I turn at the sign for the caverns.

"What are you doing?" Nellie jerks to watchfulness.

"We're not in a hurry, and I thought it would be nice—"

"No." She shakes her head. "Not that."

"Why not?" I brake to a stop in a parking space. "This is one stop in this wasteland that I'd like to see."

"You want to see it, go." Her shoulders are hunched, her fingers clench the armrest like she's afraid I'll drag her from the car. "The Duchess and I will be right here."

My irritation dissipates like smoke in a wind. "What is it, Nellie?"

"I don't like closed-in places."

"Why not?"

She looks so small and for the first time, vulnerable. This morning has taken too much out of her. I'm not pushing, and I'm sure not leaving her in the car alone. "Okay, we're off." I put the car in reverse.

"Thank you, Jacqueline. You always were a good girl."

Old bitterness boils in my gut, but I'm letting that pass. There's been enough heaviness today.

After miles of rolling empty miles, a gas station comes up on our right, and I pull in. "We need gas."

Nellie's head snaps up from her chest. "I've gotta pee."

"Well, all right, then." I pull up to the empty gas pumps.

She dons her sparkly sunglasses and lifts her chin. "Kybo, Baby."

I'm not even asking for a translation. If it's about a bathroom, I'm sure I'm better ignorant. I get out, retrieve her walker, and she totters off.

I pay, insert the nozzle into the gas hog's maw, and glance around while the tank fills. Wind blows dust, ancient bits of trash, and small tumbleweeds across the tarmac. This place feels like a tiny manmade spot on the vastness of the desert.

When the nozzle clicks off, I hang it up and head for the office to see what's taking Nellie.

I'm perusing a dusty display of aspirin, eyed by a grizzled geezer in a grease-smeared T-shirt, when Nellie walks out of the bathroom.

She waves a hand in front of her face. "You may not want to go in there for a while."

"That yer goat?" The old guy says, looking out the window.

I follow his line of sight. "What the hell?" A large, dirty black and white goat stands in the back seat, happily munching

Nellie's Cheese Doodles. I run through the door and out to the car. "Shoo!" I wave my arms and try to look menacing. "Get out of there, you mangy cur!"

Nellie's walker squeaks up behind me. "A dog is a cur. A goat is caprine."

Unconcerned with semantics, the goat dips his head in the bag and comes out chewing, a sprinkling of orange doodle-dust in his grass-stained beard.

I am at a loss as to how to handle this. I put my hands on my knees and pant in shallow breaths.

"He must be your spirit animal. Can we keep him?" Nellie pats the goat's rump and it farts.

I put my hand over my mouth and gag.

Nellie cackles. "Like Ben Franklin said, 'Fart for freedom. Fart for liberty. Fart proudly' Dude." She turns to me. "So? Can we keep him?"

"Don't be ridiculous. Help me get it out of there."

"Well, you know, I'm not so steady on my feet . . ." Her voice turns tremulous.

I glare at her. "Really?"

A smug smile curls the corners of her mouth. "Really."

I'm not touching that thing with my bare hands. While the beast munches, I snatch tissues from the box on the floorboard, stretch them between my fingers, then push it on the hip. It turns and looks at me with unsettling alien eyes.

"Baaaaah."

"I'm with you, Dude." Nellie says.

I poke again, and this time when the head swings around, it tries to nip me. I jerk back, a strand of orange saliva stretching from its mouth to the tissue. "Erg." I gag and drop the tissues.

Maybe the guy in the office . . . I turn to see a hand flip the "open" sign to "closed."

"Oh, for fuck's sake." I look to the heavens. "Am I the only adult in this entire state?"

No answer.

How did I come to this? I'm a business owner. A city-dweller. What do I know from goats, for Chrissake? I stand for a moment, trying to find a solution. None come to me. But I've got to do something. "Fine. So I've stepped into the back gates of hell." I open the passenger door. "Get your skinny ass in."

"Yay! What do you want to name him?" At my expression, she sobers and gets in.

"Buckle your damned belt." I slam the door, close the walker, and careful not to touch the beast, slide it in the back seat. I stomp to the driver's door, and with a mighty heave and a squeal of hinges, open it, slide in, fire the engine, and peel rubber out of the parking lot.

There's an angry bleat from the back seat, as the goat scrabbles for footing.

I smile an evil smile and floor it. A mile down the road though, revenge has worn off and I'm wondering what gets *caprine* excrement out of upholstery.

A horn sounds behind us. An ancient sun-burnt car belching exhaust gets larger in the rear-view mirror. In a moment, he's alongside.

"Pull over!" A man older than Nellie waves a skinny arm.

"Make a run for it." Nellie yells from the passenger seat and flips him the bird.

"Pull over or I'll have you arrested for goat-napping."

Oh thank you. My hero, in a rusty ranchero. I pull to a stop in the gravel, and a cloud of dust rolls over us.

He pulls ahead, stops and gets out, a hank of twine trailing from his fist. His face is red, and he's mad enough that I half expect smoke to roll out of his hair-filled ears. "Good thing

Herb at the station called, or you'da made clean off with Ralph." He glares and walks by me.

Ralph?

"Come on, we're goin' home. Belinda's comin' in heat. You got work to do, son."

The car bounces as Ralph vaults out of the back seat. The man loops twine around its neck and it parades, head high, past my door.

"Bah."

He puts the goat in the passenger seat, and when he drives off, another cloud of dust envelopes us.

I look over at my grandmother. "I want a drink."

Peach Springs is tribal headquarters for the Hualapai, but there's not much more there. Valentine and Hackberry are next, but they're virtually ghost towns. I'm thankful for signs of civilization when we reach the outskirts of Kingman.

Nellie's sparkly sunglasses turn my way. "Let's stay here for tonight. Tomorrow I'll take you out and show you something special."

"If it's special like today, I'll take a pass. What is it?" I scan the side of the road for a decent hotel. I'm sick of fleabags.

"It's a surprise. But trust me, you're going to love it."

Trusting Nellie isn't in my best interest, but the goat encounter took the fight out of me. I'll worry about tomorrow, tomorrow. I've got to call work, then I want a drink. I'm starting to get the draw of a cocktail every evening, but there's no way I'd allow myself that. The memory of my mother's downfall is too strong. But how often do I have to survive a day like today? I pull in at a national chain hotel that is two stars short of five, but a big step up from the garish cinderblocks we've stayed in so far.

"Oh, they have a pool!" Nellie claps her hands.

"Do you have a bathing suit in that pillowcase?"

"Jack, don't you know anything? You can skinny-dip after midnight."

"I've never seen a sign to that effect." We pull in under the portico in front of the office.

I now know Nellie well enough to know she's rolling her eyes behind the sunglasses. Whatever. "Let's get a room and relax."

We check in, and Nellie is napping by the time I call my office. As every day, Steph insists everything is fine there. I pull out the blooms I pressed between the pages of my novel and inhale the fading smell of hope. Given enough of these, I could extract their essence, and enhance it . . . I pull up the outline of my presentation and get to work.

"Jack, you ready for dinner?" Nellie's head pops in the door between our rooms.

I look up, shocked to see that two hours have passed. My stomach growls, and I put down my pen. "Yes, let's. I'm starving."

"Are you working again?"

"I'm working always." I snatch my purse and walk over to hold the door for her walker.

This hotel has a bar attached. One of those generic, cave-like places that serve booze all day, attracting spouse-cheaters and alcoholics. Depressing, but I want a drink more than ambiance. The waitress leads us to a high-backed vinyl booth, and I slide in, trying not to wonder what the dim light hides.

Nellie orders a whiskey highball. I order a Sangria. Without fruit. When they come, she clinks my glass. "May all your highs and lows come only in the bedroom."

I take a deep sip, and sigh. "I've been looking forward to this."

"I like hanging out with you, too."

Not what I meant, but I don't correct her. "We have to be in Vegas Friday morning. That's all of a hundred miles. What do you want to see between here and there?"

"Depends on tomorrow." She takes a sip and smacks her lips. "That's some good shit, right there."

"Where are we going?"

She wags a finger. "Still a surprise."

"As long as it doesn't involve goat-wrestling."

"I wouldn't think so, but I never rule it out, either." Her eyes narrow. "Have you ever let yourself go and just have fun, Jack?"

I straighten. "I most certainly—"

"What *do* you do for fun?"

"I go to the theatre. Classical concerts. I go to art shows. You know, things like that." Leo's rumpled morning hair and sleepy smile float through my mind.

Nellie touches the end of her nose and tips her head back. "Well, la-tee-da."

"Hang on. Who are you to judge me? I've worked hard for what I have, and just because I don't know how to goat-wrestle —"

"Now, now, don't get your tinsel in a tangle." She waves the waitress over and orders refills.

I'm about to argue that I'm not done with my first, when I look down and see that I am. "Can you bring some menus, too?" I don't want a hangover like the last time. The waitress nods and walks away.

"I'm talking about letting your hair down and trying something new. Something different. Something you've never done before."

My turn to narrow my eyes. "Like what?"

"Doesn't matter what." She waves a hand. "I'm talking about expanding your horizons. If you only do the same things all the time, how do you know what you like?"

"Because this way keeps me from doing things I won't like."

She raises an eyebrow. "No one ever died doing things they didn't like, Jack."

She wasn't there to clean up the aftermath of the alcoholism tornado that tore through our lives. "Maybe not, but I spent years doing things I didn't like, and I don't recommend it."

"Being afraid isn't any way to live, Darlin'."

Seeing the pity on her face, the pilot light of anger that always burns in my chest flares. My spine snaps straight. "I grew up afraid. You had millions of dollars. You could have fixed it. Or at least seen that there were groceries in the house." I spit the words. "But you went your merry way, doing whatever made *you* happy. Every. Single. Time." My finger hits the table with the last words.

Her voice is calm, as if trying to soothe. "Things happened the way they were meant to. You and your mother needed each other."

Words of outrage, shock, anger pile into my mouth, all trying to get out at the same time.

"Think about it, Jack. Your mom needed help. You're a doer. You've always had busy hands, even when you were little. Without a purpose, there's no telling what trouble you'd have cooked up—you may even have ended up on your mother's path." She nods. "The Universe puts people together for a reason. Your childhood made you the successful businessperson you are today. It taught you discipline, money management, and how to survive hard times."

My jaw drops, spilling all the unsaid words onto the table. It takes me a few seconds to gather them. "Well, that theory manages to absolve you very neatly, doesn't it? I bet it's easy to not feel guilty when you can blame the Universe for all your shortcomings. Aren't you worried about your Karma? You left me to flounder with the monster you created. Surely your 'Universe' won't reward you for it."

She looks down at her drink. "The path I was set on was different."

"And believing *that* helps you live with yourself."

She turns her glass in precise, one-quarter turns. "Oh, I have many things to live with."

"As do I, Nellie. As do I." If looks were daggers, my companion would be a bloody rag, but I'm not missing my chance to get answers. "Why Vegas? How did we end up there?"

"That was your mother. She came from between my legs fighting, and never stopped." She looks up at me, her eyes sad. "In that way, you and she are alike. That's the Scorpio in you —you end up stinging yourself as often as others."

"I do not."

"You do child, by not allowing yourself to experience life." She shakes her head as if to clear it. "But you asked about your mother. She was a wild-child, running around the commune barefoot, like a wild horse, strong, beautiful, untamed. Then the hormones hit, and she got uncontrollable. She was determined to be a dancer. She had a natural grace, but no patience with hours of tedious practice; she wanted to leap off a cliff and fly. So she did, the minute she found a man who would take her.

"It took me a while to find her. I tried New York and L.A. first. By the time I got to Vegas, the man was in the wind, and she was dancing in a strip club on the seedy side of town." My grandmother looks up at me. "She was pregnant."

The knowledge hits like a boulder in a rockslide, rearranging everything I've ever known. "Me?"

"You."

"The man who took her there was my father? Who was he?"

"Yes, and I don't know. She was about to graduate high school and was working in an ice cream parlor in town. She met him there, and they arranged to leave behind everyone's back. I never met him."

Something she sees in my face softens hers.

"Don't concern yourself with him. He was only in your mother's life to give her you." She reaches to pat my hand. "How can you doubt that things happened just as the Universe had planned?"

"More cop-outs to absolve *everyone* of responsibility." I throw up my hands. "If I'd bought into that, I could have walked away and left Mom in her vomit."

"Ah, but you wouldn't have." She taps a finger to her temple. "The Universe gave her a steady, responsible doer. Do you think that was by accident?"

"Good thing too, huh? Because her mother sure as hell wasn't. You'd waltz in, play Glinda the Good Witch for a couple days, then blow out of town. This is the biggest load of horsecrap I've ever heard."

"You don't have to believe it for it to be true." She flips open the menu. "What looks good to you?"

"That's it? Subject closed?"

"Jack, the past doesn't hold the answers you're looking for. Let go of the pain, you'll be free of your past. You then can look to the future."

Bitterness sheets my stomach in acid, and I push my drink away. I'm tired to death of this woman, her guiltless philosophies and endless absolution of sins. "You get what you want. Have them put the bill on the room." I scoot out of the booth to stand. "I'm going for a walk."

"I'll get you something. You can have it later."

I'm already steaming for the door.

Her voice comes from behind me. "Oh, and now you owe me two memories, just so you know."

Blinking like a subterranean creature, I push through the lobby door into the orange and gold desert sunset. I cross the parking lot to the road, and head west. How did I come to this? In the middle of nowhere, in leggings and a cheap T-shirt, my hair brittle, my skin dry, stuck in a rusted-out beater reeking of goat, with a woman related to me, yet so different she could be an alien.

For a time, I just walk, my stupid flip flops smacking my heels with every step, inhaling the oily smell of hot asphalt. It takes about a mile for the tide of anger to go out, exposing doubts. Nellie, though irritating and full of BS, isn't all wrong.

I spent my life after Vegas, climbing out of that precarious past. But I have to admit, I spend a lot of time being anxious about falling back into it. Which, when I think about it, is silly. Even if my business were to fail, I'd be all right. I'm not that homeless teen with nowhere to turn. I may fall, but not that far.

Never again.

Could Nellie be right? If I could let go of the pain and bitterness of my past, would I be free? Or would it still follow me the rest of my life, like a violet-tinged shadow?

I don't know, but I'm beginning to think this may be a choice.

Unable to focus, I give up trying to work at nine. Unable to relax, I give up trying to sleep at midnight. There are more nasty tweets about my shop, with the hashtag #UltBeautyShow. Another *why* I don't have an answer for. I'm not big enough for this kind of attention, and I have no enemies that I know of in the industry. My brain is on an agitate cycle: the business, for sure, but the memories, the new information about my name, my mother and my grandmother are like a red sock thrown into a load of whites, staining everything with its color.

I know what would help. Calling Leo. But that's not fair— I'd be using him, and we're broken up. Still, the thought tugs, urging me to pick up the phone. He did say I could call anytime . . .

"Ah, my late-night lady." His voice is smooth and calm, like a balm spreading over my chapped mind.

"Can we be friends?"

He chuckles. "You mean we're not?"

"I mean—"

"I know what you mean, Jack. I think we are many unnamed things. If friendship is what you want to call it, I'm okay with that." A heartbeat of silence. "For now."

Not going there. I can't handle one more conundrum tonight. "How's your work coming?"

There's a creak as he leans back in his kitchen chair. The one nearest the window always does that. "It's coming. I'm happy with my progress on Twenty First Century Man. But you didn't call to talk about that."

Guilt makes me blurt. "I'm a pretty crappy friend, huh?"

"Let me be the judge of that. What's Nellie done now?"

I find myself telling him about Easy, the demon goat, and what I've learned about my mother. But not how I feel about it.

"I get addiction. I had a favorite uncle, growing up. But he had a gambling problem and spent all his time at the casino or dodging bookies he owed money to."

"How awful for him. Living in Vegas, I saw lots of compulsive gamblers. Where is he now?"

"Doing a dime in the state pen for robbery."

"Oh Leo. I'm so sorry."

"Is what it is. I go up to see him once a month and take him cigarettes."

I knew nothing of this. Our relationship was based on art and sex. I've been careful to keep things light and shallow. Out here on the road, it's hard to remember why. "Tell me something fun about your childhood."

Two hours later when we hang up, I'm asleep in minutes.

Chapter 8

Toto, I don't think we're in Kansas

anymore.

Frank Baum

The morning, getting-ready-and-back-on-the-road is now routine. Seattle seems a cool, green dream. I feel like this is my life—that it's always been this way, with the road stretching ahead. I get Nellie settled, get in and slam the car door. "So where are we going?"

Nellie is perky today, leaning forward, hands on the dash like a little kid going to McDonald's. "Paradise del Soul. It's out of town a ways."

"Sounds like a resort. We probably should stop and buy some decent clothes."

"Trust me, we're good."

"Well, if you say so, but when we hit Vegas, we've got to do some shopping." My safety net's holes are widening with every mile, but the worry is blunted a bit the farther we go. I guess that means that, somewhere deep inside, I must feel I'm getting my money's worth.

"Whatever you say, Jack."

"I still wish you wouldn't call me that." The road curves between rock buttes and desert landscape.

Feeling the weight of her gaze, I glance over.

"Would you share a memory with me? There are things I want to know, too."

I want to blow her off. To tell her she has no right to my past—my pain. Her face looks so hopeful, even with her stupid star sunglasses, that I waver. She doesn't have a right. But I don't have the right to know hers either, yet she's been open with me—even the bad parts. I consider a moment, then pull off the road, stop, and wait for the inevitable dust cloud that rolls over us to settle. I turn so I'm leaning against the door. If I'm going to tell her, I'm saying it to her face.

"My senior year of high school, Mom's long slide hit bottom. She hadn't held a job in a year, and her whole life revolved around her next drink. She shook like a Parkinson's patient, wheezed walking across the carpet to the bathroom, and complained of pain when she was alert enough to be aware of it. I was going to school and working a four to midnight shift at a Stop 'n Go to keep a roof over our heads. There was no money for doctors. I thought if I could just finish high school . . . but when yellow crept onto her skin, I knew I had to do something. Do you know what paperwork for Medicaid is like?" I shake my head. "Never mind. You don't want to know. After tearing through a red tape forest, I finally got her approved, and an appointment."

I take a breath and descend into hell. "Gotta give the doctors credit, they were thorough. High blood pressure, cardiac myopathy, fatty liver riddled with Cirrhosis, Pancreatitis, Jaundice. All classic end-stage alcoholism.

"I'd researched at the library. It was nothing I didn't already know. But knowing something will happen and have it start to happen are two very different things, you know?" My voice wobbles, and G'ma's papery palm comes over mine. "They said they'd send her home if she had someone stay with her all day. They left off the *to die*, but they didn't need to say it.

"I knew this coming in, but it didn't help. Overwhelmed and afraid, I lost it right there in the office. I couldn't be with my mother while she died, because I was so busy making sure she had a place indoors to do it in." I pull a tissue from the box and make myself spew the rest. The worst. "And there was this scholarship. With that, a job or two at college, and a bit I'd squirreled away that Mom didn't know about, I planned on leaving in September. God help me. I hoped she'd be gone by then. I didn't know what I'd do, if not."

Tears run into the furrows of my grandmother's face. "Don't do that to yourself, Jacqueline. You did more than any grown-up. You were a wonderful daughter."

It would have been such a help to have G'ma to lean on back then. To have her watching over Mom at home while I was at school or working. But I'm not throwing that in her face. Not now, when her pain at missing it is so thick that I'm breathing it. "Well, I still feel guilty about it. She was a crappy mother at the end, but I remember when I was little, her dancing light as Tinkerbell across the floor, eyes sparkling to give me a goodnight kiss. That's the woman I want to remember."

"That's the woman I *do* remember. The world was too harsh a place for a free, light spirit as that."

"I'm glad you weren't there at the end." When the words slip out, I'm shocked to realize I mean them. After all, my guilt is so much less than a mother's—wondering where you went wrong, what you could have done differently . . .

G'ma swipes tears. "I think you need to finish."

"They kept her in the hospital the rest of the time, drugged, mostly. I talked to my guidance counselor at school. She said I could graduate on the credits I had and got permission for me to miss the last month, and graduation. I got an extra job and visited Mom every afternoon." I blow my nose and push the words through my regret-swollen throat. "I came in one afternoon, and she was alert, looking better than she had in a long time. She patted the bed and when I sat, she took my hands." I stop to breathe for a moment. "She told me she was sorry. That I was a kid and I was stuck mothering *her*. She said she didn't know what made her so antsy all her life, wanting things she couldn't have and drinking to cover the holes the wanting left in her. Then she did a really strange thing."

I wait until G'ma looks up from her lap.

"She told me not to blame you."

Her narrow shoulders shake with sobs.

"She said she knew that you couldn't have done anything else, though she didn't know why." I cock my head and study my mother's mother. "What did she mean?"

She's crying too hard to answer.

A week ago, I would have flung my mother's death in her face. I didn't think Nellie deserved to know her daughter forgave her. You couldn't have pried that confession out of me with a crowbar.

Somewhere on this road, like a leak in the Duchess' transmission, bitterness dripped out, unnoticed. I'm not sure about the how or why of it, or even if I'm glad.

My grandmother and I sit in the sunshine in the middle of nowhere, exhaling old pain.

Ten miles outside Kingman, Nellie tells me to hang a Ralph, and I shudder at the name of the demon goat. If I survive this trip, I'll have some good stories to tell—not that anyone would believe them.

We start up a rocky, pinion pine-covered mountain. Not a mountain by Washington standards, but for Arizona, a dizzying height. I slow on the curves, enjoying the dappled sunshine and scent of fresh pine. This stopover may not be so bad. At least we're out of the sameness of the desert.

"Slow down. It's just up ahead." Nellie's tone is an excited bird-chirp. "Here. Turn here."

I turn at a small break in the trees onto an asphalt track too narrow to be called a road. We pass under a log arch with a hand carved wooden sign:

Paradise del Soul ~ you were born to be free!

NO TRESPASSING

Sounds woo-woo, but this is Nellie, so I expect nothing less. There's a break in the trees on the right, giving a view of a placid sapphire lake. "Wow."

Nellie closes her eyes, inhales, and lets out a huge sigh. "It's as wonderful as I remember."

I pull into a clearing. There are cabins, and a large restaurant/store/office, all built of rough logs. "Oh. No. Way." I brake so fast the seat belt tugs on my lap. There are naked people. Everywhere.

"What's the big deal, Jack?" Nellie takes off her sun hat. "You brought a half gallon of sunscreen. You should be fine."

Before she finishes, my head is shaking back and forth. "Nope, nope to the power of nope. You've done some crazy things, Nellie, but this—" A very overweight man jogs by, and I try not to . . . see. "This is way past my limits. If you think I'm going to parade around—"

"Let me explain." She takes off her star sunglasses and grabs my hand. "After I found Easy that morning in the desert, I was half out of my mind. More than half, because when I became aware, I had walked miles into the desert wearing only a crop top, shorts, and sandals, the sun was a ball of fire, straight overhead."

Her eyes are deep pools of sadness I can't turn away from.

"I had no idea where the van was. The temperature was over a hundred, and I had no water." Her fingers clench mine. "I slept that night shivering in the dirt and woke to another blazing hot sunrise. I could have been getting somewhere, or I could have been walking in circles, I had no way of knowing.

"By afternoon, I was dehydrated, exhausted, and I'd lost a sandal. I gave up. This life was too hard. I'd follow Easy, and depending on which religion was right, I might have a chance of being with him again. I sat down to wait for the end.

"Easy came to me then. We argued. He said I had to fight for us both from now on. I told him that a quitter had no right to judge me. He got mad and stomped off. I sat and listened to the wind and waited. Around dusk, two people appeared. I asked if they were angels. I told them I was ready."

She looks away and studies the clearing.

I'm again shocked by the brutality of my grandmother's life. "Who were they?"

She turns back to me. "They said they were pilgrims, seeking enlightenment. They took me to town, helped me report what had happened and deal with the details. Then they brought me here." She waves a scrawny arm. "This place is a lot more than what you see with your eyes, child. You have to see past your puritanical roots to see with your soul."

"My puritanical roots have gotten me this far, and I have no —" I try to pull my hand away, but her fingers dig into my skin.

"I just want to commune with nature and worship with these wonderful people one more time." She squints up at me. "This place is magical, Jack. It replenished me and gave me the strength to go on. It will hold answers for you, too. I know it." She thumps a fist to her concave chest. "I know it here."

I shake my head.

"There's a medicine woman here." A twinkle comes to her eye. "She knows local plants. She can help you find new scents."

My brains says no. But she's plucked at a string of longing, deep inside me. It makes a lonely sound. I take in a barest hint of a tantalizing scent on the wind. Pine and . . . something. I glance around. "Well, just so you know, I am *not* taking my clothes off."

Nellie squeals, leans over, knocks my hat awry, putting her dry lips to my check. "No worries. Clothing is optional."

I straighten my hat. "Well I wish a couple of these people would take the option." Apparently, *this* is how far I'm willing to go to learn the secrets Nellie holds. But it's not like I'm going to run into anyone I know, so I can take this memory to my grave. I put the car in drive and pull up to the end of the store where a sign declares it the office.

"I love you, Jacqueline Oliver." Nellie looks at me with a fond smile.

"Oh, now you do, huh? That might have helped—Stop that!"

She's grabbed the hem of her T-shirt and is trying to wrestle it over her head.

I grab her hands. "Stop it right now!"

Her hands fall to her lap. "You're probably right. This body has changed so much since I was here, they wouldn't recognize me. Let's go in. I want to see Spike."

"If they had a dog back then, it's long dead, now." I pull the door handle and put my shoulder into it. It pops open with a squeal.

Nellie titters. "No, silly. That's the name of the Soul's leader."

I *so* don't want to see a naked biker dude. I walk around, open Nellie's door, and reach for her walker in the back seat.

"Leave that shitty thing. I want to walk in under my own power."

"Are you sure?"

She waves me off and steps out of the car.

I rush to take her elbow. She's not breaking the other hip on my watch. We take the two steps slow and easy, then cross the porch.

A little wind chime tinkles against the door when I open it. The room is a surprise—it looks like a high-end mountain resort. The interior logs are a soft gold. Across the room, a large fireplace is surrounded by cranberry colored chairs and a matching plaid couch. Through a broad doorway, is a pool table, a card table with a partially completed jigsaw puzzle, and a kitchen area.

"Welcome to Paradise del Soul." A squeaky voice comes from our left. A man stands behind a reception desk. He's short and thin, with a mustache and a tonsure of gray hair around his bald pate. All I can see above the counter is his sunken chest sporting a few gray curly hairs. He looks like a naked CPA.

"Spike!" Nellie holds out her arms.

He takes off his reading glasses to look her over. "Blue? Oh my Creator, Blue, is that really you?" He comes around the desk and takes a few hopping steps to envelop Nellie in a hug.

That cannot be sanitary.

"Oh Spike, I can't tell you how I've missed this place." Nellie clasps his bony shoulder blades and lays her head on his shoulder.

He strokes her hair.

"I don't know why you stayed away so long, silly. Wait til the others hear that Blue has returned!" He holds her at arm's length. "You haven't changed. I'd have recognized you anywhere."

Nellie actually blushes. "Oh go on, I'm ancient now."

"As are we all. The Creator has blessed us."

Still holding Spike's hand, Nellie turns to me. "Spike, this is my granddaughter, Jack."

I lift my hand to shake, then think better of it (who knows where his have been?) and let it drop awkwardly to my side, forcing my gaze to stay on his face. "Um. My name is Jacqueline."

"Jack it is, then." He steps forward and takes my hand.

Which leaves the three of us holding hands. I squirm inside, drop his hand, and step to the desk. They could at least put out hand sanitizer. "I guess we'll need a room for tonight."

Nellie steps beside me. "Two nights."

She's pushing it. She knows it. I glare at her.

She smiles like an innocent. "You said we have to be in Vegas on Friday, right? That's like a hundred miles from here."

"Ninety-seven, actually." Spike says.

A CPA would know the exact number. "Oh fine. Two nights then."

He gets us registered into a cabin. The rate is *exclusive* mountain resort-sized. Great. All this, and naked people, too. I hand over my credit card. "I'll just check in at work, and then —"

"There's no cell or internet service on the mountain." Spike passes two keys over the desk to us.

Alarm floods my stomach. "What? We're not that far from civilization."

He shakes his head. "We don't allow the outside world to interfere with our chi."

"Oh, this is not acceptable. To pay this much for a room with no internet, no phone, and naked—"

"We'll be fine." Nellie pats my hand. "Jack is wound just a little tight."

"You'll want a meal plan, then." He names an exorbitant price.

I swallow, picturing my safety net in flames. "We'll just eat in town."

He looks at me over his glasses. "What town?"

"I don't know, the nearest restaurant."

Nellie squeezes my hand. "That's where we ate breakfast."

That can't be right. "Kingman?"

She nods.

"What a racket," I grumble, and hand over my credit card. Again.

"You'll love our food. We serve only organic vegetables, grass fed beef and free-range chickens."

For what he's charging, they must be giving those chickens massages.

"So, what's on the agenda, Spike?" Nellie chirps. "First, lunch. The staff is going to be so happy to see you, Blue. Then there's volleyball on the beach, or alone time. Tonight, we'll have a group sharing and meditation session."

I've been railroaded by an octogenarian hippie. A *nudist* octogenarian hippie. Fine. Nellie will have her reunion, commune with the mountain Gods, and I'll just hang out in the room for two days. I can survive that. "Come on, Nellie," I take her arm and steer her for the door.

"You'll see a lot more of me in a few, Spike." She waggles her fingers at him.

"And I am looking forward to it." He says as I push the door open and the wind chime tinkles again.

Back gates of hell, I tell you. And my grandmother is the imp, waving me inside.

I'm halfway to our cabin when it hits me—if they can run a credit card, they have a land line. Maybe I can talk Spike into letting me make a call.

I get Nellie in the room, then go out to the car to get our clothes. When I walk back in, Nellie is naked, looking at herself in the bathroom mirror. Her skin is liver-spotted, wizened and *brown*. She has pastie-sized white patches on her nipples and the triangle of her pubis. Her butt is all tan. My grandmother wears a thong bikini. It takes me a moment to wrap my head around that. I drop the bags and raise an eyebrow. "Where on earth did you go to get a tan?"

"The Old Fart's Warehouse has an interior courtyard."

I snap my hanging jaw shut and drop onto the bed. "You mean you sunbathe almost naked in front of everyone?"

"Eh." She flips a hand. "If all those old guys threw in together, they couldn't raise a decent woody."

I put my head in my hands. "There is no way we share the same gene pool."

"If you're not getting naked, let's go to lunch."

Naked people and food aren't an appetizing combination, but I can't go forty-eight hours without eating. "I guess."

I'll be two days without calling the store. They'll think I died out here in the desert. Hell, I feel like I'm losing *myself* out here. A lonely thought floats through my mind before I can stop it.

Leo may forget me too.

The dining experience is closer to camp than an exclusive resort. The long log-sided room has tablecloth covered cafeteria-style tables with long benches attached.

"We eat family style at Paradise del Soul." Nellie says. At my insistence, she put on flip flops, sun screen and her sun hat but refused to wear anything else. Except for the small buckskin bag which she retrieved from her walker and put around her neck.

Turns out, she fits the dress code far better than I. The closest this crowd comes to being clothed is the napkin in their laps.

I peer through the long serving window. Thank God the cooks are clothed, anyway.

"Blue!" A bony old man stands and carefully extricates himself from a bench seat.

At his shout, conversations cease, and all eyes turn to us. My face flames, though why *I* should be embarrassed, I can't imagine.

"Oh my God. It's Blue!" A lavender-haired old lady with a dowager's hump shimmies off the end of her seat and hurries over, flat breasts flapping.

"Starlight!" Nellie takes the woman in a full-body hug.

"When Spike told me you were here, I couldn't believe it!"

The little old man arrives. "Blue, you beautiful thing. I'm so happy to see you!"

Nellie lets go of Starlight to clasp the man to her. "Oh Ren, you're still here!"

"I went back to the outside world for a while. It didn't work for me."

"You always were too soft for the outside." She pats his back.

"Blue!" Several people call to her.

Nellie waves both hands over her head. "I'm baaaaack!"

The crowd breaks into applause.

I take her elbow. "Let's find a place to sit."

"Oh, over here." Nellie hangs a Louie. "There's someone I want you to meet."

She leads the way to a table at the back. Luckily, there's space at the end, so Nellie doesn't have to try to balance on one foot and slide in. I help her to her seat, then step in next to her.

Sitting across the table is a woman younger than Nellie, but older than me. Probably around the age my mother would be, had she lived. Her long, silver-white hair lies in braids partially covering her breasts. Her face is handsome and tanned, but it's her eyes that hold me. Deep brown and bottomless, they telegraph calm, surety, and peace. My muscles ease their death grip on my bones, just a bit.

"Hello Blue." Her voice is quiet and melodious.

"You remember me?" Nellie's voice is calm; I wonder if she too is affected by this woman's tranquility.

She smiles. One front tooth is a bit crooked, but it adds, rather than takes away from her beauty. "Of course, I do. You are a legend here."

Legend?

Nellie turns to me. "This is Fawn. She's del Soul's healer, and the person I wanted you to meet. Fawn, this is my granddaughter, Jack."

She tips her head and offers her hand. "I'm pleased to meet you."

"Where's your mother, Fawn?" Nellie asks. "Don't tell me she's—"

"No, she's fine. Mother is going to live forever. She moved to a retirement community in Boca Raton."

"Your mother in a golf cart—that I can't imagine. Jack, when I was here, Fawn's mother was the healer, and a good one. Fawn wanted to travel in her mother's footsteps, and here you are." Nellie takes Fawn's hand in hers. "I'm so proud of you."

"Thank you."

"Excuse me, friends," Spike's voice quiets the crowd, "shall we have a few moments of reflection with your deity? And would you ask for blessings for those who, due to geography, politics or their own closed minds, don't have the freedom we enjoy?"

Everyone bows their heads. I do the same. I haven't prayed since I was old enough to realize God wasn't more real than the tooth fairy, but I send good thoughts out to those in prison. The unrightfully accused, anyway.

"Thank you." Spike says after a minute. "After lunch, there will be a lecture right here, on healing the world through the use of crystals. Oh, and there will be a non-competitive volleyball game on the beach. Enjoy your lunch."

What is the point of non-competitive volleyball?

A voice comes from behind us. "May I ask your preference for your meal?"

I turn to a clothed young woman standing with a pad and pencil.

Nellie says, "We are tippling T-rexes."

The young woman giggles. "We don't go by that terminology anymore, but thank you, I've got it." She walks away.

I raise an eyebrow at Nellie.

"We drink alcohol and eat meat. Vegetarians are Brontosauri, and Vegans are Daisies."

"Why don't we just choose from a menu?"

Fawn speaks up. "Each lifestyle has one choice per meal. But no need to worry; they're all tasty, balanced and nutritious."

Doesn't sound promising. But since there are no choices . . . "Have you always lived here, Fawn?"

"Except when I went off to school."

"You attended college?"

"University of Colorado. Double major in nutrition and philosophy."

A naked mountain shaman with a double degree. Wow.

Servers are trooping in with covered dishes, delivering them to tables.

"Told you she was the cat's meow." Nellie puts her napkin in her lap. "Jack is a perfumer who, in her drive to make money, has lost her joy."

"Nellie!"

She ignores me, addressing Fawn. "I told her you probably wouldn't mind showing her the local plants."

Fawn's eyes are warm and welcoming. "I would consider it a pleasure. Are you free after lunch? I'd planned to do a gather then."

"I'd like that, thank you." I glare at Nellie. Her mouth is like a machine gun with a hair trigger. She hasn't seen me go nuclear yet but if she keeps this up, she's going to get the opportunity.

A server sets a plate in front of me and removes the lid, then does the same for Nellie and Fawn. There's a square of sizzling meat, the rest of the plate is taken up by steamed asparagus spears, carrots and cauliflower. "What is this meat?"

Fawn looks up from a salad scattered with walnuts and sunflower seeds. "Bison. It's much healthier than beef. More protein, less fat. And I understand it tastes wonderful."

"Fawn is a Daisy." Nellie says in a theatrical whisper.

I cut off a tiny piece and taste it. My mouth floods with a flavor close to beef, but mellower. Better. "Wow."

The vegetables are perfect, the multigrain rolls dense and satisfying.

Nellie catches up on the news from del Soul. Words fly I don't know the meaning of: Metaphysical freedom, ontology, numerology . . . I tune them out. I've got electricity at least—I should be able to finish my presentation by the time we leave.

For dessert, they bring a dish of strawberry ice cream. Fawn tells us the milk and strawberries are from right here in del Soul and is churned in the kitchen.

"Worth the money, huh, Jack?" Nellie winks.

I pat my lips with the napkin. Two can play the ignoring game.

"I'll go to my room and get my things." Fawn stands. "Meet you by the lake in say, ten minutes?"

"I'll be there." I clamber out of the bench and take Nellie's elbow.

Nellie doesn't rise. "I'm staying for the crystal lecture. I'll see you later, Jack."

I turn to walk out but am blocked by a crowd of Nellie admirers.

"Blue, tell us what you've been doing?"

"Do you remember when—"

"Blue, would you help me? I'm a bit lost, and—"

I walk out, trying to get my head around the note of respect in their voices. My grandmother is *somebody* here. Granted, it's an oddball nudist colony, but still . . .

I walk down the path to the lake, focusing on the trees rather than the assorted backsides heading for the volleyball game.

She must have been here a long time to become legend. Wait. She told me there were no classes at the orphanage; how did she learn to read? Where did she go to school? It feels like I only have a few edge pieces in a complicated jigsaw puzzle.

I skirt the dirt volleyball court at the edge of the lake, and gaze across to the tree-lined shore on the other side. The sun is warm on my face, the conversation only a buzz behind me. The crows cawing, sparrows chirping loosen something wound tightly inside me.

There are huge gaps between Nellie's stories. I need to press her for more pieces. With luck, the entire puzzle will be clear by the time I drop her off at the retirement home. That seems a million miles from now, but it's not.

"There you are." Fawn's soft voice comes from behind me. She's wearing a floppy sunhat, and a yellow and white midi-dress and hiking shoes. She carries an open-ended basket and pruning shears. "I thought you'd be more comfortable if I wore clothes."

What an observant woman. "So kind of you. I imagine if I stayed long enough, I'd get used to seeing naked people." Not that I'm staying anywhere near that long.

"Tell me how I can help you."

She leads the way along the shoreline as I explain that I'm looking for fragrant local plants. She stoops now and again to clip what looks like a weed and lay it in her basket. Her silence feels friendly and somehow, non-judgmental. I find myself talking about my business.

When she stoops to snip a dried stalk, I notice the leather piece she has to hold her twist of heavy hair up. It has a Yin-Yang symbol on it in black and white. "I like your hair clip. I'm not very good at life balance."

She straightens. "It's not easy. I wear it to be mindful."

She walks on, turning at a path into the woods that leads up a rocky slope.

"I can show you the fragrant plants and trees of the mountains. There are some great ones." She flicks a shy look my way. "Do you mind my asking you a few questions?"

"As long as I can ask a few of my own."

"That's fair." She smiles and we walk on. "You seem uncomfortable with more than the nudity here."

I can't help a snort. "I'm uncomfortable with most things in my life right now."

"You and your grandmother . . ."

"Are just getting to know each other. I've never met anyone who knew her back when. Can you tell me what she was like?"

She frowns, as if searching for the right words. "When she first came to us, she was like a soldier, back from war. She lived outdoors, jumped at sounds, kept to herself, and spent a lot of time staring out at nothing. My mother and many others tried to get her to open up, but Blue ignored them. I was seven, and curious, so I followed her. Everywhere. I became her silent shadow. She ignored me too, for the longest time. But I got the feeling sometimes, that she appreciated my quiet company. Then, one day she walked to a clearing in the woods, sat on a fallen log, and without looking at me asked why I followed her. It was a beginning."

I'm breaking a sweat, leaning forward, stepping around rocks in the path. I've got to get back to the gym when I get home.

"It's not much farther." She stops to wait for me. "I guess Blue felt like anything she told a child didn't count. She didn't talk about her past, or what had happened in the desert, but we talked about everything else—we were soon fast friends. After a while, she let others in, too. Within three months, she was taking classes and soaking up all the philosophy and belief systems we offer here."

"Did someone here teach her to read?"

She tilts her head and looks at me. "She already knew how. Why do you ask?"

"No reason." If Nellie never told anyone of her past, it's sure not my place to do it—the little I know, anyway.

"I've never seen anyone learn so fast. Soon she was teaching classes. It's like she was starved for reasons why the world is the way it is. As if she were looking for a religious base that made sense to her." She steps into the sunshine.

We are in a meadow, where grasses bend in the scented breeze coming off the mountain. I understand why they call this place Paradise. If there's a heaven, I think it must be like this meadow.

Fawn gazes to the blue mountain beyond. "I always thought she'd take my mother's place as healer. She certainly had the knowledge. But one day about a year later, Blue packed up, bid us goodbye, and walked down the mountain."

"She never came back?"

"Not until today."

Chapter 9

Only when the tide goes out
do you discover who's been
swimming naked.
Warren Buffet

F awn leads the way through the meadow. The grass releases
a fresh, organic scent that would make a good base note
for a man's fragrance. The scents people find most pleasing
aren't made in a lab; they come from nature. Smell is the most
memory-invoking of the senses—it's why we love the aroma of
turkey cooking—it takes us back to when we felt secure and
loved. Well, for most people anyway.

I feel like I'm standing at the edge of the Grand Canyon
where the ground crumbled away. Opening to my
grandmother would be like leaping off that canyon wall,
trusting I had wings, despite the mirror telling me I don't.

A leap of faith.

It terrifies me, but I'm tired. Tired of doing the same things over and over and enjoying them less, every time. Tired of covering up the past when it won't stay buried. Tired of being alone in the world.

"A penny for your thoughts." Fawn's quiet voice cuts in.

I realize my feet have stopped moving, and we're standing in the middle of the meadow. I shake my head. "I'm afraid they're worth about everything I own."

"Ah, a crossroads."

"Exactly."

"Only you can choose the right path. But when I am there, I think about what Nelson Mandela said: May your choices reflect your hopes, and not your fears."

The words hit me deep, echoing back, sounding like truth. I need to remember that quote.

She stops and bends at a sage colored bush covered in yellow flowers. "This is a Brittlebush." She breaks off a stem and hands it to me. "It can be burnt as incense."

I hold it to my nose, and my thoughts are blown away as the scent awakens my senses.

As it should. After all, I'm in Paradise.

<hr />

When we descend the path to the lake, half the samples in Fawn's basket are mine. Potential hums through my veins. I feel alive in ways that I haven't in . . . I can't remember. The sun is warm on my shoulders, and my lungs are clean, drenched in spring air and ideas. "I can't thank you enough for sharing your knowledge." I touch her arm. "I'm taking away much more than good-smelling plants."

Her smile is warm. "I'm so glad."

I follow her, my limbs loose and fluid. I feel younger than when I climbed up—lighter.

I don't know if I'm brave enough to let go and fly, but for now, loosening my grip feels good.

We break out of the woods at the shore of the lake as the sun touches the tops of the evergreens on the opposite shore.

Fawn stops in front of the office. "Dinner is at six. I'll see you there?" She scoops my cuttings from the basket and wraps them in a red paisley handkerchief.

"You will." I walk to the cabin, whistling a tune from the sixties about good vibrations.

I open the door and the delicate scent of lavender meets me. Nellie is asleep on the bed, in all her naked glory, except she's added a few strands of Mardi Gras beads. She looks almost vulnerable lying there. My grandmother acts childlike, but given her past, she's anything but. Tenderness floods my chest, raising a smile. I lay the cuttings on my bed, step to the bathroom, close the door and turn on the shower.

I'm amazed at her resiliency. To have come from the dust bowl, survived the orphanage and losing her brother, then losing Easy . . . my childhood was bad, but not compared to hers. I shed clothes and step into the hot spray. And yet, she's almost always perky and optimistic. I haven't seen any indication that she is resentful, or that she holds her trials against anyone; even whatever deity she's worshipping that particular day. Is her happiness a finely crafted mask she created over the many years? Wouldn't it have to be?

But if she is truly happy, how did she manage that? Another thing to ask her. The questions are piling up. I never would have imagined that my grandmother would hold answers—not only to my past, but maybe my future as well? There's a scary thought. Loosening my grip is one thing; parading around naked and spouting new-age philosophies? There's got to be somewhere in-between.

Except I don't *do* in-between.

At dinner, a chardonnay with a slight citrus flavor compliments delicious lemon chicken pasta. Nellie chatters through the meal, discussing with others the essential oils class she took this afternoon. We linger, and when I stand I realize I have a bit of a mellow buzz going.

"Hey Jack," Nellie smiles up at me. "Wanna go skinny dipping?"

"No, I'm going to see if Spike will let me use the phone."

"He's leading a session tonight on Reiki healing. He won't be in the office."

I can't talk to Leo. The thought brings a lonely pang that I realize is not new. It seems the farther I get from him, the more he follows: in my thoughts, my sleep, my core. I'll consider that later, when my head clears.

"Oh, come on, we'll walk a bit around the lake. Just you and me. It's dark. No one will see." She raises an eyebrow. "You have skinny dipped, haven't you?"

With a challenge like that, I'm not about to admit that I haven't. But when we walk out to the star encrusted night sky, I find that I want to. I mean, what can it hurt? I decided this afternoon to loosen my grip a bit. Wouldn't this be an almost safe way to start? Tip my toe in the pool, so to speak. I giggle at my own cleverness. "Okay, you're on, Nellie."

"Far *out*." She loops her arm in mine and pulls me toward the lakeshore.

The white sand path ahead is lustrous in the bright moonlight, the grass we pass releases its smell to the night. After a hundred feet, Nellie stops.

I'm looking down, and bump into her bony back. "What?"

"This is only missing one thing." She messes with the leather bag around her neck, then, in a lighter's flare, she lights a joint.

"Oh, for cripes sake, Nellie."

She takes a deep inhale and holds it out.

"No. Thank you."

She exhales the sweet smoke. "Jack. We are twenty-five miles from a cop, on private property. We are adults. This is no more dangerous than the wine you just drank." In the glow of the tip, she squints up at me. "What's your excuse this time in your attempt to convince me you aren't afraid?"

I straighten. "I am *not* afraid. I just know—"

"It's not the pot. You're afraid of loosening your sphincter. Admit it."

"Yeah? Well screw you, Nellie Oliver." I snatch it from her fingers, put it to my lips and inhale.

"There's my Jack!" She cackles. "Let that shit go, Baby."

My lungs seize, then reject the smoke in a paroxysm of coughing. When I can breathe again, I take another hit. Call me a coward, will she? I survived the meanest streets of Vegas as a kid. This lungful settles a bit. I exhale and hand the joint back to her. "Lead on, G'ma."

She looks up at me with a beatific smile. "I love you, Jack." She turns and walks on.

That's when I realize I used her old nickname, but it doesn't seem important anymore. My head loosens on my neck, and it feels like my feet aren't quite touching the ground in the most pleasant way.

"Here we are." She takes off her beads and leather bag. When she wades in, the moonlight fractures on the ripples. "The water is delicious. Come on in."

I step out of my flip flops, pull off my T-shirt and bra. The light breeze is a lover's caress on my bare skin. Leo's artist's hands appear in my mind. I wish he were here right now. It occurs to me that I'm horny as I peel out of my leggings, laughing when I almost tip over into the grass.

Suddenly being naked doesn't seem as weird as it did earlier. In fact, I kind of get the draw. Clothes don't make you—they hide you. Hiding is good in public, but when you're alone, or maybe with someone you trust . . . not that I trust Nellie. I stand tall and stride in. The cool water sets off sparkles of surprise on my skin. The silt squeezing between my toes feels welcoming.

Farther out, Nellie treads water. "Isn't this great?"

"This is the *best*." I walk until the water covers my shoulders, then lie back and float until the water covers my ears, muffling the outside world. I'm alone with my thoughts and the stars stretching overhead. I drift, touching an idea here and there, but emotion seems blunted, softer. What would I discover if I let myself feel, without iron-fisted judgement? I lift my head. "Hey, G'ma."

"Yeah?"

"Why did you leave del Soul?"

Silence.

"I mean, since—"

"I don't want to talk about that tonight." I realize how much life is usually in her voice only in its absence. She sighs. "I want to live in the right now, hanging with my Jack and just mellowing out. Okay?"

"Sure."

"Groovy."

I'm sorry I made her sad. She's had so much of it in her life. "Hey, G'ma."

"Yeah?"

"Remember when you used to play tea-time with me?"

"Sure do. It was fun, wasn't it?"

Then I remember the day Mom tried to join us, shitfaced, and fell into the table, breaking my pretty tea set. That sure isn't cheering. There has to be another memory . . . "Hey, remember when you took me to the Ice Capades?"

"I'd almost forgotten about that."

The smile is back in her voice, and I'm stupid with happy about it. "I must've been around six or seven, right? We went to Circus-Circus, and they had all those Disney characters on ice, remember?" Mom was working, so she couldn't ruin that memory.

"I remember seeing your little face lit up in the stage lights— you were enchanted. I was enchanted, watching you." She sighs again. "You were such a beautiful child. So joyful, rushing out to meet the next new experience. God, how I cherished you."

I used to rush to meet new things? Me? I'll need to think about that. Later. I lay back and let the water cradle me. My mind drifts again to the meaning behind the stars, my tiny place among them, and the memory of the weight of a sexy man's stare from across the room.

"G'ma?"

"Still here." Her voice is closer.

"How did you know you were in love with Easy?"

There's a small splash. "Oh Jack. Are you telling me you've never been in love? Not even a little bit?"

It's the pot. Or the wine. But if you want to know, you have to ask. Even if it means trusting someone you're not sure you should. "Hey, I've been a little busy, working my way through school, starting a successful business, and—"

"Hon, I'm not being critical. Just surprised, that's all. Let me think of a way to explain it." Silence for a half minute. "It starts when you notice yourself thinking about him when he's not around. Then, when you're with him, you find you're looking for excuses not to leave. And spending all that time together, you find two opposite and wonderful things."

"What?"

"The ways that you're alike. The big stuff, like religion, philosophy, stuff like that. It's easiest if you agree, or at least respect the other person's belief system. But what keeps you together are the ways that you're *not* alike. Because that's endlessly fascinating. It gives you a chance to study and understand a life you never would have experienced otherwise."

I think about Leo and his artist's gift for seeing the world. I love hearing him talk about his exquisite creations—seeing how his mind solves problems. "I totally get that."

"You only need one more thing to cement the relationship."

"What's that?"

"Skull exploding, transcendental, down-in-the-barnyard sex."

And we're off, laughing until the ducks take off with a squawk and a flurry of beating feathers.

The next morning, after a bowl of stone-cut oatmeal sprinkled with wild berries, I tell Nellie I need to catalogue and press the wildflowers Fawn and I collected yesterday. But really, just want some time alone. I'm feeling a bit awkward.

Nellie and I are *not* friends, but we connected last night. I'm not sure how to handle it. I need to keep my distance. I need to know more about her past and why she wasn't in mine before I trust her. Again.

"Okay. I'm going to attend the Rumpology lecture, then—"

I snort a laugh. "Did you just say Rumpology?"

"Sylvester Stallone's mother is big into it. The left cheek is supposed to show your past, and the right, your future."

I roll my eyes.

"If you disregard something before you learn anything about it, how do you know you're not turning away from the last piece to the puzzle you need to understand the Universe?"

"If the secret of the Universe is in a butt crack, I don't want to know."

She shrugs. "Didn't say you had to go. I said I'm going. Oh, and by the way, I signed you up for a massage and biofeedback appointment at three this afternoon."

A massage would be heaven, but biofeedback?

"Just go to the office." She slides out of the seat. "I'm off. See you later, Jack."

I watch her flat, wrinkled behind as she walks away. How do they . . . never mind, I don't want to know. I suddenly realize she hasn't used her walker since we got here. Her hip seems better, but I worry about her walking on the uneven ground. I shake my head. She made it without me for eighty-four years. If she falls, we'll deal with it. I'm not dampening her joy of being here again.

After taking notes and pressing all the cuttings, I wash every bit of clothes we have in the sink. I take it all outside and hang them on bushes behind our cabin. I have to admit, leggings and long T-shirts sure are comfortable. Maybe I'll keep them, just for around the house.

At three, I walk over to the office and the girl behind the desk directs me to the back door. I step out onto a brick patio ringed by a dense growth of trees. Branches hang over, shading the area, making it feel an isolated spot in the woods. A massage table is set up in the center, and a young woman with waist-long black hair stands behind it in a Hawaiian print Mumu. "You must be Jack. I'm Zena," she says in a soft accent. Russian, or Eastern European.

Soft instrumental music mixed with the sounds of a rain shower come from a boom box on the bricks. I glance to the trees. Will she expect me to be naked out here? I'm not sure about all this. "My grandmother said something about biofeedback?"

"Come, sit and I'll explain." She pats the table.

I step to it but remain standing.

"What I do is very informal; I don't use machinery or electrodes or anything like that. We all hold stress in different parts of our bodies. I do a massage and then make you aware of where *you* hold stress, and give you tips on how to release it before it harms you."

That sounds logical and not as "out there" as I feared. "Do I have to be naked?"

"I don't hear that often at del Soul." She smiles. "But no, I will expose only the body part I am working on at any one time. I'll warn you though. I might mess up your hair. All right?"

"That's fine. You couldn't hurt it worse than the wind and dry has."

She hands me a terrycloth wrap and turns her back to light some incense sticks on a table behind her. I glance around while pulling off clothes. The wrap covers me from armpits to knees, secured by several Velcro tabs. When I lie down, I realize the table is not only padded, but heated as well. I close my eyes, take in the delicate sandalwood scent and listen to the rain on the CD. This is nice.

I jump a bit when Zena's hands touch my temples. "Try to relax. If you have any questions, just ask."

"Okay."

Her fingers slide over my skin in circles, trailing moisture and warmth. I didn't know the muscles in my face were tight, but bit by bit, they relax.

"You have tightness between your eyes, and at your jawline. You don't have to remember this; I'll make notes and give them to you. But can you feel that they are tense?"

"God, yes."

She moves on to massage my scalp in long, sure strokes. When she moves to my neck, I moan.

"The neck is a familiar place for stress to hide."

Apparently. When she cradles my head and works on my neck and shoulders, I become a Gumby, bendable, but with absolutely no will of my own.

She works her way down my arms. My body trusts her, the muscles going slack at her touch.

"Oh, your hands are dry."

"I'm used to humidity, and I've been in the desert for going on a week."

"I've got something for that." There's rustling, but opening my eyes takes too much effort. She massages my fingers and hands with warm oil, making me aware of how sensitive they are. She slips plastic gloves over my hands, then slides them into heated mittens.

Oh. My. God. That is amazing.

A half hour later, she's done and I'm a puddle of goo.

"You just relax while I write up my notes."

"I'm not sure I'm capable of anything else." My jaw muscles are so lax, it's hard to form words.

I'm dozing when she touches my shoulder. "All set. Get up slowly, to give your body a bit to acclimate."

I sit up. My body feels light and supple and . . . happy is the only word for it. Like I'm a kid again, only I'd forgotten what that felt like until right now. Then, before I've had an opportunity to revel in the feeling, my body falls back into my familiar adult shell.

I liked the relaxed-child version better.

Maybe I'll find a good massage-therapist in Seattle.

"Here are my notes, to read at your leisure." She lifts a couple college-lined sheets.

I'm out the door and back in the cabin in a minute. Nellie is still gone. I sit on the bed and open Zena's notes.

Your major problem areas for stress are: between your eyes, your jawline, the cords of your neck, your shoulders and upper back. These are the areas I see with issues of self-esteem. They tell me that you are trying hard to maintain a façade that is not natural to your psyche.

Wait, what? Does this woman have a degree in psychology? Psychiatry? She doesn't even know me.

I scan the rest, and at the end, there are tips for how to rid my body of stress. I stalk to the bathroom, turn on the shower, determined to wash off that woman's touch. The warm water does its magic, relaxing my muscles again. I notice that the places that snapped to attention first are the areas she named: between my eyes, jaw, neck, shoulders, upper back.

Any decent massage-therapist could have discovered that.

But the rest . . . how did she know that? If it was a guess, it was off-the-charts lucky. And I have to admit, my reaction is proof that her assessment pressed several nerves. Alone, with the water pouring over me, cutting out the real world, I have to admit, she's right.

I step out of the shower calmer, more relaxed. After all, how can you ever hope to fix something if you're not willing to admit it's a problem? It's not like I didn't know it, deep down. A dog may bury a bone, but he *always* remembers where he put it. I pull on my clothes, lay on the bed and pick up her notes to read them again.

"Jack." My shoulder is shaken. "Jack, wake up."

"Huh?" I open an eye to see Nellie leaning over me.

"It's time to go to dinner."

"You're kidding." I sit up and check the clock on the nightstand, shocked to realize I slept the afternoon away. "Okay. Just let me brush my teeth and change."

She chuckles, and plops on the bed. "Only you would worry about changing at a nudist colony."

I step to the bathroom.

"So how was the massage?"

"It was wonderful. Just what I needed. Thanks for setting it up." I run a brush through my hair, which is completely mashed down on one side.

"I agree with her assessment."

I step out and snatch the papers from her. "That's private."

"You're uptight and anxiety driven. Well, duh. That's what I've been trying to tell you—"

"You want to eat? Let's go." I step into my flip flops. I swear, my cracked and dirty flats are going in the first dumpster I come to when we get to Las Vegas. Tomorrow, thank God.

"Tonight is a luau, on the beach."

"Really? That should be fun."

"Yeah, they are epic. Great food, then we sit around and share."

I pull open the door and stop. "Share what?"

"Just a discussion about our belief systems. No big deal. You don't have to share if you don't want to."

Well, the food will be good, anyway. I can duck out, after.

I wish I could call Leo. At this hour, he's probably working in his studio. I love watching the muscles in his forearms flexing as he works tin snips. His intent focus, a jaw muscle flexing while he thinks. One lone curl, falling onto his forehead. Why didn't I ever tell him that? This far away, all my reasons seem excuses.

But I feel the magnetic pull of him in my core. He's somehow gotten under my skin, to nestle somewhere inside me. I've *never* been tempted to delve into a relationship before. Even more startling, the thought doesn't make me want to run and hide, for fear he'll see the real me under the façade.

I'd planned on mining my grandmother's secrets on this trip. But it seems I'm discovering as much about my own.

Chapter 10

The things we fear the most have
already happened to us.
Unknown

No pig on a spit at this luau. I imagine, not to offend the herbivores. The volleyball net has been taken down, and barbeques are set up in a line by the trees. The air is laced with the mouth-watering smell of grilling meat and vegetables. Naked people lounge in towel-covered beach chairs or stand talking in groups. Nellie and I head for the wine being dispensed from the "bar"—a two by four on cinderblocks with a palm-frond roof.

"Blue, come talk to us!"

"No, over here first. We want your opinion."

In the light of the tiki torches, G'ma's smile warms my heart.

"You go. I'm fine." I see why she loves it here. She's valued and held in high esteem. This is her *place*. I realize I don't really have a place.

I take a plastic glass of a very good cabernet and wander to the beach. The moon hasn't yet risen but there's a yellow glow of potential over the trees on the opposite side of the lake. The babble behind me is white noise that only makes me feel more alone.

I've always made big decisions by looking at the worst that could happen. If I can live with that, I can use logic to make the right decision.

But what if I can't live with the worst that could happen? In this case, letting people in, and being at the mercy of their casual regard. Or disregard.

The past days have made me take a hard look inside, and what I saw scared me. I've built a persona, layer by layer, like armor made of decoupage. I saw an exhibit in a museum once, of Chinese armor made from paper—you add enough layers, and it's impenetrable. No one I know would ever guess where I've come from. Hell, in my busy, insulated world, even *I'm* able to believe I'm safe in my armor.

But strip away all those layers, and that lost, terrified teen is still there. If I let people in, they could *see.*

"Jack, come on." Nellie's shout comes from behind me. "They're serving dinner."

We eat from recycled paper plates in our laps. Laughter is frequent and loud. These people seem as comfortable with each other as they are with their nakedness. Maybe the two are related—clothing as armor and all that. I may loosen up a bit, but parade around without a shred of armor? I shiver. Not me. Not ever.

When I'm done, I take my empty plate to a garbage can and drop it in. A young woman with a beautiful body raises an eyebrow and offers me a hit of a thick joint. I shake my head, then change my mind and take it from her fingers. This is my last night to relax. Starting tomorrow, things will move like a brakeless train. I inhale a lungful of smoke and hold it. Chest hitching, I hand it back, tipping my head in thanks.

"Friends, could I have your attention?" Spike stands in front of a large campfire, where several people are roasting marshmallows on sticks. "Let's have a night of sharing, shall we?"

There's an excited buzz from the crowd.

"Oh, these are the *best.*" The woman's voice rasps from beside me. She passes the joint back.

"What's this about?" I take a hit. The thick pungent smell that fills my nose and mouth doesn't seem as foreign as it used to.

"Spike chooses a subject and whoever wants to, shares their views on it. I've learned so much from these sessions."

Great. More new-age babble. "Groovy." I hand the joint back. "Thanks." I return to my chair, head buzzing. I sit and lay my head back, watching the fire's embers float up to play among the stars.

"Okay, tonight's subject is," he pauses for effect, "what comes after this life? I know many of you hold different views on the subject, and no one will ask you to change them. We are here to explore. I only ask that you keep an open mind. Can you do that?"

Several "yes's" from the audience and many nods.

"Who wants to share?"

The Great Religion Debate. Second only to politics. I glance from the dark sky to the fire. Wouldn't Spike's bare butt get toasted like a marshmallow so close to the fire? I snort a laugh, and slap a hand over my mouth to keep the rest in.

"I believe in Christianity." A young man with long hair and a mustache stands. "If I live a good life and keep the commandments, I go to heaven. I'm looking forward to having great conversations with Jesus and his dad."

A voice comes from over by the grills. "I think Hell can be a place on this plane."

"I don't know how anyone can believe anything." A fifty-something woman standing at the edge of the trees says. "We have no proof. In all the centuries, no one has come back to tell us what happens next. I'm a scientist. I believe in only what there is evidence to support."

"But man once believed the earth was flat," the wannabe friend of Jesus says, "the facts didn't change; we just got better data."

Spike jumps in. "But there are commonalities in all religions. We can go back to the earliest recorded cave paintings, and see that . . ."

I tune out the conversation that's pretty close to the ones I had in college. Most moved on from those freshman level discussions, focusing on making it in *this* world. Religious arguments always boil down to faith anyway. Either you have it or you don't. I was inoculated against that with all my other childhood immunizations. I believe you get what you work for. No more, no less. I'll leave what comes next to the theologians and philosophers.

I drift for a time, watching the fire, my thoughts shifting as aimlessly as the embers, and winking out just as fast.

My grandmother's voice brings me back.

"I believe in reincarnation. I hope to come back as a hawk, or an osprey. But that isn't really pertinent." She's standing on the left side, right up front. "I think the real question is, why are we here? I believe we are put on this plane to learn. Each life is a quest to learn a new aspect of the experience: charity, love, pain, and self-worth are just a few examples." She glances over the crowd. "Have you ever met an 'old soul'?"

Several nods.

"My theory explains Jesus, Mohammed, or any other prophet you care to name. They have been here many times and came one last time to learn about teaching and giving, and in doing so, imparted precious wisdom to the rest of us."

The Jesus dude raises his hand. "But what's the end game? What happens when you learn everything?"

Nellie shrugs. "Some say we become pure energy. I don't know if they're right or not."

"That kinda makes sense." The woman who shared her pot with me speaks up. "My mother was stubborn to the max. When my dad left us, she sunk into herself til she wouldn't even leave the house. Within two years, she got cancer, and was dead a year after that. It's like she was stuck. She couldn't go forward, couldn't go back. Maybe the Universe decided she'd have to learn some other way and took her out." Her voice gets softer as she goes. "Maybe she's come back in a different situation, so she can try again."

"Yes, just that." Nellie says.

"What are you here to learn?" The words are out of my mouth before I realize I've said them out loud.

"Great question." Someone in the crowd says.

Nellie thinks for a moment. "There is much pain in the world. But suffering is optional. I believe that when I fully learn to accept that lesson, I won't need to be here anymore." She turns and she finds me in the crowd. "What are *you* here to learn?"

Her gaze is a laser, burning through my paper mâché armor. My insides go to ice. The cold shoots down my limbs, flash-freezing me in place.

"I think I'm here to learn to be a mother." A woman says, and the conversation moves on.

I unlock my neck muscles and my head falls against the chair back. I try one of Zena's suggestions, slowing my breathing and concentrating on my heartbeat until it slows from a panicked gallop.

What is with me? Hanging around my grandmother has me questioning the meaning of the Universe? I miss my sane, orderly life, where my most philosophical challenge is whether to attend a Choral Christmas Concert.

The Milky Way stretches overhead, a reminder that not everything needs to be answered tonight. I stand and walk back to the room.

I have no idea what I'm here to learn. But from her look, my grandmother thinks she does. And knowing her, I'll be hearing about it. Soon.

The next morning dawns overcast, with pewter clouds hanging low over the lake. I polished my presentation last night, and I'm antsy to get on the road, but we're delayed by the crowd that surrounds Nellie, wanting to say goodbye.

They stand around chatting, patting, and hugging. There are only a few old-timers who knew her when she lived here, yet her admirers are all ages. How did she get that close to these people in two days? They do share their philosophies, and she probably met a bunch of them in the classes she attended, but it's more than that. She behaves as if everyone is good and means her well, and people react to her trusting child-like openness, coming close, opening up.

Yet her childhood should have made her the opposite: guarded, untrusting and closed-off.

I realize with a flush, that I mean . . . more like me. How has she managed to stay open in such a hard, cruel world? Her words of last night come back to me: *suffering is optional.*

Could that even be possible? I shake my head, my mind reeling at what a huge paradigm shift that would be.

My stomach burn reminds me of what's ahead, Vegas, and adrenaline-laced potential buzzes under my skin. I have confidence in my speech, but I need clothes, and some time to get my head back in business-mode. "I'm sorry Nellie, but we've got to go." I pull open my door and slide behind the wheel.

The people swarm, pulling her into a huge group hug.

"Don't stay away so long, Blue."

Nellie just shakes her head and shoots me a glance. She made a promise, it seems a lifetime ago, that she wouldn't try to run away again. She won't be back.

The woman who extracted that promise seems mean and cold to me now. Maybe next year, I'll treat her to a trip here for her birthday. Wouldn't that be a wonderful surprise?

Spike hugs her last, and longest. "We love you, Blue. You always are in our hearts, even if you're not in our arms." He lets her go and opens the car door for her.

She gets in slowly, taking his hand to ease onto the seat.

Is she hurting today? She's been so much better the past few

—

"Let's blow this pop stand, Jack." She raises her arms, and waves at the group. "I love you all! Always!"

I twist the key. It cranks and cranks, and just when I think the beater won't start, it does, with a roar and a backfire.

"Old ladies fart a lot." She says, patting the dash. The people laugh, but I see the sheen in her eyes.

I put it in reverse, execute a Y-turn and roll onto the tree-canopied trail, Nellie waving madly to the crowd behind.

The mountain road is deserted when I stop at the intersection. I look left, remembering everything that brought us here, then right, thinking about Vegas. My stomach takes a roller coaster's dip and flip.

I've always hated roller coasters.

The bruised clouds belch a rumble of thunder. It's sure not going to get better sitting here. I crank the wheel to the right and hit the gas.

Only two miles from del Soul, I pull off the flat road that will lead down the mountain. A narrow strip of meadow ends where a dense tangle of evergreens takes over.

Nellie jerks from her reverie. "Why are we stopping?"

"I've *got* to put the top up. This storm isn't going to hold off much longer." I put my shoulder to the door, and it pops open with a squeal.

"Jack, the top—"

"I know, you don't like it up." I walk to the back and lift the sunburnt plastic lid that covers the rag-top. "But Nellie, it's going to rain." As if to underline my statement, a fat drop plops on the top of my head. I've got to hurry.

"But Jack . . ."

I peer into the compartment. Something's not right. There's way too much metal, and not enough . . . I pull, and the framework unfolds. There's *no* "rag" to this rag-top. "Oh, you've *got* to be kidding me," I say to the back of my grandmother's head. "You bought a car with *no* top at all?"

I drop the metal and the lid slams shut with a bang. We are going to arrive in Vegas looking like drowned rats, when I have to look my very best for the presentation. I stalk to the passenger door, plant my fists on my hips and glare. "Another lie. What do you have to say for yourself?"

She shrugs. "If I'd told you, you'd made me take the Duchess back. The chances of rain were slight."

"No, they're about to be a hundred percent." The rain patters, leaving dime-sized splats in the dust. The smell of goat wafts off the back seat, reminding me what a folly this entire trip has been. I knew better, but I let her Glinda the Good Witch looks lure me in. I jog to the driver's seat, slide in, and crank the key. "We'll discuss this when we get somewhere dry."

Rawr, rawr, rawr . . . Then nothing.

I turn the key back, pump the accelerator twice, and twist it again.

Rawwwwrrrr . . . Silence.

Lightning flicks vertically over our heads, and the sky lets loose a torrent of rain.

"Shitshitshitshit!" My voice is drowned out by a clap of thunder that concusses my eardrums.

Nellie sits like a pound puppy in the passenger seat, sad, wet, bedraggled. Her fault or not, I've got to get her to a dry, safe place.

I stand in the seat and step over the door, scanning the trees, remembering news stories of golfers who have been struck by lightning, sheltering under a tree. Water runs into my bra. Shitshitshitshit.

Think, Jacqueline!

I open the trunk, dump out a plastic trash bag of my belongings, take the few steps to the passenger side and hand it to her. "Here, keep the rain off your head. I'll be right back."

"Yes, Jack."

Now she's agreeable. I pull my phone, wondering how long it'll take AAA to get here. I've only got maybe an hour's leeway. I'll just have to shop fast, that's all.

I pull up the phone number and dial. When there is no ring, I pull it from my ear and check the bars. None. The extended network's got nothing, either.

Lightning cracks again, and the thunder booms in my chest. We have *got* to find shelter.

The rain is hitting so hard it bounces off the pavement, creating a mist that obscures the road. We haven't seen a car since we left del Soul.

Chilled and frantic, I swipe hair out of my eyes and scan the tree line once more.

Wait.

There's a darker spot, deep in the trees. A line that seems more manmade than natural. I jog to the edge of the trees, my flip flops slipping and squelching in the sodden grass. *Yes!* A moss-covered roofline takes shape in the gloom. It doesn't look inhabited, but I don't care—it's shelter. I slip and slither my way back to the car. "Nellie, come on." I jerk open the door.

She peers from under the plastic she holds over her head. "Where?"

"Somewhere safe. Hurry."

Crrrack!

Boom!

Dang, that was close. A hand under her elbow, the other around her shoulders, we go slow as fast as we can. The only thing worse than the fix we're in is if she fell. Water drums off my skull to drip into my eyes.

As we step into the trees, the wet underbrush scratches and pulls, as if trying to keep us out. For some stupid reason, I remember every campy horror movie I've ever seen. *Don't go in the woods!* I shake off a shiver.

When the dilapidated cabin appears through the trees, Nellie stops, just as another roll of thunder hits. "No."

"What? It's shelter. If anyone's there, they'll have a phone. If not—"

"No-no-no-no-no." She falls out of my grasp into a heap at my feet.

"What is it, Nellie? We've got to get out of the open. Lightning—"

A high keening escapes her and she rocks back and forth. Her chest rises in a deep breath. "NOOooooooo!"

The primal desperation in that word slices through me. I crouch and put my hand on her back.

She shivers from under my touch. "Don'ttouch-don'ttouch-don'ttouch meeeeeee!" The terror contorting her features hits a primitive part deep inside, making my head swivel, looking for danger. "What? What is it?"

Staring to the tiny cabin's shadows, she shrinks back, turns on her hands and knees, and scrabble-crawls away.

Is she having a break with reality? Hallucinating? It doesn't matter—I have to get her to safety. I grab her ankle to stop her and crawl until I'm alongside.

She's whimpering like a beaten puppy.

"G'ma. G'ma. It's okay. We don't have to go there. Do you hear me?"

She stops struggling. I lower her to the ground and wrap her in my arms. "It's Jack. I'm here. I'll keep you safe. I promise." I hope I'm not lying. I search my mind for a more secure place, but short of the cabin, I can't think of one.

We are now at the mercy of Nellie's "Universe."

I pull the trash bag up to protect her wet head and cradle her shivering body close to mine. I'm almost afraid to find out what could have reduced my happy-go-lucky G'ma to this hysterical, shivering husk.

Tenderness melts my anger like a Chinook wind, and I rub circles on her back, whispering words of calm and safety and love. Slowly, so slowly, she stops shivering, and lies still.

I drift, miserable yet soothed by the sound of the rain and the comfort of company. In fifteen minutes, when chirping birds signal the end of the storm, I raise my head and pull my phone. It's been over an hour since the car broke down.

Barring a miracle, there's no way I'm going to make that presentation.

I shake her awake. "G'ma, roll over. I'm going to get you to the car."

Her whimper tears something in me, and the last bit of bitterness spills out, draining away in rivulets, like the rain. I gather her in my arms and struggle to my feet. It's not too hard; she weighs next to nothing.

Her arms come around my neck and she clings to me.

"It's okay. I've got you now. You're safe, love." I rest my cheek against her thin, plastered-down hair, and carry her across the grass to the car.

I set her on her feet by the trunk and open it. I wish I had a blanket to wrap her in, but there's nothing. I sort through the clothes and pull out a cardigan I haven't worn since the plane flight down and drape it over her shoulders. I know it's useless, but I check the bars on my phone. *No service.* I feel minutes ticking by like a manic metronome. Fifteen more precious minutes gone.

I glance back the way we came. It's only a couple miles to del Soul. I could run there in twenty or so minutes. G'ma is hunched over, staring at the pavement, lost somewhere in the past. Love for this rag-tag old lady bubbles from deep inside me. She may be odd, and not always truthful, but she's my G'ma, and even if a run to del Soul would mean I'd make it to that presentation, there's no way I'm leaving her.

I put my arm around her shoulders. "Okay, let's get you in the—" Hope lifts at the sound of an engine echoing through the trees. In a few seconds, a battered sedan comes around the curve, from the way we came. "Hold on, G'ma. Don't move."

She's shivering again, and I have a hard time forcing my hands to let her go. But we *have* to get out of here. I step into the road, looking over my shoulder to be sure she's not following. If this driver is not in the mood to stop and help, he's going to have to run me over.

I glimpse a shock of straight-up hair and widened eyes behind the wheel. The car slows, to stop beside me. The heavily tinted window rolls down.

The driver can't be over sixteen, with a gold ring in his nose, huge black discs distorting his earlobes and green tendril tattoos winding up from his collar. "Geez, lady, you trying to get killed?" His hair defies gravity, the ends a deep sapphire blue.

"We need help."

The door pops open and he gets out and walks over. "That storm was bad. Why didn't you put the top up?"

I bite back the snark. We need this ride. If I have to beat him up and steal his car to do it, I will. "Will you give us a ride?"

"I'm on my way to work in Bullhead, will that work?"

Bullhead is ninety miles from Vegas. I open my mouth to tell him that would be great, but then glance again at Nellie. Her eyes are sunken, haunted. She will probably snap out of it when she gets dry and warm. But can I take that chance? The best place for her is del Soul—Spike and Fawn will know how to help her. If not, they have a phone to call an ambulance. I sneak a glance to the right; the way down the mountain, and my chance to put Heart's Note on the radar. Loyalty to myself vs. obligation to my grandmother war in my brain.

I shake my head. Nellie isn't an obligation—she's *family*. I point left. "Can you take us back that way? It's only two miles or so out of your way."

"Of course." He heads to the driver's side. "Would you put this in the trunk?" I point to her walker and he's quick to obey.

G'ma doesn't resist when I lead her to the car and settle her on the seat. I snatch my purse from the front seat of our car, take a dry set of clothes each, grab my cuttings and my laptop, then glance around. There's nothing else worth keeping. I'll buy us decent clothes in Las Vegas.

He's back in the driver's seat by the time I slide into the car beside G'ma. "I can pay you."

"My dad would kill me if I took money to help stranded old ladies."

Whatever, kid, just drive. "Would you mind turning on the heater? My grandmother is chilled." I put my arm around her, press her head to my shoulder and within seconds, she's asleep, breathing in shallow breaths.

I direct the way back to del Soul. Luckily the rain has driven all the naked inside—I'd hate to be the one to corrupt the young man. He seems more a country kid than the badass he tries to pull off. He pulls up next to the lodge, jumps out and runs around to help.

He offers to lift G'ma out of the car, but I shudder to think if she woke with a stranger holding her. "I've got her." I lift her out of the back seat without waking her. "Thank you so much. You saved us, you know."

Red spreads up from the green tendrils at his collar. "It's nothing. But I've got to git if I'm going to be to work on time." He pulls out the walker, then tucks the end of the garbage bag of my clothes into my hand.

"You go. Thanks again."

He runs to the car, and in a minute, is gone.

I take the few steps to the door and kick it.

Seconds later, Spike opens it. His eyes go big. "Blue!"

He reaches for her and I let him take her from me.

"Jack, what happened? Was it the storm?"

"The car died, and we were caught out in it, and . . . Spike, there's something wrong. She had a breakdown or something . . ." My voice wobbles to an end.

He carries her to the couch in front of a roaring fire in the fireplace and settles her in his bare lap. "Hand me the throw, will you?"

I grab a plaid blanket from the back of a chair and wrap it around her.

He looks down into Nellie's sunken face and pallid skin. "Do you know which cabin is Fawn's?"

"Yes, I'll get her."

In minutes, I'm back, Fawn on my heels. G'ma is awake and crying into Spike's hollow chest.

I take a step, but Fawn's hand on my arm stops me. "We'll take good care of her, don't worry. Why don't you get into some dry clothes?"

Spike struggles to a stand, G'ma clinging to him like a limpet. "Use the same cabin you were in."

"Here are some dry clothes for her." I dig in the bag and come up with a T-shirt and leggings that are only damp.

"Thank you." Fawn pats my shoulder. "You know she'll be in good hands."

"I do." But still, my hands circle each other in a wringing dance.

Spike walks to a door in the back wall, and Fawn follows.

"Could I make a phone call?"

Spike nods to the desk. "Just come around. There's a phone under the counter." They go out and close the door behind them.

I walk around the registration desk. The clock says I'm due to start my presentation in two hours. I could make it if I found someone to race me down the mountain. Adrenaline hits my bloodstream, until my gaze snags on the door G'ma was carried through. Just as fast, a balm of calm coats my frayed nerves. I'm not going anywhere. I made my decision on the side of the road. I'm not leaving my grandmother. Pulling up the number with shaking fingers, I dial Scott Rodgers' cell.

"Jacqueline. I was getting worried. If you'll come down to the convention floor, I'll show you—"

"I'm sorry to tell you Mr. Rodgers, I'm not going to be able to make it."

Silence.

"My grandmother, she had a, well a medical emergency, and I'm—"

"Are you kidding me? What am I supposed to do at this late date? No one is prepared to discuss—"

"Sir, this is important to my business. If there was any way I could, you have to know I'd be there. This was unavoidable."

"Well, that's what I get for trusting a *small* business owner. You can bet I won't be bothering you in the future. If I were you, I'd have more concern for my reputation. Once destroyed, it's gone."

"I'm so sorry—" I'm talking to dead air.

My knees lose function, and I plop into the chair, drop my head onto my forearm and try not to cry.

And, as with everything else I've attempted today, I'm unsuccessful.

Chapter 11

*Your future needs you. Your past
doesn't.*

m.r.

I allow myself a few minutes to wallow but then take a deep shaky breath and lift my head and let out a from-the-gut sigh. A huge opportunity lost. I don't regret my decision, but in the scent business, you're either on your way up, or you're nowhere.

I'm in the middle of nowhere in more ways than one.

Spike tiptoes out of the back office and gently shuts the door behind him.

Worry jerks me to my feet. "How is G'ma?"

He gives me a smile. "Fawn gave her a tea to make her sleep. She should feel much better when she wakes, but we'd like her to stay overnight to be sure."

I let out a breath and walk back to the customer side of the desk. "Did she tell you what happened? Why she was so terrified?"

He steps behind the desk, shaking his head. "Blue has never talked of her past, but I'm sure it was a shade from then. I recognize the signs."

That thuds into my consciousness. "You mean she has been like that *before*?"

Head down, he gives me a sad nod. "Why don't you go change and get warm? You're shaking."

Not from cold, but he couldn't know that. Pulled by the life-preserver need to talk to Leo, I look longingly at the phone, but I'm not doing it with Spike hovering. Instead I go to the cabin that almost feels like coming home. I strip and steep in a hot shower until the shivers are banished, then fall on the bed into oblivion.

The next morning, Spike offers to drive us to Bullhead City where I can rent a car. When they bring G'ma out, it's like a dimmer switch has turned down her normal sunny disposition. Our leave-taking is different too. Only Fawn is there to send us off. She hugs G'ma a long time, whispering in her ear. Finally, she steps back and I help G'ma into the back seat and get in beside her.

"Are you all right? Warm enough?" I put an arm around her shoulders, just in case.

"I'm fine." She looks up at me, pain swimming in her tears. "I'm so sorry, child. You've missed your presentation."

"That doesn't matter."

She looks at me like *I've* lost my wits. "Your business is the most important thing to you."

"I don't need that show to be a success. " I can't quite meet her gaze. It's one thing to recognize that she's worth more—it's another to admit it to her. I still need to guard my heart.

She pats my hand. "Whatever you say, Jack." I catch her small smile before she turns to the window.

She sounds like Leo, knowing more than I've said. Missing him hits like a whirlwind, and I spend the rest of the ride chasing my wind-blown emotions.

In less than an hour, we're saying goodbye to Spike outside the car rental at the Bullhead City airport.

The woman at the desk looks askance at my stained clothes, but not at my credit card.

Five minutes later, a young man pulls up an economy sedan, and I help G'ma in the front seat. I clip her seatbelt, walk to the driver's side and slide in, noticing things I usually don't: the soft thunk of a new door closing, cushy leather seats, and most of all, the roof over my head. Well that, and the absence of goat-funk. "You ready?"

She nods.

"Are you comfortable? Need anything?"

"Stop fussing. I'm fine." She grouses.

There's my G'ma. "Okay. Get ready Sodom, here we come." Outside of town, I hang a Ralph at Highway 95. It occurs to me that things started going wrong (not just Nellie odd) when we turned off Route 66. I'm sure my grandmother would have something philosophical to say about that, but when I look over, she's asleep.

The sun hitting her face turns her pallid skin translucent, seeming as fragile as ancient parchment. Before today, fragile isn't a word I would have used to describe Nellie. Much as I wanted to know her past when I began this trip, I've changed my mind. Whatever happened back there scared her so bad, it frightened *me*. G'ma's secrets are safe from me.

I have nothing to do but worry until we blow by the Las Vegas city limits sign. My stomach clenches to a hollow ball of heat. I realize neither of us have eaten today. That's just the thing to avoid the decision I've been giving the side-eye to since it occurred to me.

I pull into the parking lot of a national chain eatery.

When I put it in park, Nellie wakes. "Where are we?" She straightens only enough to see over the lip of the window.

"Vegas, Baby!" I shove all the false cheer I have into the words. I'm not sure who I'm trying to convince, but it sure isn't working on me.

"Like Gracie says, Feed your head." G'ma unsnaps the belt and it retracts with a clang.

Good to see she's back spouting obscure quotes from people I don't know. "Yeah, let's do that."

A half hour later, armed with full bellies and a purse full of antacids I picked up at the checkout counter, we return to the car and head into the lion's maw.

I fully intended to drive by. But when I see we're only a few streets away, I realize that my conscious has taken a backseat to my subconscious, and that bitch is taking us downtown.

"Ah, Memory Lane." Nellie says from the cheap seats. "Are you sure you want to do this?"

"Hell no." I hang a Louie at Civic Center. Downtown Vegas is the part only lost tourists see. Easy to forget among the fake grass and tinkling fountains of the strip that you're in the desert but down here, it's as obvious as a bleached cow's skull. Rain wouldn't wash away the graffiti or the trash, but it would help the patina of dust that coats everything. Homeless are camped in the skimpy shade of yellowed palms and the freeway overpasses, the prevalent color plastic-tarp-blue.

All right, dammit. If I'm here, I'm going to *be* here. Maybe then, these streets won't haunt my nights and, as I've come to realize the past week, my days. If I quit running and see it through adult eyes, maybe I can drive away and leave this all behind, like the gamblers do with their money when they go home. I roll down the window to take in the perfume of my side of Vegas: spoiled garbage, sweat, despair.

A Ralph at Cheyenne Street, and we're here. The city tries to camouflage tenements with stucco and a step-above-tacky façades, but it doesn't fool anyone, least of all the people who live here.

I wonder if whoever named these apartments was tasteless or tripping. It would take both to come up with *Chez Cheyenne.* I pull to the curb, put it in park, and let it idle.

"Are you going to get out?"

A sketchy dude with dirty dreads, torn sweats and paper slippers shuffles by. "Not without a gun."

I sit, eyes riveted to the last door on the end, ground floor. It's open, the flimsy screen covering a dark hole. But I don't need light to see the worn linoleum, filthy shag carpet, battered walls. The sagging kitchen cabinets that, when I lived there, held little more than cockroaches.

The music of this place echoes between the too-close buildings—a bad marriage of Heavy Metal and The Blues.

My thoughts come out as words, unbidden. "I was accepted to U.C. Berkeley with scholarships and loans. The day Mom passed, I came back here to find an eviction notice in the mailbox. At first, I freaked. But then I looked around in the cold light of morning and realized that aside from my clothes and a few books, there was nothing of value—nothing I wanted to take with me. That broke the bottleneck in my head. I packed what I wanted in a duffel, walked out and bought a bus ticket to Berkeley."

It's funny. After dreading this for so many years I expected this place to hold more of . . . I don't know. *Something.* In the hard desert sun, it's just a sad, run-down bunch of buildings. My past doesn't exist in this place. It exists in my *head.*

Then how am I ever going to be free of it?

"There's an African Proverb." Nellie's gaze heats the side of my face, but I can't look away from my childhood. "If you escaped from the lion's den, why go back for your hat?"

Easy for her to say. That den never held *her*.

But the thought holds only a pale shadow of my anger of a week ago. I'm done holding my grandmother responsible for my past. It was what it was. Blame and teeth gnashing won't change one second of it.

And I didn't leave anything here. Not even my hat.

G'ma is right about something else. This place forged me: my tenacity, work ethic and a not-so-healthy fear of failure.

Skills of every successful entrepreneur.

I rip my gaze away. "Keep on truckin'. Isn't that what your generation used to say?"

"Right on, Baby. You ready to bug out?"

"More than." I put the car in drive and pull away from the curb, hoping that scene stays in the rear-view mirror, where it belongs.

"Whoa. We're going high-roller." Nellie's eyes light with child-at-Christmas excitement when I pull into the rotunda, past the Roman columns and statues of Caesars Palace. She rubs her hands together. "Did I ever tell you your G'ma is a mythical force at a poker table?"

"You didn't. But forget it. We don't have money for gambling." I'm already wincing, imagining the hotel and clothes shopping charges. A fresh-faced kid opens my door, and hands me a receipt. Not to mention the cost to park. Another kid hands Nellie out the other side.

"Luggage, Ma'am?"

I think about the rags in the trash bag in the trunk. "None, thanks." I walk around to meet Nellie on the other side. "You want your walker?"

"Oh hell no." She scans the impressive marble and gold entrance, mouth open a bit. She's probably never done Vegas like this in her life. I've learned a lot about Nellie Oliver the past week. She's made the best of her life, hard as it was. I have to admit that I didn't make it easier the past few years, shuffling her off to molder in the "old fart warehouse." That place is top drawer, but it *is* a drawer. Especially to a woman who has lived out-of-doors her whole life. My free-range grandma.

I look to the glass and gold entrance doors. Screw it. I'm tired of being that scared teen, saving pennies to be sure she never is hungry again. I'm an adult, dammit. I want to give my grandmother some good memories. I know they won't negate the awful ones, but we've missed so much of each other over the years. A few good memories to share will do us both good. I loop my arm in hers. "Brace yourself, G'ma. We're about to start living large."

Her wrinkles lift and she pats my arm. "Faaaar out, Jack."

I have a room reserved, but when I get to the front desk, I upgrade to a two-bedroom suite. Thanks to the Ultimate Beauty Show ending, they had one open. We take the elevator up, and when I open the door, the look of awe on Nellie's face is worth the price.

The suite is total class, done in cream, gray, and French Blue, with replica antiques. Everything is cushy: the carpets, the couches, and when Nellie falls back onto the bed, she says it's like a cloud catching her.

"Well you take a long nap, then we'll go shopping." I pull a cashmere throw from the foot of the bed over her, and she rolls on her side. I tiptoe out and close the double doors behind me.

I pull my phone and sink onto the couch. My finger caresses Leo's number, but duty comes first. I dial work.

"Thank God. We were getting frantic here. Where are you?" Steph says in a rush.

I try to imagine my bomb-proof manager frantic but can't quite manage it. "Hi Steph. I was out of range of civilization for a couple days. In Vegas, now. Okay, fill me in. How are the fulfillment orders?"

"They're fine. Tell me how the presentation went." My chair squeaks, and I picture her leaning back in it. "Don't leave out a thing."

"Um. I'd have to leave out the whole thing."

"That doesn't sound good."

She deserves to know. If she thinks Heart's Note is a loser, so be it. Better I know now. I give her the three-minute clothed and sanitized version of where I've been this week.

"There was a goat. In your car."

Well, not entirely sanitized. That she would pull that incident out of the pile of disasters, surprises me. "Yeah, but didn't you hear? I missed the presentation."

"If Rodgers can't understand a family emergency, it just proves he's a heartless Durk."

G'ma's idioms fly over my head just as fast as the younger generation's do. "You're not mad?"

"Hey, we didn't have this opportunity a week ago, and we were doing fine, remember?"

My shoulders unhunch, just a bit. "You're not going to leave m—Heart's Note, are you?"

"What, and miss out on the ground floor of an indie success story? Do I seem stupid to you?"

"You seem wonderful to me. Thanks for believing in the business."

"Business hell. I believe in *you*."

Much needed warmth courses through my blood, and I have to wait until I know my voice will be steady before I answer.

"Remind me to give you a raise as soon as I can afford it."

"Told you I wasn't stupid."

I smile for the first time in what seems like forever. "Thanks Steph. When I get back, we're going to do that dinner you suggested."

"You're on."

"Great. Listen, I've got to jump. I have more phone calls to make."

I caress the next number for seconds, considering. Then hit speed dial.

"Hello?" His voice is as warm as sunshine in my ear.

"Leo. I'm so glad to hear your voice."

"I called your store, but they hadn't heard from you, either. Are you all right?"

His concern zips through me, leaving sparkles in its wake. "Out of cell tower range. This has been one heck of a trip."

"Tell me all about it. Where were you? How's your grandmother?"

"She's okay, now, but can I fill you in tonight? I have to get her up from a nap and go clothes shopping. The leggings and T-shirt I've been wearing are rags."

"You? In a T-shirt?" His deep chuckle is like water over rocks. "I don't believe it. Send me a picture."

"Dream on."

"No, really, I'd love to see you with your hair down."

I remember what I look like after a night in bed with him. "You already have."

"Some of my fondest memories. Speaking of that, when are you coming home?"

Home. Coming from his mouth, it seems farther than just miles and time. "Monday, Tuesday at the latest. We're taking a day or two here, then I'll need to get Nellie back and settled before I catch a plane home."

"You can call me anytime. You know that."

And knowing it forms a warm ball of something new and nameless settling in my chest. "Thanks. And Leo?"

"Yeah, Jack?"

"I miss you."

The surprised silence on the other end matches mine.

"And I miss you."

I click end and realize that conversation sure didn't sound like two people who've broken up. Does that mean we're back together? No time for mooning (if that's what this is). I spend the next hour catching up on emails. When I internet surf, I find more nasty tweets.

Screw that. I'll worry about it when I get home. I stand, step to the double doors and open them. "Time to get up, G'ma. There is shopping to be done." There's a silly lilt to my voice I've never heard before.

When we get to the lobby, I stop by the bell desk, and see that my other surprise is waiting. I contacted Mobility Store to rent her a "senior scooter" to get around on. But this is Vegas —they do overblown like nobody's business. Sitting beside the desk is a silver scooter that looks like an old Indian motorcycle with huge fender skirts, complete with red and gold flames. "Now, I'm not saying you can't walk. But . . ."

"Ooooooh." Nellie breaths "For me?"

I can't help my smile. "Well, *I* certainly wasn't born to be wild."

She hugs my waist, then sits on it, and hits the throttle to turn slow 360's on the waxed floor. The bellhops chuckle, but when a snobby chick at the concierge desk glares and lifts a phone, we head for the elevators, and down to the underground mall.

The doors whoosh open, and we step/roll out. I take in a deep lungful of leather, exclusive perfume, and rich food that combine to the heady scent of chic. My exhaustion lifts like a mainlined caffeine hit, and I can hear my charge card whimpering in my wallet. This is the most expensive shopping experience per square foot outside Dubai. The cloud mural ceiling and shopfronts create the illusion of strolling in ancient Rome—if they had tailored clothing and air conditioning.

I look down at Nellie. "You ready, G'ma?"

She glances right and left. "I don't know how I'm going to find something to wear here."

She sounds so much like me in that tacky souvenir store back in Williams, I have to laugh. "Oh, you might be surprised."

"Cool wheels, Granny." A teen in sagging jeans and a black T-shirt emblazoned with *Death Rattle* slouches by.

"Thanks. Like your T-shirt, Dude." Her chin comes up. "Lead on, Jack."

The sales racks at Armani, Gucci, and Versace later, I'm outfitted with enough clothes to last until I get home, and then some.

Nellie has yet to buy anything, despite my urging. I sigh. "All right then, I give in. Let's go."

"It doesn't matter. I can just wear what I have on."

"Hopefully it won't come to that. Follow me." She rolls behind me to the very end of the mall, where *The Vintage Vogue* is tucked away like an odd relative. I've never been beyond the display windows, but what Nellie sees there lights her face. "This place is the tits!"

I shoot a look around, but no one seems to have noticed. "Let's go in."

I try to steer her toward the retro Dior or de la Renta, but of course she heads for the bright colors and relaxed '60s styles of Thea Porter. Two flowered caftans and a searing yellow and bling jogging suit later, I find a compromise—a George

Halley's turquoise embroidered Japanese silk jacket (which she says looks like a Nehru jacket, whatever that is) and a pair of black silk chiffon Palazzo pants.

We reach an impasse at shoes. I vote for patent leather flats, she votes for the high-top converse. After a half hour disagreement, all my soft feelings for my grandmother have crisped. A cute pixie of a salesgirl saves us, suggesting Nellie get the high-tops for the jogging suit, and a pair of too-gaudy jeweled leather sandals for the dressier outfits.

"Let it never be said I don't know how to compromise," I say with a sigh, and arrange to have the purchases sent to our room as I did the others.

"Time to hit the poker table." Nellie buries the throttle and heads for the elevator.

My destroyed flats slap the marble floor, until I'm alongside. I steer her left. "Oh no you don't. Let's sit and have a cup of coffee, then I have to work."

"Oh all right. But Jack, you really gotta learn to live a little."

I sink into the cushioned seat of a tiny wrought-iron table outside a trendy bistro. "I have 'lived' quite enough in the past week, thanks." And God knows, I can't afford much more "living." I order two cappuccinos and a lovely brochette for us to share.

"You're worried about the business." Nellie gives me that curious-sparrow head-tilt.

"I'm not sure 'worried' does this feeling justice."

"But you've found your mojo out on the Mother Road, Jack. I sense it. You're ready to roll."

My half smile is rueful. "Thanks for the support. I'm going to need all I can get. But now," I sign for the charges and push to my feet. "I've got work to do."

"You go on. I'm going to wander. I haven't been in Vegas in twenty years."

I pull a spare room key card from my purse, but when she reaches for it, I pull it out of reach and glare at her. "*No* gambling. You hear me? I just don't have the money, G'ma, and I'm not kidding."

"Got it, Jack." She crosses her heart. "No gambling."

I hesitate, trying to find room in the promise that she can wiggle out of, but there isn't any. "Okay, I'll see you at dinner."

A luxurious bath later, I'm dressed in new from the skin out, and sit down to run the numbers, then research where I can advertise Heart's Note that won't put us under water.

It's close to seven p.m. when Nellie rolls in the door.

"Where have you been? I was about to call out the Saint Bernards to start a search." I close my laptop.

She parks the scooter by the front door and, Palazzo pants fluttering, walks across the floor to me, waving cash fanned out in her hand.

"Oh God, tell me you didn't rob a bank."

She laughs, and hands me the thick wad. "I told you I was deadly at five card stud."

"Nellie, you *promised*. No gambling."

She blows on her nails and buffs them on her jacket. "Babe, when I play, it isn't gambling."

I riff through the pile. "There must be five thousand dollars here!"

"Five thousand, eight hundred and forty-three, to be exact."

I should scold her. But she looks so proud and happy, and it wouldn't do any good anyway. "You are a shark, Nellie Oliver." I hold out the money to her.

She sobers. "No, you keep that. I know this trip has been expensive. That's my contribution."

"I'm not broke yet. You keep it."

She pulls up a chair, sits beside me, and takes my hand. "Please, take it, Jack. It's an inadequate thank you."

I set the money on the coffee table. "I don't need help."

I grab a couple of overpriced bottles of water from the mini-fridge (in for a penny) and hand her one before sitting.

"Jack, will you tell me one more thing?"

I give her the side-eye. "What?"

"You won't accept help, you've never been in love, and you haven't mentioned any friends in the past week." She takes my hand. "I know you had to grow up fast because of your mother's alcoholism, and my leaving didn't help, but I sense that's not all of it." She rubs her knobby thumb over the skin on the back of my hand. "Why don't you let people in?"

I study the carpet. Can I trust my grandmother with my most shameful memory? I reach inside, to see how I feel about that, but only expectant silence echoes back. Where's intuition when you need it? I look up, into the wrinkled face of my family. She lies, is inappropriate and her beliefs are far from mine. But she's also known hard times and made mistakes. If anyone could understand, she could.

"I saw Berkeley as my chance for a fresh start. I figured everything that had happened in my life up til then was up to other people—now I was going to make a perfect life for myself." My scoffing snort is loud in the quiet room. "First semester, I took Psych 101. Everybody did. The prof was the youngest on staff, and his lectures weren't dry and dull, like the others. He encouraged discussion, and I found myself drawn in and opening up. He made you feel like you weren't a clueless freshman, that your opinion was of value. And he was gorgeous, with deep brown eyes, longish hair, and a beard. Half the girls had a crush on him, me included.

"One night, after class, he asked if I wanted to go for coffee. I was thrilled and flattered and confused. What could he want with a little twit like me? We talked until the place closed, and when he dropped me off at my apartment, he kissed me. I walked on air for two days.

"We went for coffee after his lectures from then on. He told me I was special. He asked questions until I told him about Mom, and Vegas. He said I'd endured what would have taken down a lesser person. We made out in his car. The third time, he rented a hotel room, and relieved me of my virginity. I imagined I was in love." My face heats, remembering. "He said we had to be careful, because he was up for tenure, and him dating a student wouldn't go over well. By then, I'd have done anything for him. Out of all the women on that estrogen-stuffed campus, he'd chosen *me.* That had to mean I was as special as he said, right? Heady stuff for a poor girl from the slummy side of Vegas.

"Within a month, he asked me to move in with him. See, he had an infirm mother, and he traded off days caring for her with his sister. He'd been living at his mother's house up til now because it was convenient, but he wanted a space that was just for us, so he rented a furnished apartment. I had been living in a two-bedroom dorm room with three other scholarship girls. They told me if I moved out, I wouldn't get my deposit, or the month's rent I'd just paid back, but hey, an apartment with my love or four girls in a two-bedroom dorm room? No brainer.

"I lived in a bubble of bliss, studying in the quiet the nights when he was at his mother's, and making dinner for him and love to him, the nights he was home." I shake my head. "I look back on that naïve, star-struck young woman and I can't believe it was me. Seems like a different lifetime."

"What happened?" Nellie's soft words break into my thought. I'd almost forgotten she was there.

"His wife called."

G'ma winces.

"Yeah, turns out, there was no infirm mother. I don't know what story he was feeding his wife about the nights he was gone, but apparently she was less gullible than I. I had a day to find somewhere to live. But my former roommates had already replaced me, and no way I had even the deposit for anywhere else."

My shiver is from remembered fear. "I didn't have money for next semester's tuition *and* a place to live. I'd messed up the perfect life I'd planned in the first six months. All I knew was I wasn't quitting school. It was all I had. So I got a second job and lived in my car for a semester."

G'ma makes a clucking sound in her throat.

"It wasn't too bad. I showered at the gym and ate once a day at my fast food restaurant job. But it taught me. I vowed I'd never put my future in the hands of anyone else, ever again."

Her look of pity stings.

"It's pretty easy to do. I just don't let anyone matter that much."

G'ma squeezes my hand. "That is so sad. Jack, don't you see what you've done? Because you're afraid of bad things that have *already* happened, you're sacrificing your future. You're missing so much of the richness of life by being alone."

"Maybe, but I'm not risking my hard-fought security in pursuit of a maybe I've never seen."

Nellie draws a deep breath through her nose. "I have one more memory to tell you. Maybe it will help put things in perspective for you."

"You don't owe me any stories, G'ma. You were right. They won't change one thing about my past. It's okay." I pat her cool, papery hand.

"If it were just for you, I don't think I could do it." She looks out the window. "I think I have to tell it for *me*."

Chapter 12

Oh Sweetie, monsters are real,

and they look like people.

Unknown

1943-1944~

For a time after my brother's death, I died, too. I shuffled through the big, rambling rooms like the ghost I wish I were, not speaking to the attendants, not engaging with the other kids.

But trees can't keep the sap from rising in the spring, and neither can children. One day, sitting under a huge oak in the yard, I looked up and noticed the leaves had unfurled, the sky was deep blue, and the sun shone warm. Hints of green poked up from the winter-dead grass.

It was time to get back to the living.

When the little ones managed to find joy in spite of their surroundings, I found my joy, in helping them. I was twelve years and one month old when the head matron sent for me. I stepped into her high-ceilinged, library-hushed office, not sure what to expect.

She looked up from the pile of papers on her desk. "Nellie, you have been a good help to us the past few months. We are going to miss you."

Ma! Excitement coursed through me, and I had a hard time keeping my feet from a happy dance. Ma came back for us . . . for me. I craned my neck to peer out the window, but there was just a dusty old farm truck out front. Maybe she caught a ride from the train station—

"The Vogels have come to take you to their farm."

"Who are the Vogels, and what do they have to do with my ma?"

"They're not adopting you, mind. But you'll be helping them on their farm in exchange for your room and board."

"But," my brain struggled to catch up, "you just said I've been a help." Panic swapped out the excitement in my blood, and I suddenly understood the saying, "the devil you know," down to the holey soles of my shoes. "You *need* my help."

The matron shook her head. "Lord knows that's true. But there isn't enough food for all under this roof, and with the new cutbacks . . ." She waved the thought away. "Regardless, I know you'll be a good worker for the Vogels." She stood, walked around the desk, took my hands, and pressed them in hers, as if we were praying. "God be with you, child."

"But they haven't even met me. How do they know—"

"I recommended you, and they agreed. Please don't fight this. Just go and make us proud."

There was a knock at the door and another matron ushered in a couple. They seemed old, but they were probably in their early forties. They reminded me of that painting—that farmer couple, American Gothic. Only more worn-down. Sterner.

I gathered my few belongings including my touchstones: the Saint Anthony medal my mother had given me and all I had left of my brother—one of his socks. Before I could think, I was loaded into the battered farm truck between these two silent strangers and the man drove us away.

The air was chilly that day, so the windows stayed rolled up, trapping the smell of motor oil and body odor. Dust billowed out the back window and we bounced in silence on sprung springs.

After fifteen minutes I asked, "Where are we going?"

"The farm." The man said.

"How far is it?" If I didn't like these arrangements, maybe I could find my way back to the orphanage.

The man shot me an irritated glance. "Down the road apiece."

The woman stayed silent.

With nothing else to do, I watched the man's hands on the steering wheel. They were big, with long knobby fingers with dark hair on the backs with dirt embedded in the skin. They were as spare and ugly as turkey feet.

"Apiece" turned out to be four hours away. They never stopped, never said a word the whole time—either to me, or each other. By the time he pulled into the dusty dooryard, I was about to bust with the need to pee. I climbed down from the truck and asked the woman where the outhouse was.

She looked at me like she'd expected a worker and got a blithering idiot instead. "Where is an outhouse ever?"

I didn't have time to argue. I ran around the side of the clapboard house to find the privy out back. Once I was done, I stepped out and looked around. The house was squat and square, the boards a wasp's nest gray color, as if harsh weather had beat all the color out of them.

When I walked around to the front, the couple were gone. My burlap sack of clothes was in the dirt beside the truck. I lifted it and walked to the front stoop, then stopped, not knowing what to do next. Knock? Walk in?

"You gonna stand out there til dark?" The man's rusty voice came from the shadowy inside.

I figured it was rusty from not being used. I pulled the screen door and walked in.

It was a darkened parlor with faded wallpaper and not-new furniture that looked like it had never been used. I kept walking through a doorway and into the kitchen. The man and woman sat at a spindly wood table only big enough for two, waiting.

"Sit." The man said, pointing to a stepstool.

I glanced around at the old cabinets with white paint aged to ivory and dark smudges around every knob. The black and white tile underfoot was well-worn and dingy. That was the best word to describe the house and its people—dingy.

I sat.

The man began. "We'll feed you and you'll have somewheres to sleep. You'll get shoes when winter comes, and new clothes once a year, or when you grow out of 'em. For that, I expect an honest day's work out of you. The lady at that charity house swore you were a good worker." He squinted at me like he was trying to see through my skin. "Was she lyin'?"

"No."

"No, *Sir.*" The woman gave me a dragon glare. "He's Sir, I'm Missus. Got that?"

"Yes . . . Missus." The cold emptiness in her tone slapped me. There would be no caring in this house. No joy. As I saw the dingy days stretching before me, one after another, the hope I'd garnered the past month shriveled like leaves with the frost, darkened, then fell away.

"Show the girl her place." He said to his wife without looking at her. "Then you come out to the barn." That part was for me. He stood and walked out the back door.

Life there was pretty much as I'd imagined. I had a pallet on the floor in a tiny closet-like space, and Sir would wake me with a terrifying kick to the door beside my head each day. I jumped every time, my heart banging the bones of my chest, as if it too, wanted to escape.

I'd wriggle into a shirt and overalls, and by the time I got to the kitchen, Missus had breakfast ready. Meals were silent, save essential information exchanged (between them) and barked orders (at me). I ate fast and headed out for barn chores: feeding and milking cows, shoveling manure and caring for more damned chickens. Then I screened the milk, and churned it—a monotonous, back-breaking job.

Then I went in the house and did chores there, cleaning, mostly. But no matter how many rugs I beat, no matter how much dusting and washing, that house stayed dingy. It was as if the years of hopelessness had seeped into the walls, and when I washed them, it oozed out again.

But I had a roof to sleep under, a change of clothes, and food. I told myself it was more than many had, comforting myself with the thought that I'd only stay until I was old enough to make it on my own.

That worked for about a year. Things began to change, so slow it took me a while to realize. Sir started watching me like a fox watches a mouse. First, when Missus wasn't around, then when her back was turned. He'd find reasons to brush against me in the barn.

I had no idea what was wrong, only that it didn't feel right. It gave me a jolting, staticky warning, like when a twister's coming.

I woke in the middle of the night, hearing breathing right outside my door. Scared me spitless, but after a time, there'd be shuffling steps away. It was him.

The clenching wrongness in my gut increased as the weeks went by. I thought about running away, but I knew I didn't look old enough to get a job. Besides, winter was coming. Hog butchering time had come and gone, and there was frost on the ground every morning. Spring. I vowed I'd leave as soon as it was warm enough to give up my shoes for the year. Until then, I'd just stay to myself.

A month went by. One night I woke to his heavy breathing but this time, my door was jerked open and a hand came over my mouth, squeezing hard.

"Quiet." His rusty whisper came out of the dark on stale onion fumes. "I have a chore for you. Follow me."

Wondering what the heck could need doing in the middle of the night, I put on my overalls, scratchy winter shirt and shoes, and followed him through the dark kitchen, snatching the Missus' old winter jacket from the peg by the door on my way out. It was cold. I could see my breath in the light of an almost full moon. I didn't need a flashlight to get to the barn; my feet knew the way.

But when he reached the barn, he kept walking. The smokehouse was behind the barn a ways, a safeguard against losing outbuildings if it caught fire.

I'd never been inside, for the same reason I made it a point to be busy with other chores at slaughter time. The thought of those pigs, hanging from hooks . . . I shivered, only partly from the cold.

The closer we got, the dread rose in me like cold pond water. My fear forced words from my lips. "What do you need me to do out here in the middle of the night?"

He turned on me. "If I'da wanted you ta know, I'da told you." He backhanded me across the mouth. "No more cheek outta you."

I stood frozen, mouth open. Sir had been scornful and sharp, but I'd never been hit before. I looked to the house, but the windows were all dark. Not that I'd expect much help from the Missus, but—

"Come on. Or do you want more?"

I sniffled, bit my lip and followed.

The smokehouse was a small building; no more than eight feet square, with a steep pitched roof. He led the way to the back where there was a small door with a padlock. He flipped on a flashlight, handed it to me, telling me to keep it trained on the door. He pulled a ring of keys from his overall pocket and used the smallest one to unlock it.

When the door swung open, my light caught the dull shine in the pigs' eye sockets. They hung from hooks through their necks, suspended from the rafters. There were six of them. They swayed in the light, seeming alive, until I realized it was just my shaking hands, moving the flashlight.

"Gimme that." He held out a hand, and I put the light in it.

In the center of the dirt floor was a pit, with the charcoal of a long-dead fire.

"I dropped my jackknife earlier and just woke up and remembered." He pointed. "That back corner there."

That made no sense. The door was locked, and it's not like someone was going to be way out here, looking to steal a jackknife. Why not leave it til morning?

"Git."

His raised hand convinced me. I stepped in, keeping my eyes downcast so not to see the carcasses. I skirted the pit and peered into the dark corner.

He rushed me then, grabbing me from behind. I fell, cracking my face on the rock-hard floor. My head spun, and I saw fireworks. When I came to a few seconds later, cold air brushed private skin. He'd pulled down my overalls, and I was lying on my back. The flashlight leaned against the wall, spotlighting the blackened pigs.

He messed with his fly.

I scuttled back, blood from my busted nose trickling down my face and into my throat. I almost tipped into the pit before he grabbed my ankle and jerked me back. I'd never seen a man's business before, and when he pulled it out, long, hard and pink, I fought harder, though I still didn't know what he meant to do. I opened my mouth to scream.

He grabbed my jaw in one hand and pinched. Hard. "You yell, and I'll gut you and hang you from a hook like them pigs. You lay still now, and you'll live."

I didn't move. Not when he lay on me. Not when he pushed it in. I felt a vicious tearing inside and I whimpered, but he didn't seem to notice, just pushed and grunted and moaned. I stared up at the pigs, the shadows turning them into a gaping horror.

In a few minutes that felt like a year, he collapsed on top of me. When he caught his breath, he pushed onto his knees and shoved himself back in his overalls.

I lay as he left me, frozen in pain, fear and loathing.

"Now that weren't so bad, eh?" He squinted down at me. "You'll get used to it." He pushed to his feet. "Now you stay quiet until I come back. If you yell or bring notice to yourself . . ." He pointed at an empty hook in the corner.

"But the Missus. She'll—"

"She won't. See, you ran away tonight."

At his leer, my stomach rebelled, and I rolled over and emptied it into the pit of charcoal.

"Remember. Shhhhhh." He held a finger to his lips, picked up my shoes and the flashlight, and walked out. The padlock clicked, then rattled as he tested it.

I was left in the pitch black with my shame, the smell of burnt flesh and the memory of glinting eye sockets.

He came, usually at night, sometimes during the day. At worst, several times a day. He brought me a bucket to use as a toilet, water, and small bits of leftover food from the table.

And he raped me. Every time. After a black eye and bruised ribs, I learned not to fight, just to lay there, looking up at the roof, trying not to see my cell mates. I began to believe the pigs were the lucky ones; they were beyond pain.

It was frigid-cold. I wrapped myself in the Missus' coat, but the ground leached heat and it was hard to sleep from shivering. I tested the board walls, but they held firm. I tried the door, but it was solid. Years of fires had baked the floor hard as cement. If I'd had something to hit him with, I'd have used it, but there was nothing except the pigs, and they were too heavy for me to lift. I had nothing to do all day but try to stay warm and dread the rattle of the lock.

I realized I had three choices: death, insanity, or escape.

Then, one day maybe ten days into hell, a miracle happened. He was between my legs, grunting like an animal, when something clunked the outside of my thigh. I felt around, and my fingers closed over something. I didn't know what it was until he was gone.

His jackknife. I covered my mouth to muffle my crazed laughter. The excuse he used to get me here was going to get me out. The rest of that day I planned, gripping that knife so hard my muscles cramped.

He came that night. Though I was expecting it, the rattle of the lock startled me so bad I saw stars. The door opened out, and as he stepped in, I met him, plunging the knife in at the waist, and pulling up, ripping that man the way he'd gutted those pigs. He fell, and the moonlight through the door showed the surprise on his face. I stood over him, blood dripping from my hand, watching until he died. Then I turned to the pigs and said, "That was for all of us."

I dragged him inside the door, closed it and put the padlock on, then rattled it to be sure it locked. With luck, they wouldn't find him til the smell gave him away.

I ran barefoot over the frozen ground, not even feeling the cold or the stones, freedom whistling past my ears.

Chapter 13

*To ask the right question is harder
than to answer it.*

Georg Cantor

I sit motionless, devastated for the girl who became my
grandmother.

"I appreciate the support, Jack, but you're about to break
my fingers."

I look down to see I'm squeezing her hands so hard my
knuckles are white. "Oh, sorry." I loosen the death-grip, but
my fingers refuse to let go all the way.

She pulls her hands from mine and pats my cheek, a tender
look in her faded eyes. "Thank you, Jack."

"For what? Oh my God, G'ma—"

"For this." She takes her hand from my cheek and holds it
up. The palm is wet.

That's when I realize tears are sheeting my face and dripping
off my chin. I wipe my nose on the sleeve of my dress. "Please,

can you talk about the rest? What happened after that?"

"Well, it could only go up from there, right?" She gives me a sad smile. "I ran to the city, figuring it would be easier to disappear there."

"Why didn't you go to the police? It was self-defense. No court would—"

"It would have been an orphan's word against a landowner's, in 1945, that meant something. And remember, the state hadn't done me any favors so far. I wasn't going to take the chance."

"But even if—"

"Hush, Jack." She puts her hand over mine. "Let me tell the rest. I think it's time I did."

I want to argue, but if listening is all I can do, I will.

"I got odd jobs, sweeping out stores, running errands. Then I lucked into a full-time job, setting pins in a bowling alley. They didn't have machines to do it back then. I think the owner hired me because I'd cost him way less than an adult. And I'd be out of sight, so no one would know he was breaking child labor laws." She snorts. "Not that I knew anything about that. I was just happy to be able to eat once a day."

"Weren't you afraid?"

She nods. "Whenever I'd see a cop, I'd duck away, feeling sure they'd see the guilt on my face."

"No, I mean being all alone in a big city. The bad things that could have happened . . ."

"I don't remember being afraid about that. I was just doing what I could to survive. I changed my name. Back then, records weren't great, and kids had no I.D. I called myself Nellie Blue. No one knew different, so that's who I became."

I have to smile. "That's where 'Blue' came from. I wondered."

"When the bowling alley owner asked me my last name, I blurted the first thing that came to me—my favorite color." She shrugs. "Hey, I was thirteen."

"You never were caught for . . . you know." I can't even say it.

"No. I figure the Universe had a hand in that, too."

"Well, that's the *least* it could do."

"Things got better when I discovered the library." Her eyes crinkle at the corners. "I wandered in just to get warm one day. I was gobsmacked. All those books! A librarian saw me standing slack-jawed, dripping melting snow on her floor. She asked if she could help. I told her I wanted to learn to read.

"I spent every spare hour there for the next four years, working my way from primers to reference books. I never got over it—anything you wanted to know was in that building, and it was all free. My library card was my first I.D."

My stomach interrupts with a growl, and I check my phone. "How'd it get so late? I'll tell you what. Let's order room service and just hang out the rest of the night."

"Sounds like a winner. I'm kinda tired."

"I should think so." Did we really wake up this morning at Paradise del Soul? It seems a lifetime ago. "You call and order us whatever you want. I'm going to run you a hot bath."

"That would be lovely." She lifts the receiver.

I walk to her bathroom, the past, present, and future shifting inside me like I'm one of those cheap kaleidoscope toys, with colored pieces falling into constantly new and unexpected patterns. I turn the hot spigot, and it hits me. "Oh, G'ma."

I walk back to sink down at her feet. "You said you wanted to stay. With me and Mom. But you couldn't." I swallow the hard chunk of truth that has crawled up my throat. "Is this why?"

She nods and runs a hand over my hair. "For years, I couldn't sleep indoors. The bowling alley was huge, so that wasn't so bad. I made up a pallet in the back, and they turned a blind eye." She sighs. "My fear of enclosed spaces has gotten a bit better over the years, but that dark cabin gave me the same reaction as those tiny apartments you grew up in . . ." A shudder rips through her, making her fingers dance on my scalp. "I hated leaving you. I wanted to take you with me, but what kind of life would that be for a child? Living on the road, sleeping outside? You wouldn't have had an education, and never having had one, I couldn't take that from you."

"I'm so sorry." I shake my head, dislodging more tears. "I blamed you all those years—I made you the fall guy for everything bad that happened to me."

"Shhhhh, child. Things happened as they were meant to. Now, go turn off the spigot, or people in the room below will be treading water."

She takes a long, hot bath that I have to help her into. Her body is so frail; the opposite of her spirit. I watch her luxuriate from my perch on the marble vanity as kaleidoscope bits fall into new patterns.

"That's why you don't eat pork."

"Yes. The smoked pigs terrified me at first, but in the long dark hours, I whispered to them. They became my co-conspirators. You don't eat your friends. Chicken on the other hand?" She flips her wrist, and suds fly. "I'm all down with that."

I think for a few minutes. "Did you and Easy marry? You never said."

"Yes, and no. We didn't believe in that. But he took me to a courthouse and handled the legal documents to give me his name. To keep me safe."

"Did he know . . . about the smokehouse?"

She shakes her head. "He knew something happened, and that I was on the run, but he never asked. He knew I couldn't talk about it."

"But he believed in you. Even not knowing."

She cocks her head. "Of course. That's what love is, child." She sits up straight. "Now, while you get me out of here, tell me about that nice man you whisper to late at night on the phone."

"I don't . . . how do you know about that?"

She winks at me. "I'm old Jack, not deaf."

I try to put my thoughts together while I help her out, dry her off, and wrap her in a thick, white velveteen and terry robe. "His name is Leo. He's a metal artist who does the most amazing work. I'll show you pictures on my phone, later."

"Is he sexy?"

I chuckle at the twinkle in her eye. "Yes, but I'm *not* discussing my sex life with you, so just forget it."

She snaps her fingers. "You are a killjoy. I've told you that before, right?"

There's a knock at the door, which turns out to be our dinner: Roasted chicken, mashed potatoes, asparagus, and devil's food cake for dessert.

We're eating when she picks up the subject again. "So, tell me three good things about this Leo of yours."

"He's not mine. But let me think." I take a bite of chicken and think while I chew. "He doesn't ask permission. He assumes what I'd like, and most times, guesses right. I've never been with a man like that."

"Ah, observant and caring enough to put you at the center of his world."

"I wouldn't put it that way." But he kind of does, doesn't he? I'll think about that later. "He's different from me in so many ways. He makes me see that mine isn't the only way."

"Wow, a brave man."

"Stop." I swat at her arm but am careful to barely touch it. She bruises so easily.

"And the third?" She gives me that curious bird head-tilt.

I think for a few moments. My cheeks heat, but I give her a wicked grin. "He is fantastic in bed."

"Woo hoo!" She pumps a fist in the air. "I knew you had my genes in there somewhere."

We laugh and talk for hours, as if we're two women exploring a new friendship. Though it sounds odd to say, it feels like I'm getting to know my grandmother—the real person—for the first time.

When I see her wrinkles slacken, I stand. "Let's get you to bed. I'm exhausted. I can't imagine how tired you are."

"It has been an amazing day, that's for sure." She lets me help her up, and I cradle her elbow all the way to the bedroom.

I pull down the covers and turn on the lamp on the nightstand. "Can I ask you one more question?"

"I have no more secrets, child." She sits on the edge of the bed.

"Given your horrific childhood, and the hard life you've led, how can you be so open and happy?" I know her well enough now to know her optimism isn't faked.

"I *am* happy. I've had a wonderful life, Jack. An amazing life." She lays back in the bed, and I help lift her legs and tuck her in. "When you have awful things happen, it teaches you how amazingly special the average days are. You've got a longer yardstick to measure by than most people. You *know* what bad is, so whatever is better than that is cause for celebration." She frowns. "I should have died in that smokehouse. How would it honor the miracle the Universe granted me, if I wasted the rest of my life, being angry or afraid?"

How indeed. My childhood was a party compared to Nellie's, and yet the past week I've come to realize how much I live in fear. Fear well disguised, but fear, nonetheless.

"I'm so proud of you. I know I give you a hard time about your business, but the will and energy and intuition it took to start that from nothing," she puts her hand out, to touch my heart, "I feel like that part of you came from me."

"It *did,* G'ma." There's a vise in my throat and my voice comes out wavery.

"But you've got to loosen the reins on yourself. I hope you see that. Oh, that reminds me." She reaches to the nightstand, lifts her soft leather medicine bag and hands it to me. "This has held all my secrets, all these years. It will hold yours, too."

"Oh, I couldn't. That's a part of you." I try to hand it back.

"You'll need it more than I. You hush now and take it." When she's sure I'll keep it, she nods. "Good."

"That's enough now. You need to get some rest. We have all day tomorrow to talk." I try to stand, but she grabs my hand.

"You've done a wonderful thing, Jacqueline. Thank you for pushing me, and for listening. That mess feels so much better out than in. Maybe now I can finally put it behind me for good." She kisses the back of my hand. "Thank you."

I sink onto the bed again and wrap my arms around her thin shoulders. "I'm glad, G'ma. But you've given me so much more . . ." My voice cracks, and I stumble to a stop.

"Shhhhh." She pats my back. "Now can we get a goat?"

I sputter a laugh through my tears, then walk to turn on the bathroom light, and still laughing, walk out.

Chapter 14

Pain is universal.

Suffering is optional.

Nellie Oliver

When my phone alarm buzzes the next morning, I come instantly awake, despite getting—I squint at the screen—two hours sleep.

Once Nellie was in bed, I called Leo, filling him in on our watershed day. His quiet understanding was butter on my burned places. It makes me want to reciprocate more, no matter how scary that seems. When he asked if he could meet us in Vegas, I actually considered it. I'm proud of my grandmother and would like to have him meet her. But I'm also selfish; I want her all to myself for a bit longer. Maybe later. If things work out with he and I.

When I hung up, I lay there for hours, the kaleidoscope still turning, fitting my past together in new ways, snapping together like jigsaw pieces, making a brand-new picture. G'ma loved me. The reason she left wasn't me . . . it wasn't even Mom.

Knowing that changed the topography of my past like a tsunami changes the land it scours. But it sent ripples into my present, too. Then the tide went out, laying bare what I couldn't bear before. I thought the bad things that happened were a punishment—because I wasn't enough. Instead, they were just things that happened. No one abandoned me on purpose. Mom had her demons and it turns out, G'ma did too. The prof from college? He was just a stupid mistake, and what he gave me wasn't love.

Now that I don't have to be the girl carrying a heavy backpack of guilt, who am I?

Who do I *want* to be? The realization that I can choose shoots sparkles through me.

For maybe the first time in my life, I'm not seeing the future as a potential for disaster. Overnight, a tentative surety has crept in to curl up next to my heart. Dammit, that little girl dealt with more than most kids, and not only survived, but had the guts to put herself through college and create a business from nothing. I'm pretty proud of that little scrapper.

I throw the covers back and call in an order for room service, and for once, don't feel guilty. How can a shift in the past make such a change in my present? I don't know, but I am so light I can't feel my feet touching the floor as I head for the shower.

An hour and a half later, Nellie and I are ready for whatever the day brings.

I check us out in the full-length mirror by the door. We're casual but not tourist-trap, bargain-bin casual. "Don't we look like women to be reckoned with?"

"To the max, Baby." Nellie winks at me.

"What do you want to do today?"

"I'm going to teach you how to have some *fun,* Grasshopper."

"As long as it doesn't involve gambling. Or getting arrested."

———— *ele* ————

"Where are we headed?" I hold the door to the lobby for G'ma's scooter.

"Insanity." She hits the throttle and rolls past me.

"You've been headed there for years."

"Very funny. You oughta show respect for your elders, whippersnapper."

I suppress a smile. "Yes Ma'am." She really is fun. "Seriously, where are we going?"

"Be patient. You'll see."

It's ten, and the town is only beginning to resurrect itself. We only pass a few people, and most of them look like they haven't been to bed yet. Though the sun is raising the temperature it's still bearable, and shopkeepers are out, washing down sidewalks. G'ma slows, and we window-shop our way down the strip. I'd love to get something for Leo. But what? It can't be some tourist tchotchke. And it can't be too expensive, in case he thinks it means something more than what it means. What *would* it mean, exactly? I shake my head. It's too early to figure that out.

A woman steps out of a shop, releasing the heady smell of good leather.

"G'ma, wait." I pull open the door and take a deep breath of luxury. "I'm just going to step in here a second."

"Something for your mystery man?" She waggles her eyebrows.

My face heats. "Just stay in the shade. I'll be right back."

A saleswoman in an expensive double-breasted dress looks up from behind the counter, managing to look down her nose at the same time. "May I help you?"

"I'm not sure. Let me look . . ." A sculptor can't show his body of work easily. I'm thinking an artist's bag to hold oversized pictures of his sculptures. In a lighted cubby I find a beautiful black pebbled portfolio. Almost afraid to look, I pull the price tag. Holy wow. Is this made of dinosaur hide?

"That is lovely. And we can personalize it with your name sewn in gold thread on the inside for free."

They should, for this price. I lift it. It's sophisticated, stiff, substantial. Professional—it's perfect. But the money I've spent this trip . . . then I remember G'ma's take from the poker table last night. It wouldn't be such a large step, if the money didn't come from my safety net, would it? Screw it. I don't even care what he thinks the extravagance means. He deserves this. "I'll take it."

"You've made a wonderful choice."

She looks pleased, which tells me she just made a nice commission. I follow her to the cash register, pay, ask her to personalize it to Leo, and have it delivered to our hotel when it's done. I walk out to G'ma's knowing look. "Shut up."

"Hey, loosening up looks good on you. The next stop will help, too."

"Lead on, oh Sage one."

She pulls in at the lobby of the Stratosphere Hotel. I'm worried she'll want to gamble, but she rolls past the poker tables and heads to the elevator. Once in, she pushes the button for the top floor.

"We're going to the observation deck?"

"Yup."

"Not a huge fan of heights, G'ma."

"That's the loosen up part, Jack."

When the doors open she rolls out. Oh no. *This* is what she meant by Insanity. A ride where octopus arms dangle you over the edge of a thousand-foot drop, spin you to 3G's, then extend, so you're looking straight down.

"Come on, Jack."

"You're the insane one if you think I'm getting on that thing. And you have no business doing it either."

"Jack." She parks the scooter and comes to take my hand. "This amazing trip ends soon. I'm going back to the old fart warehouse tomorrow. This is my last chance to really live. And it's your chance to start."

"By dying?" She's pulling the guilt card, and it's not working. I'd do almost anything for her. But not this.

She looks up at me, her stupid sunglasses sparkling in the sun. "Please, Jack? It's the last thing I'll ask you for, the rest of my life." She licks her finger and crosses her heart with it.

The contraption looks solid, and I've never heard of an accident . . . If an octogenarian is up for it, it makes me look like I have a stick up my butt if I'm not. It would prove Nellie's opinion about me has been right, all along. "Oh hell. But if I die, I'll haunt your skinny butt for eternity. Just so you know."

She shoves her fists in the air. "Faaaaar out!"

"Yeah, well try to remember you like me when I hurl on you."

The man loads us in, securing our bodies, sealing my fate. My stomach takes cover in my throat, there's chunks of ice in my intestines, and my heart is running the Indy 500. "I think I'm having a panic attack."

"You're gonna be fine. How bad can it be, if they let an old lady like me on?"

My head whips to her. "You mean you've never been on this?"

"Nope. But I already know I'm gonna love it."

Rock music blares from speakers over our heads, and the thing jolts. I squeal, and my fingers meld with the metal bar. It inches out from the deck until we are hanging with nothing under us but a looooong fall.

"Ohshitohshitohshit." I close my eyes. I should have called Leo to say goodbye. It starts spinning, slow at first, then speeds up. "I'm too young to die!" I wail.

"Woooooohoooooo!"

I sneak a look at G'ma. Her arms are up, her mouth is open with glee. "Let 'er rip!"

"Hang on for God's sake!" Inch by inch, the beast's arms ease out. The music thumps my eardrums.

"Open your eyes, Jack, this is incredible!"

We're spinning fast now, almost perpendicular. I crack an eyelid. The strip spins like a top, so very, very far below. My sphincter loosens. I slam my eye shut and concentrate on keeping all orifices clamped tight.

An eternity later, the spinning slows and the arms begin to retract.

When the man touches my arm, I scream.

"It's okay, Lady. It's over."

"Are you okay Jack?" G'ma can't be too concerned; she's standing on the deck, grinning ear-to-ear.

"I think I believe in God now."

"See? Told you it would open your mind."

I take the man's hand and clamber out to stand on rubber knees. "I'm not talking to you. I need a bathroom."

"You mean you don't want to do it again?" At my look, she wanders to her scooter and sits. "Okay, fine."

After a bathroom, we stop at a bistro on the way back to the hotel. I get coffee, G'ma gets a huge slab of cheesecake.

"You sure you don't want to share? This'd go great with coffee."

"It'd go great with an elastic waistband." But my stomach has calmed, and my mouth is watering. "Okay, hand me that other fork."

"See? Insanity shook loose your iron grip on life. Told you it would."

"You know, I can't help but compare us. I've lived within the lines my whole life, afraid to step outside for fear of losing what I had. You had a much worse childhood, but you're the polar opposite. How did you get so brave?"

"I've made it my goal to banish fear from my life, but as you've seen, I'm not always successful. All of life is a chance, Jack. You can live in fear, or without it, but either way, you'll die in the end." She shrugs. "Why not suck the marrow out of every day while you're here?"

She makes it sound very logical, but I know fear is the opposite of logic. After living with G'ma this week though, I do recognize that it's a choice. A choice I'm going to try to make more often. "G'ma, will you answer another question for me?"

"Fire away."

I pick up and discard beginnings, trying to word it a way that won't sound accusatory.

"Just ask, Jack. I told you I don't have any more secrets."

"Well, I looked it up, and Woodstock was years after Easy died. You have been a bit . . . loose with the truth at times, about little stuff that doesn't matter and big stuff, too. Why do you do that?"

I expect her face to fall. Even clouds of anger to gather. Instead, she smiles.

"Well, when you live on the run like I did, 'truth' is a fluid thing. After all, I made up a new name, and it became the truth." She looks at her fork, pushing what's left of her cheesecake around her plate. "I make things up to correct reality to be what *should* have happened. Easy and I should have been at Woodstock, dammit."

I take her hand to still it. "You're right. You guys should have been. I'm so sorry."

She swipes a tear, but when she looks up, their sparkle is back. "But today isn't about sad things. Today is about us. Let's get at it."

My phone rings. I pull it from my purse, surprised by the number. "Leo? Is everything all right?" He never calls in the daytime.

"Better than all right. I'm at the airport."

"Seatac? Where are you going?"

"No, I'm here. In Vegas."

"Here?" I gulp down a mixture of thrill, trepidation and sparkly anticipation.

"Mystery man?" G'ma whispers.

"I know I shouldn't have. But I wanted to see you, and I so wanted to meet Nellie. I'm not going to take all your time. I'm only here for a few hours . . . Are you mad?"

I'm not sure how I feel, but mad isn't part of it. "Nope. G'ma can't wait to meet you. Come on down the strip. We'll meet you inside the doors of Caesars Palace."

"On my way."

I hang up. G'ma grabs my hands. "By this evening, I'll know if he's right for you."

"I'm perfectly capable of deciding that for myself." I leave money on the table and stand.

"Then why haven't you yet?" Her laser stare sees into me.

"Okay, you have a point. Now, get your scooter and let's burn rubber. I don't want to keep him waiting." The day that started slow and meandering has sped up. How many hours will he be here? I didn't think to ask.

On the way out, I stop at a rack of brochures of local attractions. "What should we do this afternoon? Tour of the Hoover Dam?"

"Boooring." She pulls a fold-out. "Hot air balloon trip over the strip!"

"You're kidding, right? I've seen enough of the strip from that vantage point to last the rest of my life." I pull another. "How about a Jeep tour of Red Rock Canyon?" An artist would love that. And maybe I can find the plant with that elusive fragrance I've been looking for.

"That'd be the tits."

I hope she doesn't talk like that around—who am I kidding? Of course she will. And the realization hits me that I no longer care. Nellie is the real deal, and if he can't see that, then . . . I don't know what, but it will tell me something I'll need to know if he and I are going to move forward to whatever's next. A shower of jitters shoots down my nerves. I don't need to decide that now.

"Okay, floor it, G'ma. We've got a date."

Leo looks the same, from his topsiders sans socks, to his coming-untucked shirt, and two-day beard scruff. There's no reason the sight of him should melt my insides. But it does. Especially that half-cocked smile that reminds me he's seen me naked. My nether-regions spasm, and it's everything I can do not to throw myself at him. Instead, I stand staring like a star-struck fan-girl.

He doesn't move either.

"You must be Leo." G'ma rolls in like an ice-breaker on Lake Superior. "Jack only told me a few things about you, but

I can see they're true."

He bends at the waist to take her hand. "Really? What did she tell you?"

Oh God, not the sex. Please, not the—

"Mostly that you're an animal in the sack."

Leo bursts into surprised laughter. "I am so happy to meet you, Nellie. Jack has told me a lot about *you.*"

G'ma fluffs her cotton candy hair. "Well she wouldn't know, but I too, am dynamite in bed."

"Of that, I have no doubt." He straightens, steps to me, slides his hands up under my hair, and kisses the hell out of me.

All the yearning from the past week of late-night phone calls somehow breaks loose, and I'm lost.

A throat clear burns off the smoke fogging my brain.

"Excuse me." A man with a large brown-wrapped package stands waiting to get in the door.

I step aside, embarrassment mingling with sexual heat until I feel like I'm going to spontaneously combust right here in front of Caesars.

G'ma winks at Leo. "See? She takes after me."

"G'ma, behave yourself." I turn to Leo. "How long are you here for?"

"Well, I didn't want to bust into your time together. I just wanted to—"

"Oh no," G'ma says, "stay as long as you like. This could get very interesting."

"I don't have a flight booked. Figured that way I could tuck tail and run if you weren't glad to see me."

"Well, I guess that's off the table." I fan my hot face. "We thought maybe a Jeep trip through Red Rock Canyon. Have you ever spent time in the desert?"

"Flown over, but that's about it."

I tuck my arm in his. "Well you're about to get up close and personal with some of the most starkly beautiful land you'll ever see. Taxi!"

Three hours later, we're back in town, having a late lunch at the hotel before Leo has to catch a cab back to the airport.

"That was incredible." Leo sips his iced tea. "This has given me so many ideas. The colored cliffs in that canyon . . ." He shakes his head.

"Don't get too excited. It sure isn't like this in the summer. Or any other time. Except these few magical weeks in the spring."

"Oh, don't listen to her." G'ma spears a forkful of her éclair. "The desert is always beautiful."

He turns to her. "Thanks for the tour, G'ma. Your point of view gave me good insight."

He dropped "Nellie," an hour in. They're firm and fast buds now. "And thanks for identifying more plants for me. I still haven't found that one with the fragrance I need though. I'm beginning to believe that it's the key to my next scent, and it's bugging me."

"Ruh roh." She pats her mouth with the napkin. "Have you noticed she can be a bit obsessive about her business?"

"Um. I am still here at the table, you know."

Leo pats my hand. "Yes, but I'm probably worse, so we make a good pair."

I have to admit, we kinda do. I tune them out and study the guy I've decided I'm letting all the way in, as of today. The phone calls tunneled under my icy walls, linking us in ways I didn't realize until later. Then the heat in his kiss melted the rest. Besides, who could resist a guy who loves your quirky, inappropriate grandmother? When my cheeks ache, I realize I've smiled most of this day away.

He signals the waiter over and hands him his credit card.

"No, I'll get it." I reach for the check, but Leo waves the man away.

"I've had the honor of two beautiful women's company today. It's the least I could do." When the waiter returns, Leo signs the check and returns the card to his wallet. "Now, I really do have to get to the airport. I have a project at home I can't wait to get to. See me out?"

"Yes, but first, will you take a photo of G'ma and I? We don't have any, yet."

"Of course." I turn over my phone, and I lean over G'ma in her chair, and hug her neck, inhaling her unique scent of sandalwood and dusting powder.

The waitress stops and sets a carafe of coffee down. "Do you want me to take a photo of the three of you?"

"Oh heck yes." G'ma smiles and crooks a finger at Leo. "You come over here, beefcakes."

"G'ma, you behave." But I'm laughing.

She takes several photos and hands back my phone. "Thank you. You ready to go, G'ma?"

"You two go. I'll finish dessert, and meet you outside, Jack."

"You sure?"

"Go, go." She waves us off. "Lay one on him for me."

Leo steps to Nellie, takes her hand, and raises it to his lips. "It has been an honor to meet you." Then he takes my hand and leads me out. Once on the sidewalk, he pulls me into his arms. "I mean it. This day has been wonderful. You were right, Nellie is a kick."

"Yeah, it's funny how my opinion of her has done a one-eighty in the past week."

"Well I'm glad, because I'm looking forward to hanging out with the two of you when she visits." He touches his lips to my temple. "And I hope the past week means I'm going to see a lot more of you when you get home."

"Try to keep me away." I kiss him, and it's harder to step away than it should be.

He signals a taxi. "When will you be home?"

"A few days. I'm driving G'ma to Arizona tomorrow, and I want to be sure she's okay and settled before I catch a flight home."

"You take good care, and I'll see you in a few days." A cab pulls to the curb, and he pulls me into his arms for a kiss.

Which flips every switch I've got.

"Hey, buddy, you want a cab, or you gonna get a room?"

I step back, laughing. What a difference a week makes.

The sun has gone by the time G'ma wakes from her nap. She admonishes me for working and sends me off for a hot bath while she orders food. I request a bottle of wine.

In a half hour soak I discover the delight that is a bath bomb. I luxuriate, reliving the perfect day, and Leo's kiss. I'm not sure how to do this relationship thing, but a week ago, I wouldn't have believed I could respect my grandmother, so I now know anything is possible. Nervous? Yes, but—

"Stop mooning about that sexy man and get your butt out here." G'ma barks from the other room. "The food's hot."

And the wine should be cold. A glass or two with dinner sounds divine. But maybe I shouldn't. Alcoholism runs in families. "Oh, lighten the hell up, Jack. You've drunk less in your entire life than Mom did in one day." I stick out my tongue at my reflection, pull the belt on the fluffy robe tighter, and march out to the sitting room.

Dishes cover the table, and when I step in, G'ma lights a candle on a chocolate cupcake. Champagne is chilling in an ice bucket beside the table.

"What in the world?"

"We're celebrating." She smiles and steps over to envelop me in a hug.

"What, exactly?" After all, there's lots to choose from.

"You, my love." She pours us each a glass.

Emotions flood my chest, the tide rising to my eyes. "I heard a German saying, once. Too soon old, too late smart." I sigh. "I learned I have an amazing grandmother who loved me all these years. I shut her out, and I have no way to get those years back."

"Oh Jack. Don't do this to yourself." She hands me a glass, then pats my cheek. "We only know what we know, until we know better. If I'd been able to tell you years ago, things wouldn't have happened this way."

I take a gulp. "Let me guess. The friggin' Universe again?"

"Now *that*, I'll drink to." She drains the glass, pours us both another, then sits across from me at the small table. "Suffering is optional, remember? Look at me. It took me until last night to understand what that really meant." She uncovers the food. "Seventy years! You want to talk about stupid . . ."

"Don't you say that! After what happened to you? I think you're incredible."

"And given your childhood, wouldn't an outsider say the same about you?" She raises a brow. "Pain is pain, Jack. You can't compare yours to anyone else's. It all just hurts." She hands me a plate with a thick cheeseburger and fries. "The important thing isn't the pain of our pasts. It's what we're here to learn from it."

"A cheeseburger?"

"Nothing better than grease and carbs. Now shut up and listen. I'm imparting wisdom nuggets here, dammit."

I take another gulp of champagne. "Yes'm."

"Your past was there to give you a lesson. Have you learned it yet?"

"Not sure you should ask me that with booze in my hand."
I suppress a giggle.

She gives me a stern look. "I asked you at the luau what
you're on this earth to learn. Do you have an answer yet?"

I sit, trying to gather words that scatter like chickens when I
try to grab them.

She rolls her eyes. "I see this is not the time for lessons. Just
eat."

"We'll talk in the morning, promise. Just for tonight, I want
to carb overload and party with my grandma. Okay?"

"Sounds like a plan, Stan." She lifts her dripping burger and
takes a bite.

She is so darned cute. "Hey G'ma. What if you moved in
with me? We'd have a blast."

"We would." She gives me that bright-eyed bird look. "You
could move to the desert."

A week ago, I'd have been horrified by the idea. Now? Since
the desert is no longer my nemesis and my old haunts no
longer do . . . could I? I don't know. "Let me get my company
back moving in the right direction. Then we'll talk. Okay?"

She beams like a kid on her birthday morning. "Outta sight,
Baby."

I wake to the sun pouring in the window and stretch, surprised
to feel a smile on my face. Apparently, the carbs and
champagne did their job; I'm bursting with energy, optimism,
and anxious to get back to Seattle. This trip has given me ideas
for new fragrances, and I'm dying to get to work on them.

I'll let G'ma sleep in. This past week has taken a toll on her,
but I know neither of us would have missed it. Well, I could
have skipped the goat, but last night we giggled like high-

schoolers on a sleepover. What I imagine those are like, anyway.

I head for the shower, mind whirring with what suddenly seems possible.

A half hour later, I pack the suitcase I bought, wheel it out to the door, then walk to Nellie's bedroom. I'll help her pack while she gets ready. It's only a four-hour drive to Paradise Springs, then I'll get Nellie settled and catch a flight home. I don't want to think now about how hard it's going to be to leave her there. Maybe I'll stay an extra day, just to be sure . . .

I pull the doors open. "Come on sleepyhead. One more road trip for us today." I step to the window, pull back the curtains and look down onto the sunlight reflecting off the crystal pool. "It's such a pretty day, I almost wish we still had the Duchess, so we could ride with the top down." I walk to the bed. "Sans goat funk, of course. Come on, G'ma, daylight's burn—"

The tether that holds my heart in place snaps and I'm in free-fall.

Her eyes are closed, her face slack, and oh so white.

My knees let go and I sink onto the bed, *willing* the rise and fall of the bedsheets. "No. Oh no." I take her wrist to check her pulse, but the chill of her skin proves what I already know.

My grandmother has taken her last road trip.

"You can't go, G'ma. I just found you!" It's a desolate child's wail. I lay my head on her frail chest. "Not now. Please, not now. We're not ready."

I close my eyes and feel a rumble in my mind, my own personal earthquake. It's my world cracking, opening a deep crevasse between the world with my G'ma in it, and the arid desert of a world without her. I crawl into bed, wrap my arms around her, and press my ear to her chest, hoping to stop the shifting, but reality is a cold-hearted bitch.

Most tears are like summer rain, warm, and cleansing, washing away the tumult of emotions I can no longer hold in. These are stingy, stinging things, like blood, dripping from my eyes. They don't cleanse—they burn.

When they end, I feel hot and feverish, with the bitter taste of ashes on my tongue.

After some unknown amount of time, I kiss G'ma's cheek and rise, trying to think of what comes next. Instead, I drop into a chair in the corner, memories of the past week running like a movie in my head.

I thought my growing up was hard.

I thought my solitary existence was hard.

But discovering you're not alone after all, to have that person wrenched from you after a *day*?

"That's not *fair*." The anger comes out on a shudder, my voice in a whimper.

Chapter 15

If you don't like something, change
it.
If you can't change it, change your
attitude.
Maya Angelou

The sun slips below the hills as the red-eye flight to Seattle leaves the ground. From my tiny window, the lights of the strip seem to brighten, as if claiming the approaching night. I watch until there's nothing but unbroken desert below. Last time, I left this town running. This time, I had to rip myself away.

I lean back with a sigh. The flint-edged emotions of the day have left me battered, my insides scoured by loss. I'm hollow down to my bones.

Tomorrow, I'll have to turn to my uncertain future, but for tonight, I'm living in the space between, trying to reconcile the loss I didn't see coming. It's strange, how living is so complicated, yet dying is simple. Why can't it be the other way around? I'd have welcomed something complex to do today, to keep my mind from losing her. But there were few details to take care of—after all, G'ma lived a simple life. The state requires an autopsy, but I left instructions for her to be cremated after, and her ashes sent to me.

I close my eyes, remembering our disagreements, our conversations, her cackling laugh.

The truth in her words come back to me.

There is much pain in the world. But suffering is optional. I believe that when I fully learn to accept that lesson, I won't need to be here anymore.

If she's right, I should be happy for her. She's leveled up. But I'm still too selfish. Too raw.

It's just not *fair*.

I only realize I've nodded off when the flight attendant announces the let-down into Sea-tac. The lights of my city blink into focus. I feel like a different woman in the body of the one who left a week ago. But it's like an earthquake at night; I'm not sure what has changed, so I'm hesitant to move, for fear I'll trip in the debris.

When I get back to work tomorrow, things will settle, and I'll go back to my old self, I'm sure. I trudge through the jetway to the terminal, and downstairs, to baggage claim.

"Hey, Jack."

I spin to find Leo with a handful of daisies and a sad lopsided smile. I've never been so glad to see anyone. His arms enfold me, and the muscles I've held tight all day melt into him. "You're here," my voice comes out watery and weak. I called him this morning to tell him, but . . . "Why? I have my car here, and—"

"Shhhh." He strokes my hair and whispers in my ear. "I Ubered over. I'll drive you home."

I back up until he comes into focus: too-long hair curling over his collar, two-day scruff, his soft dark chocolate eyes. How could I have been so cold to him before I left? Why? The answer feels important, but I'm too tired and heartsore to figure it out tonight. "I don't deserve this . . . you." I realize how lost I've felt all day, like a child, wanting an adult to take over.

He drops a chaste kiss on my lips, squeezes me tight, then steps back. "You deserve a lot more than you let yourself have, Jack."

G'ma's nickname on his tongue looses more tears, and I dash them with a flick of my finger. "There's my bag." I point and he nabs it.

"Let's go." He puts a protective arm around me and guides me to the door. "I'm taking you to my place, just for tonight." He looks into my face. "Okay?"

"More than okay." I've dreaded opening the door to my lonely flat tonight. "Thank you."

A half hour later, he unlocks the door to his loft and ushers me in. The tall ceilings and cement floor are impersonal, but the spotlights over the bar in the kitchen area are an oasis of welcoming yellow light. While Leo wheels my suitcase to the bedroom, I step to the long narrow windows that march down the room. It's late, but the lights of Capitol Hill's Pike neighborhood are always on—artists are notorious night-owls. "Show me your *Twenty-first Century Man.*"

Leo flips on the spotlights in his working area to my left. The figure is larger-than life, probably nine feet tall. It wears a helmet of what appears to be coconut hull. Small metal leaves cover most of the rest, a shiny green and gold gilding that shifts as I walk over, colors swirling like oil on water. In the statue's gloved hand, a delicate crystal lance.

It takes my breath. "Oh."

"You like it?"

I nod. "The lance is brilliant. It's art, not a weapon."

He smiles. "You get it."

"How could I not?" I can't take my eyes from the hundreds of shades of changing green. "I love everything you do, but this. This is . . . I don't know a word for it."

He chuckles, flips off the light, and steps over to me. "Let's hope the critics find a few nice ones. I have a show in two weeks at the Recherché Gallery."

One of Seattle's most prestigious. That in itself is a coup. I'm so proud of him. He deserves to be world-renown. "They're going to think this is the tits."

"You picked up some odd sayings in Arizona." He's smiling, but his eyebrows are buried in his curls.

"G'ma-isms." In the shadows, there's a sheet-covered figure about a foot shorter than the one in spotlights. On the worktable beside it, bits of white metal shimmer pearlescent in the lights. "What's that?"

"Oh, just something I'm playing with." He takes my hand and leads me to the far end of the loft, where warm light spills from his bedroom. "I'm so sorry about your grandmother, Jack. I'm so glad I got the chance to meet her."

And if he'd left it to me, he wouldn't have. What other things in life have I missed by my knee-jerk no? "She was a kick." I sink onto the bed with a sigh. "It feels like I've been gone a lifetime."

"A lot has happened, that's for sure. Here." He takes off my shoes, and runs his hand up my calf, kneading, trailing heat.

We've gotten to know each other better in the whispered conversations in the dark—I feel closer to him than I've been to a man . . . ever. He's been the quiet strength following me through the desert. And tonight, he was there for me when I didn't know to ask; didn't even recognize how desperately I needed him until I saw him standing there, waiting for me. I lift his chin. "You are the most amazing man."

Smiling, he bends to kiss the inside of my knee.

His giving makes me want to give. "Come." I tug his hands. "Let me show you what I mean."

Later, tangled in sheets and moonlight, my head on his shoulder, he strokes my hair. "You're different."

"I feel different."

He's quiet long enough I think he's drowsing.

"You told me Nellie's story in bits and pieces along the way, but you never told me yours. Why were you so mad at her all those years?"

I sift through the earthquake debris, to see how I feel about telling him. Walls have fallen, but which ones? There's too much to sort through. Should I take a chance? "What was your childhood like?"

"As different as my life now as possible, I think." He snorts. "I grew up in Pittsburgh. My dad was a steel worker, blue collar and proud of it. My mother was a cashier in a grocery store. My brother was the quarterback for the Southside Steel Slingers. Me? I was an artist."

"Wow."

"Yeah, I fit right in. I created scenery for all the plays, designed floats for the homecoming parade, and took every creative class that school had. I was bullied, but never beaten up—only because my brother was the local hero. He got a football scholarship to Penn State."

"And you?"

His chest rises on a deep breath. He holds it, then lets it out, long and slow. "I worked my way through high school and saved every penny. I applied for scholarships and grants, but I was still short what I'd need for U Penn, the best art school in the state. I went to my dad for a loan. Not a gift, mind you, a *loan*. To be paid back with interest."

"What did he say?"

"He told me if I majored in something that could actually support a family, he'd find the money but if I insisted on embarrassing him with my 'sensitivity,' I could forget it."

"Your *father* said that?"

"I'm pretty sure he thought I was gay, but he'd have died before he used that word."

Leo is so sure of who he is, and where he fits in the world. I wouldn't have guessed that surety was forged in fire. I should know better, after G'ma's reveal. I rub circles on his chest, as if I can soothe the old wound. "What did you do?"

"I moved out. My mother's sister lived close to the school, and she took me in. I worked during the day and went to school at night. Took me six years, but I got my degree." He laughs, but it has no humor in it. "Seems stupid now. The art is the important thing, not a piece of paper. But at the time, all I could think about was proving him wrong."

"What does he think about your success now?"

"He died of a heart attack at work the year after I graduated."

"Oh, I'm sorry."

"No reason to be. He wouldn't have had it any other way."

Leo and I have more in common than I knew. Our childhoods were very different, but like G'ma said, pain is universal.

"That's enough for tonight." His voice rumbles through his chest into my ear.

I lift my head, but his face is a composition of shadows. I can't read it. "I want to hear the rest."

"And I want to hear yours. But you've been through a lot today. The last thing you need is more emotion tonight." His lips touch my forehead. "You need sleep more."

"How do you know what I need before I do?"

He chuckles and pulls my head back down to his chest. "You're home. You're safe. Sleep now."

If he said more, it was lost in my dreams.

I'd planned on running home before work, but we slept until the sun edged over the windowsill to fall on our eyelids. I catch a quick shower, throw on clothes I bought in Vegas, and meet Leo at the door, where he holds out a cup of coffee.

"Tonight?" His eyes challenge me.

"Maybe. I'll be working very late." The lead apron of my uncertain future falls back onto my shoulders. "For like six months or . . . lots more."

His touch is soft when he lifts my chin. "We'll work it out."

I smile, remembering last night. "I'd like that." I drop a kiss on his lips and scoot out the door.

The storefront is a warm, welcome-home hug. I'd hoped that when I walked in this door again, I'd have business cards of buyers from big retail chains. If I could have talked just one of them into stocking Adam and Eve for this year's Christmas season, Heart's Note would be on the way up by this time next year. That's the problem with dreaming; when you come down, the reality that was fine before, isn't enough.

What the hell, I've made my own luck with sweat equity. There's a huge market for my scents; I just have to find a way to let the market know about them. When I unlock and pull open the door, the jingle of the little brass bells makes me smile, and I take in a bracing breath of mingled scents. My scents.

This is going to be okay. I'm going to make it okay.

No one will be here for an hour. I flip on the lights in the back room, set down my bag of cuttings from the trip, and power up my computer. My first stop is the show's website, to see what I missed. The schedule is listed, with a hole where my workshop was to be. "It couldn't be helped. You know it." My words sound loud in the big echoey room. Yeah, I know it. But it would have been—"What?"

There's a sidebar displaying tweets with the hashtag, #UltBeautyShow.

Sorry to miss Jacqueline Oliver's startup talk. Totally unprofessional.

I talked to a reporter who wanted to interview her. #EpicFail

That's what's wrong with Indies— come up fast, gone faster.

Heart's Note—hould have named it Noob Note.

The tweets have to be from a wannabe, a nobody in the industry . . . but still, it hurts. I close out and go to email. My heart thuds at Scott Rodger's address. I take a breath and click on it.

Ms. Oliver,

This is to inform you that Heart's Note will not be invited to full membership in the Perfumers Guild. As you know, we don't endorse most small operations, and I must say, you let down more than myself by your disregard of the opportunity we offered; you let down your business.

Scott Rodgers

"Why you arrogant, entitled little man." I knew the offer would be withdrawn, but to send an email informing me is a slap in the face. An old familiar shame rises to burn at the back of my throat. I wish I were one of those self-confident women that don't let the judgement of others affect them. Well, I may not be, but I'm master level "fake it til you make it." I click out of email, turn on classical on Pandora, and pull out my cuttings.

When I open the sealed bags, the smell brings my grandmother into the room so strongly that I feel her at my shoulder. "I know what you'd say, G'ma. Screw him and the horse he rode in on." A watery chuckle dribbles from my tight throat.

Wouldn't that show that smug rodent if I could come up with the hit of the Christmas season? The flowers I found in the desert are going to amount to something, I just know it. All I need is that last piece to the puzzle.

Juggling grocery bags, I fumble the key into the lock of my apartment, and walk in. They refurbished an old warehouse into twelve apartments near Pioneer Square, and I fell in love with the open floorplan and old brick walls inside. A stale smell smacks my nose, like an old abandoned house. Or a tomb. It's certainly cold enough for it. I drop the bags on the kitchen counter, then open the sliding glass door to my balcony. Even colder sea-tinged air rushes in. I cross my arms over my chest and step out.

The lights of Seattle wink a welcome-home. My skin drinks in the damp. This is exactly what I longed for all those long nights in Arizona, yet being here feels off, in a way I can't decipher. With a shiver, I walk back inside.

What is it? Nothing here has changed. Same cheap Swedish furniture, same art posters on the wall. So why am I unsettled? I walk to my bedroom, flipping on lights as I go. Nothing different here, either.

So why does it feel like something's missing?

Then I realize both what it is, and why it took me so long to figure it out. Because what's missing is nothing that was ever here to begin with.

Me. That's what was missing.

No personal photos in the long hall.

No mementos from places I've been, or things I've done.

No "favorite" anything on display.

I turn in a circle. I remember my pride the day I moved in. It didn't feel like home then (which made it a good thing), it felt like safety.

Now it feels as if I've stepped back to my past, and it's a cold, faceless place. Maybe I'll have some of the photos from the trip blown up. For sure the ones of G'ma and I in the restaurant, and the one of each of us kissing Leo's cheek, his arms draped around us. I hug myself and step to the wall to turn up the heat before returning to the kitchen to put away the groceries.

What I'm feeling is lonely. I didn't used to feel that. But I haven't been alone in over a week, slept in a bed without someone within feet of me. Had someone to talk to . . .

The antsiness seizes me, and I realize with a start, that's what drives me to walk the suburban streets after dark—loneliness. I feel like a fool for not knowing, but who names what's been your norm as far back as you remember?

I glance to my car keys, at the edge of the counter. Nope. Not tonight. I pick up the phone and dial Leo's number.

Chapter 16

*If we can share our story with
someone who responds with
empathy and understanding, shame
can't survive.*
Brené Brown

The next days are a blur. Leo and I have spoken on the phone, but I haven't seen him since the night he picked me up at the airport. I wouldn't be good company anyway, since most nights I fall asleep over my fast-food dinner.

I'm working eighteen hours a day, mostly researching plants on the internet and working in the lab I've set up in my kitchen. Steph has been great about handling everything at the store. That reminds me. I hit speed dial.

"Nothing has happened since we talked ten minutes ago." There's a chuckle in her voice.

"I'm calling to set up our dinner." Busy or no, the week with G'ma made me realize I need to reach out more. Let people in more.

"Oh, great. Thought you forgot."

"Never. You pick the day, but I'm picking the place. Dockside Table."

"Ohhh, I've heard a lot about it, but haven't been. How about Thursday, to miss the Friday crush?"

"Perfect. I haven't been there either, but the reviews are fantastic." I hang up, ignoring the guilt of a two-hundred-dollar divot in the safety net. I glance to the ceiling. "Did you see that G'ma? I'm walking the talk."

Her delighted cackle echoes in my head.

Hey, I'm on a roll, so . . . I speed dial Leo.

"I was just thinking about you." His deep voice pours over me like warm wax, making me wonder how I've stayed away this long.

"I know you're crazy-busy, getting ready for the show, but I have something for you. Mind if I stop over this weekend?"

"How about Saturday? I'll fix dinner—I'll bet you haven't eaten anything that didn't come in Styrofoam since you got home."

"Do you have cameras in my apartment?"

"No, but now that you mention it . . ."

"That's creepy."

"But hot, you gotta admit."

"I'm not admitting anything." Was that a *giggle* that just came out of me? I do not giggle. "You're on. And I haven't forgotten, you owe me the end to your story."

"And you owe me yours."

Telling would change things. It's one thing to fall into . . . whatever this is becoming, but I've never given anyone a window into my past. I hit end, wondering if I really have the guts to tell him.

The sidewalk at the waterfront is a high tide of people enjoying a gorgeous Thursday night. I pause to take a breath of spring: Primrose, fresh popcorn, yeast from the brewery down the way, and Seattle's signature salt-water base note.

Steph winds her way through the crowd to me, her red hair like a beacon, flashing in and out of the yellow light spilling from windows along the quay. She's young, charming and ambitious. She probably gets job offers all the time. I'm lucky to have her.

"Hey stranger." She smiles up at me. I always forget how petite she is.

"Glad I made reservations. Who knew it would be so busy on a weeknight?"

"Beginning of tourist season." She leads the way, cutting through the crowd to the door.

We decide to sit on the upstairs patio, for the view of the bay. The bit of nip in the air is negated by the heater glowing orange over our heads. "This is amazing."

"It is." She looks up from her menu. "Thank you for inviting me."

"I probably should have done it a long time ago."

"Oh, we all know how you pinch pennies." She scans the menu again.

I ignore the little bee sting the comment brings. Where she grew up, restaurant meals like this were probably the norm.

The waitress brings the bottle of wine Steph ordered. What the hell. I tip my head to have her pour me a glass, too.

Her eyebrows disappear into her bangs. "I thought you didn't drink."

"I changed my mind on the trip."

Once we order, she leans in. "Okay, no more being all mysterious. What happened to make you miss the show?"

"My car broke down where there was no cell service."

"I know, but why were you out there to begin with? You never said. Why didn't you just fly back here, and fly to Vegas, like you'd planned?"

I may be trying to loosen up, but I'm not going into my family dynamics with an employee. "Personal problem. It's over now." Missing G'ma rolls over me with the onshore breeze, prickling my sinuses, thickening my throat.

"But what—" She notices. "Okay, never mind. The important part is what we're going to do to get past the fallout."

"Agreed. I thought the nasty tweets would die down after the show, but they haven't."

"I can't imagine who'd bother trying to tear us down."

Bother? Poor word choice. "But luckily, the consumer couldn't care less about tweets, or little spats in the trade. They want a good product. We have that."

"Good point." She raises her overpriced glass of wine. "Here's to Heart's Note"

I lift my glass. "Here's to us." Was that a wince? "Are you okay?"

She swallows. "Fine. The wine is a bit bitter."

It doesn't seem so to me, but all I know of wine is how to consume it. And pay for it.

Leo opens his door at my knock. "Perfect timing. Dinner's almost ready."

I hand him the bottle of wine I bought with the help of the liquor store clerk.

THE ROAD TO ME

"Only if you join me."

"I could do that."

"Wow, the BV Jacqueline didn't drink."

"BV—Before Vegas?"

"Smart girl."

His dark tousled curls, strong stubbled jaw at odds with soft skin, make me want to touch. I lean in, awash in the rich outdoor scent of sage. It's not cologne, it's him. I burrow my nose where his neck meets the slope of his shoulder and inhale. His breath tickles my ear, sending shivers shooting down my nerves. I kiss him, long and deep.

He releases me with a surprised look and a smile. I've never been one to show affection. "Come on in."

I lift the portfolio, step in and am enveloped by the scent of tomatoes and garlic. "Smells heavenly."

"It's just Pasta puttanesca."

"I can't even pronounce that, much less make it."

"Are you saying you don't cook?"

Is this some kind of test? If so, he might as well know now. "I cook. But my repertoire leans more to cheeseburgers than cacciatore."

"You won't hear me dissing burgers." He adjusts the flame under the pasta. "What's that?"

"It's for you." I hold it out.

He steps over, takes it from me, and holds it up to the light. "I don't own a portfolio."

"Now you do." Smug slips out with my words. "Open it."

He opens it, takes a deep breath of rich leather, then runs his fingers over the gold embossed letters of his name. "This is top shelf." His arm comes around my waist and he pulls me to him. "It's way too much. But thank you."

His kiss telegraphs his appreciation, and I spend a while basking in it. Who knew that when giving isn't obligation, it becomes fun?

Probably only every other person on the planet.

I step back. If I don't, we'll end up in bed, and dinner will be ruined. "You so deserve it." I look around to distract me from the hormones heading south. "May I?"

He follows my line of sight to where the Twenty-first Century Man stands, complete and bathed in a spotlight. "Of course."

Walking over, I'm fascinated by the swirling greens and golds and the light fractures off the crystal lance, throwing sparkles up the wall behind it. "This is the most amazing thing. The critics are going to love it." I turn as he walks up. "They're going to love you."

He hands me a stemless glass of wine. "As my grandma used to say, 'Your mouth to God's ears.'" He raises his glass to touch mine.

I take a sip, and notice the canvas covered structure in the shadows. "What's that?"

"Just something I've been playing with."

I take a step toward it. "Can I see?"

"When I'm farther along." He takes my elbow. "Come, dinner's ready."

We talk about everything and nothing over dinner. What he's been doing the past weeks, reminiscing about his day in Vegas. He speaks of G'ma with warmth. "When you went to the restroom, she asked if I was a good poker player."

"What? Why?"

"Because she said if I played my cards right, I could have you."

Blood pounds up my neck to burst onto my cheeks. "You know better than to take her seriously, right?"

His warm gaze caresses the contours of my face. "Oh, she was dead serious. And I believed her." He shakes his head.

"Too bad I suck at poker."

I can't help my smile. "Sounds silly to say, since we were only together a week, but I miss her so."

"I know you do, and it's not silly at all." He stands and lifts his plate.

"Oh no, you cooked. I'm doing the dishes." I stand, pile the rest of the plates and follow him to the kitchen.

"No way. We're going to leave these in the sink. We have catching up to do." His look makes me think there may not be much talking involved in "catching up."

"But that's going to congeal like superglue. It would just take a second . . ."

He takes my hand. "Let's get comfortable. Grab the glasses. I have the wine." He leads me to the balcony, where we settle on his wicker couch.

The lights from the street below are enough to see by, and an Italian aria flows from Vissielo's, across the street.

It's time. But I'm nervous, and the speech I'd planned has flown out of my head.

Just tell him how you feel, child. You can trust him. G'ma whispers in my head.

I touch the back of his hand. "I have so much to tell you, I'm not sure how to start." I put my hands in my lap.

He takes one in his and waits.

"Maya Angelou said, Do the best you can until you know better. When you know better, do better." I take a sip of wine. "I find myself wanting to apologize, but I won't, because I didn't know better . . . about so many things. But mostly, I'm sorry for the things I said before Arizona. Saying I didn't want to see you anymore. It was cold, and—"

"I knew it wasn't about me. Not really. You were afraid."

I'm surprised again by how much he knows I haven't said. I stop fidgeting and look into the chocolate depths of his eyes.

"I want you in my life. I'm not making plans or expecting outcomes. I'm not sure what happens next." I swallow the fear, allowing the words to slip past. "But I want you to know, I'm going to do better. Be better. You've been so patient with my bumbling around, trying to figure this out. You may not even like where this leads me, but If you'll hang in there a bit longer, it would make me so happy." When the words run out, I stop. My nerves have settled with the telling, and it dawns on me that I've already changed, because I was worried about laying out my feelings in words, not what he'll say in response.

Because that's nothing I have control over.

His face lights with his smile. "I've known who you are from the first, Jack. I don't know how; I've never been able to do that with anyone else. But how could I be afraid of what you'll become when I already know what's underneath?" His smile is soft.

"I've had no experience with what a good relationship is." The muscles in my chest release the tight squeeze on my heart. "My mother was a dancer. A Vegas cocktail waitress. An alcoholic. A lost woman, full of so much pain."

The past flows out of me in soft, healing words that sound like a door creaking open.

Relief relaxes my shoulders and neck, as if a pressure valve has released.

He hugs me, long and hard. "That's for that young girl who bore so much more than her shoulders could bear." He settles back and squeezes my hand. "I have a present for you, too. But it has a story, as well."

I pull his hand into my lap. "I'm listening."

The lights go off in the restaurant across the street, and warm darkness presses in, insulating us from the rest of the world.

"I told you my dad refused me a loan if I insisted on an art major. I left to live with my aunt. I wasn't at all like him, except for one thing; we were both stubborn as only two men can be. I felt like he didn't accept who I was, and he felt . . . well, I don't know how he felt, because we never did come back to each other." He stares at the brick building across the street. "After he died, my brother and I were going through his things. I found this." He reaches in his pocket and pulls out a piece of metal and hands it to me. He pulls his phone and turns it to give me light.

It's a pendant. A circle of gold holding a circle of turquoise, and on it, rendered in tiny leaves of silver, a dove. "It's beautiful," I breathe.

"It's one of my earliest pieces from back when I was just starting out, and broke. I remembered it sold for way more than I was asking, but the gallery owner told me the buyer paid cash, and there was no way to trace him." When he looks up, his eyes are full of the weight of regret carried all these years. "My dad helped me the only way his pride would allow. Mom didn't even know he'd bought it."

"Oh Leo. I'm so, so sorry. For you, and your dad." I hold the gorgeous piece out to him, but he takes my hand, and folds my fingers on it.

"I want you to have it. I've already learned its lesson." He's still holding my hand in both of his. "I gave up on my father. I'm not giving up on you. I think we can have something special—maybe even something amazing. I'm patient. I'll wait as long as it takes."

I try to speak, but all the emotion I've locked down is loose, careening inside me, and only a choked sound comes out. I stand, and he has no choice but to follow, since he still holds my hands. I extricate myself and throw my arms around his neck, inhaling his scent. It centers me. I settle.

He pats slow circles on my back. "It's okay, Jack. You do what you gotta do. I'll be here. But can I ask one thing?"

I back up enough to see his face. "After this? Almost anything."

"You'll be at my show on Friday, won't you? I know what you're doing is important, but please say you'll come."

I smile and dash a tear. "I wouldn't miss it for anything." I bite my lips to hold in my secret; I've been on a mission to advertise Leo's show. Perfume isn't art, but I have a few contacts, and they promised to spread the word. Every art critic on this coast should be there. "You're going to be a smash hit."

He takes my chin in his hand and leans in to give me the sweetest kiss. "I think the time for talking has passed, don't you?"

The metal in my hand is warm. I take his proffered arm, and we stroll to the bedroom, turning off lights on the way.

I've realized a truth since I came back from the desert. I crafted a mask and wore it for the world to see. But underneath was another. A mask I wore to hide from *myself.* One I didn't even know I was wearing. I made up a persona and wrapped it around myself to keep me safe, then forgot that wasn't me.

I may not know exactly who I am yet, but for the first time, I'm not afraid to find out.

Chapter 17

Trust is earned, respect is given, and loyalty is demonstrated. Betrayal of any one of those is to lose all three.

Ziad K. Abdelnour

Despite three cups of coffee, I can still feel the tug of tired. But I wouldn't miss tonight for anything.

I turn to check out my dress in the bathroom mirror. The strapless black roses on cream jacquard comes to my knees in the front, to the floor in the back, flaring in beautiful folds. I could never have afforded a designer gown, but I wanted something special, so I rented it. It's perfect for tonight.

My hair is up in a smooth chignon so not to detract from Leo's gold and turquoise pendant.

I glance to the ceiling. "I know you'd approve, G'ma, even if it's not tie-dyed." I sink onto the bed and slip on my black peep-toe satin shoes, then grab my matching clutch, push off the bed, and head out for Leo's show.

Seeing the Recherché Gallery packed, a thrill shoots through me. I walk in, feeling the disjoined clash of the lost teen and the grown woman. Only recently have I come to be proud of them both.

Women in rhinestones, silk and sequins, and men in tuxes mill in a colorful palette. Cologne and expensive perfume mingle to the heady aroma of the elite.

The Twenty First Century Man is in the center of a sea of people, and I wade into the surf.

"This is amazing."

"Too expensive for my blood, but I saw a wall sculpture that would be perfect for—"

"How have I not heard about an artist of this caliber?"

Leo stands nearby with the owner of the gallery. Cameras flash like heat lightning.

Smiling, I skirt the crowd to circumnavigate the room. The wall art is lustrous in the spotlights. I recognize several art critics with their heads together, sipping champagne.

I pass through a doorway into another room and my feet stop. In the center is another statue—one I've never seen before. Lights reflect off leaves of the shimmering white cape that covers it from a deep hood to drape the floor. The clear plastic face is a woman's. The raised arm is transparent as well, the hand holding a crystal scepter. She is cold. Separate. Unknowable. But where the cape parts, encased in her transparent chest is a small, red bird, caught in mid-flight. People shift around me as I step closer. The plaque at the black base reads: *The Queen of Winter.*

I peer up at her features. They could be anyone's, but I feel the warm nugget of truth drop in my chest. Is this how he sees me? Saw me?

I'm not sure how to feel. Emotion is a watercolor wash, red, yellow, blue, and indigo, painting my insides. She is what was under the sheet in his studio. He worked on it before I got back from Arizona. Before he knew of my changes. So that beautiful bird—the soft part beneath, trying to get out—that was something he knew before I showed it to him.

Leo spots me over the heads of the crowd around him. He excuses himself and walks over. I've never seen him in a tux before, and the contrast of his three-day beard and hair curling against the formal attire hits my hormones. Hard. "You should dress up more often. You have the eye of every woman in the room." I touch his bow tie.

His gaze takes me in from head to foot. "And you have every man's." He touches his pendant.

I smile. "No, that's the Queen of Winter."

His eyes flick between mine. "She's you, you know. But you're the only person I'm telling that to. Do you like her?"

"You are such an intriguing man." I study him. "It's like I'm a moth to your flame. I've tried to stay away, but then you say something, or do something, and I'm captivated again."

"You, a moth?" He takes my hands and holds them out from my sides. "Never. You're a rare butterfly."

I take my hands back, to clasp them in front of me. "How do you know that? I'm only now beginning to crawl out of my chrysalis."

"Because to me, that chrysalis is as transparent as the Winter Queen's skin."

"The red bird. You're the first to see it that way."

His smile is warm as firelight. "Then I'm the lucky one."

"Excuse me, Leo?" His agent touches his elbow, but he doesn't respond. His attention is on me.

"You go. This is your night."

"Will you stay? I'd like to take you to dinner, after."

I crave sleep. This . . . relationship couldn't come at a more inopportune time. But how could I walk away from a man who sees through me, to *me?* Nellie would tell me to grab on with both hands and hang on for the ride. And for once, I agree. "I would like that."

Heart's Note: Seattle's worst.

If you like Heart's Note scents, DM me. I can point you to better ones.

That's it. Up til now, I've figured this Twitter troll would have their fun and then wander off when they didn't get a reaction. But this hasn't gone away. And I'm mad, dammit. I spend an hour researching how you track down an internet troll. The easiest way would be if he posted a photo—I could track where it was taken. But I've been through their timeline, and they've never posted one.

What I need is a hacker. But they don't advertise. They probably don't need to. I work my way through wormholes in the internet, and on a chat board, there he is: DarkHorse. And there's an email address. I send him an email about my problem. I hope this info isn't old . . . or a plant by the FBI or something. But I'm not planning murder. I only want to make it stop.

I spend the rest of the morning working with petri dishes of failed perfume experiments. I've recreated all the scents from the desert, but no matter how I combine them, there's still something missing. It's not going to work until I find that heart note.

The intercom buzzes and a male voice booms, "UPS, Ms. Oliver. I have a package you'll need to sign for."

"I'll be right there." When I trot downstairs, the man hands over a package but doesn't meet my eyes. When I read the return address of the funeral home in Las Vegas, the air whooshes out of my lungs as if something very heavy dropped onto my chest.

It's one thing to know she's gone. It becomes real on a whole other level when you hold all that's left of her in your hands.

"I'm sorry for your loss, Ms. Oliver." He's read the return address too. His eyes are kind.

I can't speak, so I just nod.

I walk up, feet dragging, open my door, and find a knife to open the box. Inside is the deep sapphire blue urn with veins of black smoke running through, giving the illusion of depth. It seemed beautiful when I picked it out; now it seems grotesque. I can't bring myself to open it. It would be an invasion of G'ma's privacy.

What did I think I was going to do with her ashes?

I didn't look that far ahead. I was in shock. I think I still am. I swipe an arm over my eyes and sniff. G'ma doesn't belong here, in this land of salt water, verdant green, and rain. She belongs in the desert that was so much a part of her. I need to take her back. To take her home.

I walk to the framed photo on the wall, of she and I in Vegas. "Soon G'ma. Okay? As soon as I can." I wipe my nose on my sleeve. "I miss you." I hug the urn, put it back in the box, walk to my bedroom and set it on the dresser. "You rest easy now."

I need to get to the shop. I change, straighten the kitchen, and close my laptop, but just for the heck of it, I open it and check email. DarkHorse responded! He will get me the info within minutes of me sending him fifty bucks via an international payment website I'm familiar with. It's legit, and secure. But how do I know he won't take off with the money and fade into the ether without getting my information? I sure wouldn't be able to chase him down.

The answer is, I don't. Is it worth possibly losing fifty dollars? I check my internal pissed-off-meter. Oh yeah, it so is. I follow the instructions and pay his fee. Nothing to do now but wait. I close my laptop and head for Heart's Note.

My second longest employee, Penny, greets me at the door. "So good to see you, Ms. Oliver. You just missed Steph. She went to lunch." Penny's young but has old school manners along with a Texan drawl.

"How're things here?"

"Lunchtimes are always busy."

"Glad to hear that. How's school?" She's in her last year of a marketing degree.

"It's a slog, but I'm looking forward to June."

"Well, keep at it. I'm hoping you'll stay on and handle the marketing it's going to take to take us nationwide."

"Wow, is that a job offer?"

"It is. Think about it." I head for my desk in the back. After paying bills that have piled up, I check my email. DarkHorse said he'd have the info in minutes . . . I click on his *confidential* email. I read it, my blood pressure shooting up like a thermometer in Arizona in August. I read it again, heartbeat thudding in my ears. This can't be right. But the email makes it impossible to deny. I mean, how could DarkHorse possibly know who my manager is? The anger that has been simmering spits, boils, then overflows, burning everything it touches.

I don't know the why of it, but I plan to find out.

I stalk to the front, where Steph is helping a high-schooler pick out a fragrance for her mother's birthday.

"You made a good choice. She'll love Eve. It's really special. Now, would you like to try our youthful scent, Flirt?"

I step to Penny. "Would you take over for Steph? I need to talk to her. Now."

Penny's eyes widen at my tone, and she hustles over, whispering to Steph, then leads the teen to the counter, chatting all the way.

A lightning flash of something crosses Steph's face, too fast to catch. I tip my head to the back room, and she follows.

"I'm sorry I was late back from lunch, but the traffic on—"

"Why?" I turn on her.

"Like I said, traffic—"

"The nasty tweets. Why?" My fingers curl to fists. I've never hit another person in my life. But I've never wanted to this bad, either.

Eyes open wide, she takes a step back. "How did you . . . you can't prove that was me."

"I have the proof. What I want to know is *why*? How could you do this? I *trusted* you."

Her mouth turns down and her bottom lip comes out, like a recalcitrant child. "I thought this would be a great place for me to learn the ropes, while I developed my own scent." She scoffs. "You think manager of a one-storefront indie is something I aspire to? I have *plans*." She flips her hair over her shoulder. "I've learned everything I can from you and I don't have years to waste around here. I've talked to several people who think my scent is great." Her voice is gelling, solidifying to something like justification.

"What did you think you'd gain by trying to ruin Heart's Note's reputation?"

"One less competitor." She shrugs. "Hey, I gave you first shot at a piece of my new scent. You turned it down. Big mistake."

And she assumed I'd never find out. How could I be so clueless? If I stand here, I'm going to slap her. "Do not move."

I walk around the desk, compute her time up to her lunch hour, plug them into my payroll program, and hand write her a check. I hold it out. "You're fired. Please, feel free to use me as a reference. I'd love to warn other business owners about a snake. I'll walk you out."

She snatches her purse from her locker and steams for the front door, ignoring Penny's questioning look.

Luckily, there are no customers. "Good luck with that scent, Steph. I don't want to see you on the premises again."

With a scathing backward glance, she goes out, slamming the door behind her.

I take three deep breaths to calm down, and when I think I can talk without fury shaking my voice, I turn to Penny and give her a quick rundown of what just happened, and why.

"Oh wow, Ms. Oliver. I had no idea, or I'd have told you, I swear." She crosses her heart with a finger.

The child's gesture cools my rage. "Thanks for that." I take another deep breath and head for the back room.

Once there, the careening emotion won't let me sit. I wish I could go running, but I need to figure out what's next. Penny would be the obvious answer as manager; there are other employees, but Heart's Note is only a side hustle for them.

But Even if Penny would take the job, which isn't a given, because of her night school demands, how do I know I can trust her? I thought Steph was a poster child employee and look how that turned out. My "people picker" sucks. That's why I've kept everyone distant all these years. Thoughts tumble, wrestle and merge in my mind. Hell, how do I know I can trust anyone? Leo? My gut rejects that idea, but it rejected any thoughts about Steph in the beginning, too. What do I do? I'm like a blind person, trusting a stranger to walk them across a busy street safely. How could they ever do that?

G'ma's strong spirit drifts through my mind. How did she stay so open all those years? She had better reason than most to not trust.

The logical thing is to just assume the manager role myself. But I can't avoid a trip to the desert much longer. I've *got* to find that missing ingredient. And G'ma's waiting to go home.

Speaking of my grandmother . . . I open the bottom drawer of my desk and pull out my big purse. I've been carrying G'ma's medicine bag around because it makes me feel good to have a bit of her with me, but I've yet to open it, not wanting to bleed again.

I pick up the leather pouch and remove the contents, one by one. Her little pot of sandalwood—saving that. Three sample vials of essential oils—they're not labeled, but I smell them: eucalyptus, lavender and frankincense. A few fragile purple flowers that fall apart in my fingers. They give off a scent like grape Kool-Aid. A worn disc, the size of a silver dollar. I hold it up to the light. Hard to tell, but it appears to be a robed man. This must be the Saint Anthony medal Nellie's mother gave her outside the orphanage. I rub my thumb over the image, sensing it's weighty import. This is precious.

I think that's all, until my fingers brush a folded piece of paper. I pull it out and unfold it. It is a receipt, but on the back, in G'ma's spidery handwriting:

"Don't forget to put yourself on the list of people you trust. If you don't trust yourself, you trust no one."

Emotions and facts twine in my chest to rise to my head, breaking in a blinding blast of rightness. "You're right, as usual, G'ma." Fingering the note, I raise my eyes to the ceiling. "And stop laughing."

I lost the old Jacqueline Oliver in the desert. When I was with G'ma in Vegas, I was sure I'd changed. But have I? Really and indelibly? "No" echoes in my head. I'm like a unique fragrance, made up of pieces of my heritage, pieces of my past, and just maybe, Leo could be a piece of my future. But in what order? What portions?

Well, I lost myself in the desert—maybe it's possible to find myself there, too.

Can I make that leap of faith? I must, because I'm beginning to believe I may find more than one missing ingredient out there.

Before I can change my mind, I tuck everything back in the bag and go talk to Penny.

"When are you leaving?"

Leo's deep voice calms the whitecaps on my agitated emotions. "Tonight, if I can get a flight."

Do it, Jack. Take a chance. G'ma's scratchy voice whispers in my ear.

"I wondered . . . do you want to come with me?" I take a breath. "I know it's last minute, and, well . . ."

"I can't think of anything I'd rather do. But I can't, and it's all your fault. I've had frantic calls from my agent this morning, along with people wanting interviews and photo shoots. The gallery owner is ecstatic. They sold everything."

"Wow." The price tags may have made me blanch, but I'm glad not everyone did.

"I heard what you did, helping to market the event. Thank you. It was a great thing to do."

"I wanted to do something. You were my anchor when I felt lost in the wilderness of Arizona. I don't know how I'd have made it without those late-night calls."

He laughs. "I hardly think the two compare. If this makes me as renown as my agent thinks, I'll have you to thank for it."

"You will be renown because of your talent and your amazing vision. You see things differently than most people. You make people think."

"If you could wait a week or two—"

"I can't. I've got to find my base note."

"There's the Jack I know."

"So, you go be famous, and I'll go searching scents, and I'll see you when I get back."

"Okay, but only if you promise to call me every night."

"I think that's a given, don't you?" I'm smiling when we hang up. I may have a bad people picker, but maybe this time, the blind squirrel found a one-of-a-kind acorn.

Penny doesn't want to tie herself to an answer about the manager position, or staying on after she finished her degree, but she agreed to hold the fort for my run to the desert, and I can't ask for more than that. I still don't have a product. I don't know what's going to happen in the desert. The future is uncertain.

All I know is, for the first time in my life, I'm rushing to meet it.

Chapter 18

We cannot change the cards we are
dealt,
just how we play the hand.
Randy Pausch

When the baggage claim doors in Phoenix whoosh open, blast furnace heat smacks me in the face. "Sweet mother of God." I trundle my roller bag to the curb, sweat beads already sliding down the knobs of my spine. The shuttle bus to the car rental comes in less than five minutes, but by then, the armpits of my linen blouse are wet, I'm wilted and can't get a deep breath.

I'd considered renting a convertible for old time's sake, but that was before I stepped into the fires of hell. "Sorry, G'ma." I pat the backpack that holds her urn, then strap it into the passenger seat of the brand-new Honda SUV. "R.I.P.,

Duchess." The sharp point at the back of my throat tastes of metal and melancholy.

I pull out into traffic on Highway 17 and head north for Route 66. Call it luck, Karma, or whatever, it just feels right to go there. Within a half hour, the houses and cars have been replaced by barrel cacti, rocks, and rattlesnakes. Maybe this wasn't such a good idea. Yes, we found aromatic plants in the desert, but it was spring. I can't imagine anything having the tenacity to bloom in this oven.

Miles of miles, all the same. I griped about Nellie, but she was interesting company. I was so used to pushing against her: her beliefs, her lifestyle, her abandonment. Once that was gone, I wasn't sure who I was, if I didn't have her to push against. Well, I'm finding out now. It's lonely.

It's not like me not to have an itinerary. Wandering out here alone is way on the other side of my comfort zone. But Nellie lived her whole life like this. Maybe I have something to learn from her yet. And I think to find who I am going to become, I'm going to have to forget black and white and get close and personal with the spectrum of gray.

The road rises, shimmering in the heat before me. I may not have a planned route but I do have an agenda. I'm antsy to get out and look for plants, but I'm not dumb enough to wander in the desert all alone. A road sign for Highway 179 sparks my interest. I've heard of Sedona. It's supposed to be an amazing artists colony, and a great outdoor hiking spot. I'm not to the Mother Road yet, but it feels right—like what I'm looking for. Good news about not having an itinerary, you can't make a wrong turn.

I hang a Louie and hit the gas. As I gain elevation, the landscape changes from flat scrub to red rock formations, open vistas, the sky is a huge bowl of blue overhead. The temperature falls to more human sustaining temps. This is more like it.

I roll onto Main Street. The buildings seem to squat to offer an unobstructed view of the ochre, gold, and buff-colored hills rimming the horizon. At a beep behind me, I pull my focus away from them to the brisk traffic and pedestrians teeming like ants to a picnic. Art galleries, jewelry stores, and boutiques outnumber the few souvenir shops. My mood lifts on the hope they could have a hotel made of something better than cinderblock. I pull in the first empty parking spot, in front of a cute little café. It's flirty awning skirts flipping up in the breeze.

Inside, I order a civilized lunch: wild caught white fish tacos, mango salsa, with cabbage and organic mixed lettuce. And coffee—a dark roast they import from Seattle. I'm liking this town better all the time. When the waitress refills my coffee, I ask her for hotel suggestions.

"Are you looking for economy? Not that anything here is inexpensive."

I should go on the cheap. Every dollar I spend is a dollar outside the budget, which is as tight as a cheerleader's skirt at a twenty-year reunion. Splurging goes against every survival instinct I own. But another feeling is almost as strong; I can't grab the future with my hands full of the past. "I'm looking for something nice, maybe with a view?"

"Ah, then I'd suggest The Allure Resort. It's out near Cathedral Rock. It'll cost you, but it's more than worth it."

"Sounds great, thanks." When she walks away, I call the resort. The only thing they have available is an exclusive room. I push back worry and book it.

The road to the resort winds through red rock canyons filled with bushy brush and wind-tortured trees. The resort is shaped in a horseshoe, snugged up against a cliff wall. I walk in and inhale the lofty perfume of luxury. I take in another deep lungful. Lord knows when I'll smell it again. I check in and am escorted to my room, which turns out to be on stilts over the canyon, a deep half-circle balcony with a fire pit, fronting a compelling, yet terrifying view. "You don't have earthquakes around here, do you?"

The bellhop chuckles. "No Ma'am. These rooms were built fifteen years ago, and we've never had a problem."

"Okay then." I tip him and he leaves. I eye the balcony. "It'd be silly to have paid for it, and not use it." I step out and inch my way to the railing. My stomach plummets even as my spirit blows out the top of my head, to soar over the canyon. Standing here, it's hard not to believe in *something*: God, Buddha, or Nellie's Universe. I mean, something created this, right? The clean scent-laden desert air rushes up to greet me. Pinon pine, with a hint of sage. I recline on the lounger, watching the skimpy clouds dance together.

Guess the long hours and late nights caught up to me, because when I wake, the sun is balancing on the line at the horizon. I wander down to the lobby. The doors of the spa whoosh open as I walk by and I'm enveloped in a mist of humidity. My skin sighs in relief. What is that smell? I step in and glance to the wall, where flowering yellow and white Plumeria put off a cloying scent. Too cloying to be *the* heart note, but it could be a piece of the puzzle. Why hadn't I thought of Plumeria before now? I walk out to the lobby, wondering what it must cost to keep tropical flowers alive in the desert. Seems kind of silly; the desert holds beautiful things, too.

Stacy, the girl at the concierge desk is a hiker. She gives me several choices of trails to try to look for plants. When I tell her I'd like a range of scenery and no crowds, her face lights up and she glances around like someone might overhear, though we're alone. "Are you a good hiker?"

"Sure." That stretches the truth a mile or so, but I'm young, and I have my hiking boots with me.

"Then, Long Canyon is what you're looking for. It's less crowded, but if you go at sunrise or sunset, it's almost deserted. Lots of plants, and great views: Wilson Mountain, Maroon Mountain, Steamboat Rock."

She hands me a map of hiking trails, and I go up to my room. I work a while, check in at the store, then fall onto the bed, and know nothing until I wake at four a.m., my stomach settled, my brain quieted, and my body rested.

Today is the day. I feel the answer waiting inside, like a word you can't remember, but you can feel the shape of it.

I lay out my clothes, moisturizer, sunscreen, and G'ma's Panama hat with the pink Route 66 ribbon. I still have mine, but I brought it in her honor. After a quick shower, I dress, gather some fruit and oat bars from the bar in my room, along with several bottles of water, and head for the car. It's still dark when I pull out of the lot, though there's a lighter shadow to the east. My message icon is flashing so I hit speakerphone and listen to a day end report from Penny, and at two a.m., one from Leo.

"Hey Jack. I'm sure you're sleeping. You must be exhausted by the travel and the climate change. Call me."

I check the clock. Five here is four in Seattle. I can't wake him that early. I have to admit, I miss him already. How fun would it have been to have him beside me this morning, sharing all the beauty of sunrise?

I daydream all the way to the trailhead, my spirits higher than the altitude. I pull into a dusty deserted lot and eat a second orange between sips of water and slathering on sunscreen. The sun hasn't made it over the scrub pines by the time I'm ready, but it's close. I get out and lift my backpack to my shoulders, glad I've gotten a head start on the tourists.

Water? Check. Hat and Sunglasses? Check. Sunscreen? Check.

I head up the abandoned Jeep trail. The air is fresh, it's maybe seventy degrees, and I glimpse a powder-blue sky between the branches that overhang the trail. I'm aware of the contraction and release of the muscles of my calves, the even expansion of my lungs, and under it all, the steady tumping of my heart. I'm happy to be alive, and right where I am.

Before long I break out of the trees, and the sandy trail winds between straggly bushes. Buff and ochre rock formations rise ahead. I stop to take a sip of water. The path looks level, but must be rising, because my lungs are laboring a bit. My stomach flinches at a hot poker strike. Dammit, I knew better than to eat citrus. But the birds are chirping and the trail ahead is empty. I snap photos, and forge on.

Down the trail farther—God knows how much farther, because there is zero Wi-Fi signal out here—it's getting hot. The sun is stronger at altitude, and there's not a cloud to block the searing rays. I'm sweating like a warthog, slapping gnats, and my hiking boot is rubbing a blister on my left heel. The pain in my stomach is relentless. Coffee *and* oranges? What were you thinking, Jack? I still haven't seen another person though, and that means I'm keeping a good pace, so I press on.

After a longer trudge, there's the tiniest hint scent of citrus in the air, and—is that grape bubble gum? What the heck would that be doing out here? It's coming from my left. I glance around but I'm alone. I step off the path and ski down a little scree of shale bits, proud that I keep my balance. The smell is leading me to a shady copse ahead, straggly branches overhang the broken rock beneath my boots. I shoot a look over my shoulder. If I stand on tippy toe, I can barely see where I left the trail. Wait. One thing I do have . . . I pull my phone. This compass app I downloaded claimed it needed no internet connectivity. Yes! Okay, the path is north by northeast. Or is that north by east north? It's closer to east than —oh screw it. As long as I remember the point on the compass, I'll be fine.

I crouch and duck-walk under the branches. The difference between full sun and dappled shade is delicious. I sit to gulp some water. God, my stomach hasn't been this bad in—ever. I can hardly think past the pounding pulses of pain. I figured it would let up when I digested the orange, but it seems worse. Maybe I should start back?

No. I've *got* to find that scent. Heart's Note may depend on it. I stumble to my feet and wade farther into the bushes.

Within a couple hundred yards, I break out into an open area at the edge of an arroyo. On the other side are several tottering monolith spires that steal what little breath I have. I sit on a rock to mop sweat and appreciate the striations of nature's watercolor before me. My hand steals to my stomach, Damn. that hurts.

Color drifts in the corner of my vision to land on my shirt. It's a desiccated flower. I lift it to my nose. *That's* the grape scent. There are a few blue-purple blooms still on the branches overhead. They spark a memory, something about how their waxy leaves march down the branches like hands, open to the sun . . . The bar! Where I ended up drunk on G'ma's Sangria fruit. This is the same bush. And she told me something—I close my eyes to pull it from my memory. Your recall had better be good when you major in Chemistry. *Texas Mountain Laurel.* I don't remember the Latin name, but she said the Natives used it in ceremonies and . . . to cure stomachaches!

I snatch a leaf from overhead and study it. I'd feel better if I could research this—I check my phone—zero bars. But I trust G'ma. She lived out here her whole life, and even Fawn said Nellie could have become the Healer at del Soul if she'd stayed. Maybe my stomach will settle. I've *got* to find that heart note. I swipe the leaf on my shirt and raise it in a toast, "Here's to you, Nellie," put it in my mouth and chew. Tastes like a leaf.

I gulp more water. A bottom-heavy bumble bee lumbers by. My gaze follows it to a tiny spot of color at the edge of my vision. What is that? I turn and crawl under the branches to where a blooming cactus teeters on the edge of the arroyo wall. A delicate pink daisy-style bloom perches on a spine, its splashy yellow stamens covered in pollen. Beautiful. And the source of the sweet citrus smell. I take several photos. "Score." I push to a stand, feeling smug. Nailed both scents with this little shortcut. I carefully detach the bloom, slide it in a baggie I brought and bury it deep in the pocket of my cargo shorts. My stomach has loosened a bit. I can head back, marking this hike in the "win" column.

I turn and the world cants beneath me, twenty degrees off its axis. "What the—" I shake my head, but that makes the world spin. Every muscle in me goes liquid, and I drop to the ground, falling on my back, so close to the edge that my heels dangle off. I lie there, trying to gather facts. My thinking seems fine, but the sky shouldn't be fuchsia. Should it? The edges of everything look sharp enough to cut. My arms, legsand torso have gone numb, as if I had a full-body Novocain shot. Dizzy, I close my eyes, then lift a hand to brush away a gnat. My hand doesn't obey. *What the hell?* Panic races down my nerves, but it helps not at all.

I. Can't. Move.

No one will venture this far off the trail. Stupid. I'm so stupid. Will they find my bleached bones, next season?

Breathe. Just breathe. You can figure out the rest later.

A shadow crosses over my eyes, and I manage to pry one open a slit. A nimbus of white hair surrounds a planet with silver sparkle stars. I blink several times. "G'ma?"

She leans over me, Hollywood sunglasses spreading sparks of light across my corneas.

"What in the name of Timothy Leary do you think you're doing, Jack? Did you really eat a Mountain Laurel leaf?"

"You said it was good for stomach problems, and—hey, what're you doing here? You're dead."

"Master of the obvious, as always. Nice hat, by the way. Now, come on, roll over." She may be dead, but she's in better shape than last I saw her, because she kneels without a wince and flips me on my side.

"Sorry about this, but it's for your own good." She shoves two fingers down my throat.

I recoil, but nothing much moves except my gag reflex. Water and bits of leaf and a few ragged oats splash onto the gravel by my head. When I can breathe again, G'ma is examining the remains like a Russian tea-leaf reader.

"That's about all of it."

"Why did you *do* that?" I choke out.

"Because it's not time for you to join me. Mountain Laurel is a powerful hallucinogen and narcotic, Jack. It's *poison*."

"Why the fuck didn't you tell me that before?"

She rolls me on my back, glances around, then puts her hands under my armpits and drags me away from the ledge, to lean against a rock in the shade. "Because, if you remember, you cut me off. You wanted to know about your grandfather."

I find that, with effort I can just hold my head up. "Which you never told me about, by the way."

"Only because I don't know."

It dawns on me why, and I slam my mind shut on the thought. "G'ma, you slut."

She sits cross-legged and shrugs. "It was the free-love generation, Baby."

I try to take this in: My dead grandmother, looking all the one-week-short of eighty-five years she had on the planet, is sitting across from me, pulling herself into a Lotus position. "Hip's coming along, huh?"

"This is the best. I can do stuff I haven't done in decades. But I don't have time to talk about that now. Jimi and Janis are gonna be jamming in a few, and Easy and I—"

"Oh! I'm so glad you're with Easy."

"Yeah, the sex is as good as it ever was. We've decided to put off returning for our next lesson down here, and take a little R and R."

"Well, you certainly earned it." This is one hell of a hallucination. I'm talking to her like this is really happening. She even *smells* like my G'ma.

"But I had to come back." She leans in to study my face. "You don't learn very fast, do you?"

"What are you talking about?"

"Didn't you learn anything that week we were together?"

"I thought I learned a lot. You never told me there would be a quiz."

"Well, there is. Look at you, Jack." She flips a hand at me and sits back with a look of disgust. "The Universe had to practically paralyze you to get your attention."

I try to roll my eyes, but they only move side to side. "I'm listening."

"Have you decided what you were sent here to learn?"

I can still feel guilty in a hallucination? "I am going to. As soon as I get the business—"

"Business, schmizness. You've been going on about that forever."

"It's my baby."

"No." She points a bony finger at me. "It's not. And you'll never have real babies if you keep messing with surrogates. What comes next? Cats? You gonna be a crazy cat lady?"

"What the hell are you talking about?"

"Are you telling me you came here to learn how to run a successful business?"

"Well, I—"

"Because the Universe doesn't set up trade schools you know. Your life isn't OJT."

"But—"

"Look, I'll give you a clue, then I've got to blow this place." She unwraps her legs, and stands, without putting her hands on the ground.

Even I can't do that.

"It's real simple." She smacks dust off her skinny butt. "You decide what's important." Her face gets big as she leans down to look me in the eye. "Then you do that. And *that* can be more than one thing, but it is *not* a business." She leans a bit farther, and plants a kiss on my forehead, straightens and turns on her heel. "I'm comin' Easy, cool your jets."

I'm panicked realizing I'm losing her again. "G'ma!"

She turns to look back at me.

"Does this mean that everything you believed is true? About the afterlife?"

"Sounds logical. Until you add the fact that you're trippin', Jack."

There is that. "Oh G'ma, I so miss you. I love you, you know."

She gives me her softest smile. "And I love you, Jack. Remember what you learned. You'll do fine. You got my genes." She walks off the edge of the arroyo into a magenta mist.

I close my eyes and fade out.

When I wake, the sky is again blue, and the sun is touching the top of my boots where they hang off the edge of the arroyo. I'm not leaning against the rock where G'ma dragged me. I sit up, grateful that my body seems to be working again. There are the bits of dried leaf in the dirt where I lay, and I scrub dried vomit from the side of my face.

Was G'ma a hallucination? Probably. But that doesn't mean I'm not glad to see her. I feel like I've gotten some closure. I got to tell her I love her one more time. That almost makes this horrific experience worthwhile.

I crawl to my backpack and gingerly drink a half bottle of water. My phone says it's 1:30. I'm hungry, but I still have to get out of here. I sit on a rock for a bit, slathering on more sunscreen, trying to gather my scattered beliefs. What *is* my thing to learn? Even if G'ma was a hallucination, it's still a good question. And it's time I stopped putting it off and find the answer.

Shouldering my backpack, I crawl through the Laurel branches and find my way back to the trail. I'm no longer alone. Hikers pass every few hundred yards. The heat presses against my skin as if it wants in. My head pounds with every step.

I know what I don't want about this life. I don't want the chaos and poverty I grew up in. Looking at my life these past few years, I realize I ran to the opposite: hard work, structure, and discipline. But those things haven't fulfilled me either.

I have a nice apartment, a decent nest egg (well, I *did*), and then I sat on it, all alone, and wondered why it didn't make me happy.

"Man, how clueless can one person be?"

I ignore the odd look of a passing hiker and head down the trail and back to civilization, to find my place in it.

When I pass the spa on my way through the lobby, I notice there's a station set up in the waiting area. It looks like a manicure table, but with different equipment. Stacy, the girl from the concierge desk, is in a chair, chatting with a woman who leans over her thigh with a Stylus that emits a small humming.

I step up quietly, so as not to disrupt whatever it is that's going on.

Stacy looks up. "Oh hey, Jacqueline. How did the hike go?"

I can't tear my eyes from her leg. "Not at all what I expected, but I have returned with what I went out there for, so it's good."

The woman sits up and runs a cloth over Stacy's leg. The buzzing stops.

"What's going on?"

"I'm getting a tattoo."

"Oh." I take a step back.

"Not what you're thinking. It's a white tattoo. Brandy, this is Jacqueline."

The lady turns, holding up gloved hands to show she can't shake. "Nice to meet you."

I lean in a bit. Pale script spells out, "Roam far, wander wi." I can only assume the last word will be "wide." "That won't show up much."

"That's the whole point. It's subtle." Brandy says. "Depending on your skin tone, it may be hard to see at all."

Stacy touches her chest. "But *I* know it's there. It's not for other people. It's for me."

Intriguing. "I'd never get a tattoo, but if I did, it'd be one like that."

Stacy pats the chair beside her. "Come sit. You can look through the designs, just for fun. Brandy is the best artist in Sedona."

"Oh no, I'm all sweaty. I just stopped to thank you for the hiking suggestion."

She pats the chair again. "Come on. It won't cost anything to look."

I have to admit, I'm intrigued. Ten minutes. Then I'm out of here. I sit, and Stacy hands me a notebook full of designs. I leaf through the pages.

"She can do them so they're kind of raised, so when it fades, you can still feel it, like braille."

Nothing catches my eye. I close the book and think. *If I were to do this, it would need to be a reminder of my lesson for this life that G'ma talked about.* A fresh scent flows through my head, and an idea tugs in my mind, but the harder I concentrate, the more elusive it is. I follow it like a wandering butterfly floating just out of reach. I stand and pull the pink cactus flower from my pocket. This is a part of it—more than the scent—part of my answer, too.

"I'll be back." I walk through the lobby and out the doors. I want the canyon backdrop, but not from my window. I walk around the hotel, to the canyon side. There's a fence around the drop off, so I lean my forearms on it and stare down to the tumbled rocks below and start from what I know.

A cactus is prickly, but not to hurt you, it's for its own protection. That's what I've done. Built spines to keep people distant, to keep me safe. And it worked. It helped me survive neglect and abandonment. But the antsiness that drives me to haunt neighborhoods at night proves the spines are in my way, too. I want more.

The kaleidoscope pieces that have been shifting since Vegas tumble again, forming the other answer I've been chasing.

I can't have the joy of connection, of *belonging* that I yearn for, without letting the world in. That means opening up. Being *vulnerable.* Panic hits with the word, telling me that this is it. This is what I'm supposed to learn. What I'm supposed to *do.*

Jesus, couldn't it be something easier? Well, I have to admit, that would kind of negate the whole point, but I can't think of anything that could more strike terror in my soul. It would be like walking into a battle, swordless and naked, and yelling at the opposing army, "Bring it on!"

I chuckle. I understand Leo's Twenty First Century Man on a whole new level.

G'ma's lesson comes unbidden. "Pain is universal. Suffering is optional." Given her background, was that lesson any easier for her? I remember the smokehouse, the rape, the glinting sockets.

I'm sure not.

My stomach takes an Insanity Coaster dive. Am I really considering this? Exposing my soft parts to the world? When it seems the only people I trust are ones that I shouldn't? Like when the Universe bumped me onto Route 66 with Nellie Oliver—I realize I've been feeling the push at my back again, bumping me toward this.

I pull the cactus flower once more from my pocket. The cactus bears the heat, the lack of water, surviving incredible odds just to stay alive—and yet, once a year, it has the courage to open this beautiful fragile flower. Expose its softest self, for a fleeting few days to see the sun, before it wilts and dies.

I know what tattoo I want. I stride for the front of the hotel, hoping I can live up to the courage of a cactus.

Chapter 19

Authenticity is the daily practice of
letting go
of who we think we're supposed to
be
and embracing who we are.
Brené Brown

A few hours later, I'm showered, checked out, and on the road. The inside of my right wrist itches, and I look down to the red outline of the cactus flower formed by many white dots under my skin. Brandy said the irritation would be gone in a week. When the white fades, I'm hoping it's almost invisible. But I'll be able to touch the raised design when I need to remind myself.

Vulnerable as a cactus's flower. That's me.

I hope.

Within twenty miles I take a Louie at Route 66 and keep going.

G'ma was a hallucination. I know that.

But it felt so real—so *her.*

Does it mean I'm going over to her new-age dark-side if I believe it *was* her?

Whatever. My gut tells me it was my grandmother. And as long as I'm picking and choosing what I want in my life, I'm choosing this.

A mist of nostalgia fills my eyes as I blow through Williams, then Seligman. I wish things could have been different—that I'd have appreciated those days at the time. But I have the memories—like the tattoo, I'll be able to touch them when I want to remember.

I'd thought to scatter her ashes where Easy died, but when I slow at the turn, the wrongness of it smacks me like the scent of a roadkill skunk. She wouldn't want to be at one of the saddest places from her life.

Then I know the perfect place to scatter her ashes. I throw my head back and laugh. I never planned to return to del Soul, but I never planned to get a tattoo, either. It'll be interesting, finding out other changes as I sift through the rubble inside me.

On the two-hour drive, I consider how I'm going to handle tonight, choosing and discarding ideas based solely on what *feels* right. Another new thing.

I turn off the highway and roll through the tunnel of trees that leads to the colony. When I pull into the clearing, the nude people strolling by don't seem as odd as they used to. I park and head for the office but hesitate at the door. It doesn't seem fair to bring such sad news. If I drove on, they'd be spared—secure in the thought their beloved Blue is safe and happy.

But she *is* safe and happy. And if anyone would understand that, it'd be these people. I turn the knob and walk into the lobby. Spike looks up from behind the desk. When he recognizes me, he smiles but then it falters and slides from his face. "I can think of only one reason you'd return here alone, Jack."

I nod. "She went peacefully, in her sleep, only a few days after we left here."

He steps around the counter and takes my hands, his eyes full of sadness. "I am not sorry for Blue. But I am so sorry for all of us who loved her. A bright light has gone from this plane."

"It surely has." I sniff. This is only the beginning of the hard things I've chosen to do this day. "Can I get a room for the night? And do you have a few minutes to talk? I have ideas for a memorial of sorts."

"Of course. Your food and lodging are on us." He squeezes my hands, then lets me go. "Come on, let's get you settled."

Word has spread by the time I sit down to dinner. Many bring me condolences, sorrow, and stories of Blue.

"Excuse me, everyone. Could you take your seats?" Spike waits until the room is quiet. "You've probably heard by now our beloved Blue has left this plane. Blue's granddaughter Jack is here. She'll be speaking at our night of sharing after dinner. Enjoy your meal, and we'll see you in a bit."

Fawn sits across the table from me with wise eyes. "I am going to miss your grandmother. She taught me so much about strength and joy."

"I miss her so much." I take a sip of water to mend the crack in my voice. "I so regret all the years I stayed mad at her for something I didn't understand."

A soft smile lights her face. "You know what Blue would say."

I smile back. "That things happened just as the Universe meant them to happen. And I'm no longer arguing with that. But still, I wish it could have been different."

It's dark by the time we gather by the lake. The fire is blazing. I'm standing between Spike and the fire, the urn with G'ma's ashes in my arms. The guests are fanned out in lawn chairs before us. My blood races, hotter than the fire, and the jitters skitter just beneath my skin. What made me think I could do this? A six-point earthquake hit Vegas once when I was ten, and the beginning felt like this—when it hits your awareness that the ground you always took for granted has betrayed you—and it's just a matter of how bad it will get. This shift feels like a nine point five.

I can't do this. What was I thinking? Stand up in front of a bunch of nude people and talk about emotions and woo-woo beliefs? I finger the inside of my wrist, a reminder that I can be whatever I want, now.

But showing emotion in public? One of my biggest fears.

Spike claps for attention. "Tonight, Jack has asked to lead the discussion. But first, let's have a few moments of silence for our dear friend."

Quiet falls over the crowd.

I stare into the fire. *I know it was right to bring you here, where you belong. I know you're happy, and only I can sort myself out. But I'm afraid, G'ma. Please help me.*

I lift the lid from the urn, and twist open the plastic bag that holds the part of G'ma she left behind. I take a shaking handful of ashes and toss them on the fire, then pass the urn to Spike. He does the same. Fawn is next. She sprinkles something over the ashes in her hand, then flings it onto the fire.

The flames flare in a hundred hues of blue.

The audience gives a collective "Ohhhhh."

The urn comes back to me, and I empty the bag onto the fire.

Spike speaks softly, but his voice carries over the crowd. "Thank you, Jack, for bringing Blue back to us. From this night on, these nights of sharing will be called, 'Blue's Fire,' in honor of our wise friend. Sweet dreams, Blue. We love you." He steps to a lawn chair and sits. Fawn backs into the shadows.

I look over the expectant faces. I'm terrified, still not sure what I'll say. But if I can't do this, it proves I can't change—that I can't live up to what I have to learn. Closing my eyes, knees quivering, I turn off my brain and search my heart.

A wrenching grief wells. I feel my mouth pull down into a rictus of pain. A sob convulses my chest and I clamp my muscles to hold it in. Tears leak past my squeezed-tight eyelids.

Time stretches like razor wire. I have to say something or run away, and I'm caught between, capable of neither.

Fawn's soft voice carries in the silence. "It's okay, Jack. Whatever comes, it's okay."

I take a breath and speak my heart. "Blue asked me that last night, what I was here to learn. I didn't know at the time. I know now." I'm sharing the deepest part of me with naked strangers. I stand outside myself, watching the tears stream, marveling.

"I thought the only way I could survive childhood was to try to control the world. I believed you only got what you worked for, and I was the only one I could depend on. I got so good at it that the world narrowed to a small tunnel of things I felt safe with. I only accepted black and white in my life.

"But G'ma helped me see that we *have* no control, except over ourselves. I was given amazing gifts that I never had to work for. My creativity and strong sense for scents. They are a big part of me—I shaped my entire career around them. But the Universe is a jokester, because my gifts, they don't live in black or white. They are made up of every shade in the palette. I am learning to open myself to them.

"My grandmother taught me by how she lived every day joyful and unafraid, even knowing how hard and uncaring the world can be. She didn't cling to the earth, fists in the dirt, trying to hold on. She threw herself off cliffs and flew, riding on updrafts of hope and belief.

"I'm going to be more like her." I take a breath. "I want to move through the world unafraid, vulnerable, believing that I have the strength, even if I'm not meant to overcome—then to accept and let go."

Spike stands. "Jack, that was a beautiful tribute to your courage and your love. It's clear you take after your grandmother." He turns to the crowd. "If anyone would like to speak, either about Jack's lesson, or about Blue, please step forward."

I cross to an empty lawn chair and sit, my mind a blank slate.

After the sharing, people wander off in clumps. I'm too keyed up to sleep. The future I was bent on has also been tumbled by the seismic events of the past month. I wander down to the lake and walk the path around it. Cricket mating calls rise from the meadow around me, and frogs join in, with a toad's bass croak adding emphasis. The stars stretch overhead like diamonds tossed on black velvet, and the lake shimmers their broken reflection.

One by one, I shed my clothes, and the water welcomes me with a cool embrace. I lay back and relax into it. Easy to be vulnerable when you're alone. But it's also a safe way to practice. I open my heart, my mind, and my soul to whatever comes.

What comes first is Leo. I want him with a fierceness that shakes me. A man who saw through Jacqueline, the persona even I believed, to the person underneath. To Jack. You can't hide from a man like that. That's why I instinctively broke up with him. If you are ashamed of who you are underneath, you sure don't want anyone around with X-ray vision.

I'm no longer ashamed. Could I one day fit into one of those dioramas I've haunted?

It now seems possible.

Joy bursts from my mouth in a delighted laugh. "It's possible!"

The next morning, it's a tear-filled goodbye. Not afraid to admit, some are mine. I won't be back. This was Nellie's place, not mine. But I'll have fond memories of del Soul.

Eyes straight ahead, I blow by the site of our breakdown in the storm. Despite the warmth of the sunny day, the dark woods bring a shiver, and I'm happy to put it in the rearview mirror.

Two hours later, I cruise the Vegas strip, having no urge to make a detour to Chez Cheyenne. Now that I've reconciled my past, I have no need to revisit it. The same is true for this town. I won't avoid it, but I can't imagine myself returning.

Goodbye.

Goodbye.

At McCarran, I drop off the rental and catch a seat on the next Seattle flight with only minutes to spare.

I purposely haven't called Leo. What I have to say needs to be said in person, but I send him a text: *Be in by two. Can I see you?*

The reply comes within seconds: *Come to my place. We'll talk.*

I settle into my seat and buckle the belt. What about my business? Do I still want to work fifteen hours a day to drive Heart's Note to the next level? And if I don't, what then?

I don't know, but now that I'm open to them, options appear.

I spend the rest of the flight making plans. I can make my choice. But for maybe the first time in my life, my choice depends on someone else. My stomach drops like at the top of a roller coaster. I refuse to take this ride the way I did Insanity, with a death grip on the safety bar, screaming in terror. I'm going to raise my arms and squeal my thrill. That's what G'ma would do.

I'm going to fly.

I swallow a shiver that slithers from my core. At least that's the plan.

And hour later, Leo opens his door at my knock. He steps aside to allow me to enter. "How was the trip?"

"Amazing and sad and joyous, but I'll tell you all that in a minute." I look into his dear scruffy face. This is right. I know it. "I love you."

He stands frozen.

"It's okay if you don't feel that, but you deserve to know that I am in love with you. I'm saying it out loud. If you don't want—"

His hands come up to cradle my head and his lips give me his answer. I lean in, feeling the wind rush past my ears. I'm flying.

Afterword

You must learn to let go.
Release the stress.
You were never in control anyway.
Steve Maraboli

Three months later . . .

From *Monthly Perfumer Magazine:*

Jacqueline Oliver clearly made the right decision, closing her storefront and coming to an arrangement with *Fleur de Montagne* to take her scents nationwide. It's allowed her to focus on creating new scents. You heard it here first—her two new fragrances will be the hit of the Christmas season.

First, there's Route 66, a distinctive men's fragrance that captures the spirit of that historic road. The bold scent is reminiscent of a time when men were men yet is somehow unique to each wearer. The blocky bottle with the amber *liquid is beautiful, but the label with a photo of the sunset touching the center of a straight, cracked-asphalt road will make it a collector's item.*

The women's fragrance is Forever Blue. It's floral, but not like any flower you've ever known. It's earthy and familiar, yet elusive. You'll have to test it to understand. The bottle is chunky and rectangular, a rich cobalt blue, with a deep curving well of perfume. The label is silver, with a delicate tracing of a falling leaf.

Timeless. Exquisite.

Eight months later . . .

I open the sliding glass door to the patio and step out, pulling the sweater around me. The pool is a glassy azure, in perfect contrast to the rust and beige palette of Courthouse Butte rising behind it. I need to start dinner, but the view holds me captive. April in Sedona is my favorite by far. I sigh and pull G'ma's butter suede medicine bag from the pocket of my sweater, tug open the strings, and select a doobie. I take a lighter from my other pocket and inhale the earthy smoke. I've found it's a good way to wind down after a productive, but long day in my lab.

"Is it that time already?" Leo's deep quiet voice comes from behind me. He moves aside the chain that holds his father's pendant to kiss the nape of my neck.

I turn into his arms. "Like Jimmy says, 'It's Five O'clock Somewhere.'"

He kisses below my ear, and heat shoots through me. "Jimmy who?"

"You gotta get with it, Beck." I smile as G'ma's laughter rings in my ears.

He steps behind, wraps his arms around me, and I hold up the joint so he can take a hit. Then we stand watching the setting sun paint the rocks gold.

"I love it here, but I'm missing green. When do you want to head back to Seattle?"

We split our time between here and Leo's loft. "After you finish your latest project. Too much hassle to carry it back and forth, don't you think?"

"You're right, as usual." He squeezes me, then steps away. "It's too cold out here for bare feet. I'm going in."

"I'll be in to start dinner in a minute."

"No rush." The door slides closed behind me.

A pair of golden hawks soar low over the roof behind me, passing over my head with only six feet between us. The male keeps going, but the female wheels around and goes over again, her screeing cry echoing off the canyon. I turn, raise a hand to shade my eyes as she dips a wing to come over again, this time, only three feet over my head. My heart bangs, wanting to break out of its cage and soar with her.

She screes once more and flaps her wings, catching up to the male who is heading for the rocky crags.

I raise a hand. "I love you, G'ma. Be happy." Then turn and walk into the house to fix dinner.

About the Author

Laura Drake's first novel, *The Sweet Spot*, was a double-finalist and then won the 2014 Romance Writers of America® RITA® award. She's since published 11 more novels. She is a founding member of Women's Fiction Writers Assn, Writers in the Storm blog, as well as a member of Western Writers of America and Women Writing the West.

Laura is a city girl who never grew out of her tomboy ways or serious cowboy crush. She gave up a corporate CFO gig to write full time. She realized a lifelong dream of becoming a Texan and is currently working on her accent. She's a wife, grandmother, and motorcycle chick in the remaining waking hours.

Acknowledgments

To the brilliant writer and sister-of-my-heart, Miranda King, who read this and, in one 4 am phone call, told me what I meant to say all along. *She* found the book's Heart's Note.

Some books are easy. This one was not one of those. It wouldn't have happened if not for generous and caring friends:

My 'critters', Fae Rowen and Kimberly Belle, and Beta readers, Beverly Rogers, Sherene Gross (thanks for the goat), Susan Donovan, Lainey Cameron, Jenny Hansen, Orly Konig, Donna Everhart. And thanks to my bud, Bruce Rauss for the pantyhose MacGyvering. And always to my constant partner on the writing road, Barbara Claypole White. I owe you a margarita.

Thank you to my super-agent, Nalini Akolekar, who read this more times than I'm sure she wants to remember, and came up with the perfect title. Thanks to Lou Aronica for taking a chance on me.

And, as always, to my dedicated readers. Thank you for 'getting' me.